THIRTY DAYS FOR HENRY
THE COMPLETE TALES OF
SHERIFF HENRY, VOLUME 6

THIRTY DAYS
FOR HENRY

THE COMPLETE TALES OF
SHERIFF HENRY, VOLUME 6

W.C. TUTTLE

ILLUSTRATED BY
SAMUEL CAHAN

POPULAR PUBLICATIONS · 2022

TABLE OF CONTENTS

THIRTY DAYS FOR HENRY

There they sit, resting their spurs on the desk of the Law—those three loco star-packers who have turned the sober workings of justice into a vaudeville routine. But men will die violently in Wild Horse County tomorrow; and Henry Harrison Conroy must stagger through another hilarious saga of Tonto Town

1

TONTO TOWN IS FALLING DOWN

"TONTO CITY," STATED "Judge" Van Treece heavily, "is on a steep downgrade, with brake-blocks busted, and a crazy driver at the lines."

Having delivered this remarkable statement, Judge raised his right foot, evidently with the intention of hooking a high-heel around the rung of his tilted chair, but found the effort too great, and let it drop back to its former position.

Henry Harrison Conroy, Sheriff of Tonto, slumped in his office chair, slowly lifted his moon-like face and looked through squinty eyes at Judge. Then, with a plump hand, he carefully massaged his huge, red nose.

"Our thought for the day," he said quietly. Judge opened his eyes, blinked, closed his eyes and relaxed again.

Sprawled on a cot in the office was the huge figure of a man, snoring lustily. He was Oscar Johnson, the jailer, whom Judge had dubbed "The Vitrified Viking." These three were known in the editorial page of the Scorpion Bend *Weekly Clarion* as "The Shame of Arizona."

Henry Harrison Conroy was short and fat, with a nose that had been publicized on vaudeville posters from coast to coast for many years. Approximately at the same time that vaudeville had expired, Henry's uncle, a patriarch of

Wild Horse Valley, had followed suit, leaving the JHC cattle ranch to Henry, whose only knowledge of the West was gleaned from a stage production of "The Squaw Man."

However, necessity forced Henry to accept this heritage, and he came to Tonto City, clad in a pearl-gray suit, derby hat, spats and a gold-headed cane. Soon he found a kindred spirit in Judge Van Treece, a whisky derelict, who had been a great criminal lawyer. Crane-like in stature, with a long, lean face and eyes pouched like those of a weary old bloodhound, Judge never permitted his dignity to be shaken by his poverty.

When Tonto City and Wild Horse Valley, in a state of extreme hilarity over these two characters, wrote Henry's name in on the ballots, Henry became sheriff of Tonto town. The whole thing was a joke, of course; but quickly the town discovered that its joke had gone too far. Henry had a taste for comedy himself; and so he appointed Judge Van Treece as his deputy and selected Oscar Johnson, the JHC horse-wrangler, for jailer. It was probably the queer-

est assortment of peace officers ever to grace the office of a Western sheriff—and Wild Horse Valley was all that the name implied.

Oscar Johnson was a giant Swede, flat-faced, with small, round, blue eyes and a button-like nose. With the strength of a Samson, the guile of a child, and a complete inability to do anything right, he was an unceasing joy to Henry Harrison Conroy.

Sitting there in the office, Henry finally shoved his sombrero back on his head, made an ineffectual attempt to elevate his boots to the desk-top, grunted disgustedly at his own beltline, and then threw a copy of the brand register at Judge's head.

Judge opened his eyes, looked reprovingly at Henry, and closed them again.

"Judge," said Henry, "you look like an anaesthetized bloodhound."

"Eh?" grunted Judge. "I—er—oh, yes. Where was I, sir?"

"You were evidently in the land of Sag and Strangle."

"I was not asleep," declared Judge. "I was merely pondering upon the plight of Tonto City. As I so aptly remarked a moment ago—"

"I know," interrupted Henry. "Busted brake-blocks and a crazy driver. You have used that phrase for weeks, rolling it around your tongue."

Judge grunted and lifted his brows. "You must admit its truth, sir," he said. "Ever since King Colt bought the Tonto Saloon and Gambling Palace, trouble has drifted into this fair valley. That uncouth remnant of the cave-age, and his cohorts—"

"I find King Colt very refreshing, sir," interrupted Henry. "The man is a diamond in the rough."

"The man is evil," declared Judge. "A devil's spawn. Look at the men he employs. Gunmen, slick-haired gamblers, female vampires in his honkytonk."

"By the way," interrupted Henry again, "that girl, known as La Mariposa, has a remarkable voice, Judge."

"I suppose she has a certain tonal quality," admitted Judge grudgingly. He stared through the window. "Those Mexican buzzards!" he grunted dismally. "Both on one horse."

"With a jug?" asked Henry quickly. "Frijole Bill said he might send in some prune whisky today."

THUNDER AND LIGHTNING Mendoza were Mexican brothers, small of stature, round-faced, ignorant and bland. Henry employed them at the JHC ranch—but for what, no one knew, unless it was for their ability to manhandle the King's English. They came into the office now, side by side, carrying a five gallon demijohn, solemn as two Colorado-maduro owls. As a matter of fact, they were as drunk as the proverbial boiled owls. Carefully they placed the jug on the floor. Then Lightning rocked on his heels, his eyes examined the blank ceiling.

"You weesh from makeeng spitch, Lightning, my leetle brodder?" asked Thunder.

"I am not spitcher," stated Lightning. "I radder seeng."

"Just a moment, gentlemen," begged Henry. "It would seem that Frijole appointed you as messenger boys—not ambassadors. Where is Frijole?"

"Frijole," replied Lightning, "ees sprad from the estable to the keetchen door."

"From the stable to the kitchen door?" gasped Judge. "What ever strung him out like that?"

"Theese leeker," replied Thunder, pointing a wavering finger at the demijohn.

"It might cramp one, thereby making one shorter," said Henry, "but do not believe that even Frijole's brew would elongate the human frame. Just how long is Frijole?"

Lightning solemnly consulted an old silver watch, which had not run for years, counted seven on his fingers, and announced: "I'm theenk 'bout two hour."

"Correctly interpreted," said Henry, "Frijole passed out two hours ago, between the stable and the kitchen."

Lightning bobbed his head so violently that he lost his balance and sat down heavily on the floor.

"You are both disgracefully drunk," declared Henry. "How many drinks did you take out of that jug?"

"I cross hees heart, I hope you die," said Thunder soberly, "we only take one seep."

"Do you mean to stand there in your shame and lie to us?" roared Judge. "You have had a quart apiece!"

"No, no, Jodge," insisted Thunder. "One leetle seep—like theese."

Thunder leaned forward toward Judge, trying to use his forefinger as a measure, stumbled over Lightning, and sprawled in the middle of the floor.

"I fear," said Henry soberly, "that this last batch of whisky needs a chemical analysis, Judge."

Judge cautiously removed the cork and sniffed deeply into the neck of the demijohn. Then he leaned back, looking at Henry. "It has a bouquet, Henry," he said. "A—a lethal fragrance. But if one little sip will do that to a Mexican, whose nervous system is calloused from drinking tequila, I really advise caution."

"At least," replied Henry, "a small drink might give us a different perspective on Tonto City. The place may not be bad at all; we may be thinking wrong of it. Get the cups, Judge."

TWO MEN WERE facing each other across a small table in the little office at the rear of the Tonto Saloon and Gambling Palace. King Colt, the owner of the Tonto, was a huge man, paunchy, and gross of feature. His thick lips were sagging in amazement, as he looked at the wizened, evil-faced cripple in the home-made wheelchair. The cowboy, who had wheeled him in, seemed ill at ease.

"Get out!" snapped King Colt, and the cowboy went into the saloon. From out in the saloon came the strains of a Mexican orchestra, the rattle of chips.

"So yo're King Colt, eh?" sneered the cripple. "Pete McLean, you—"

"The name's Colt," interrupted the big man. "Don't forget that."

"All right—Colt. My name's Tallant. Gila Jim Tallant."

"Used to be Jim Talbot, when I knew yuh. So yo're the father of Jack Tallant, eh?"

The cripple laughed harshly. "Funny, ain't it? You been here almost a year, and my ranch is only ten miles south of here. Me within ten miles of the man who crippled me for life—and I didn't know it. Over twenty years ago you smashed my hip with a bullet—made me what I am—a man who can't never walk. All I can do is set and curse the day I ever seen you."

"Oh, I know, Gila," said the big man placatingly, "it's tough. But if that bullet had been a foot higher, you'd have been dead for years. Yuh ought to look at it thataway. I—I wasn't such an awful good shot in them days."

"Yuh shot good enough on that deputy," said Gila. "They set yuh back twenty years for that bull's eye, didn't they?"

King Colt's eyes hardened and his lips twisted bitterly. Finally he nodded. "Twenty years," he said huskily. "I served every day of it, Gila."

"Yuh had it comin' to you."

King Colt nodded his head slowly. "Oh, sure, I had it comin'. But how did you happen to come here today?"

The old cripple leaned forward in his chair, his eyes burning, as he replied: "I came here to tell you to let my boy alone, damn yuh."

King Colt sat motionless, his mind racing back beyond the twenty years. For several moments he seemed to forget the old cripple, as he tried to figure a certain angle on something he had never been able to learn.

"You heard what I said, Colt?"

"Oh, yeah, I—well, now, Gila, Jack's a nice boy. You wouldn't want him to do anythin' wrong."

"So yo're tryin' to reform him, eh? Tellin' him that crime don't pay. Damn you, yo're talkin' morals to him, 'cause you figure he's hornin' into yore business. I suppose that the cattle-rustlin', cattle-stealin' all belongs to you, eh?"

"Shut up, you fool!" snapped King Colt. "Yellin' things like that. The sheriff could have heard every word yuh said, if he was out there in the saloon."

"Sheriff!" sneered the cripple. "That potato-nosed clown! He's about as much use as one pair of boots would be to a centipede."

"I know, Gila, but there's no use puttin' up signs."

"All right, then, Mr. Colt. You leave Jack alone."

"Gila, ain't a warnin' better than rubbin' a young man out complete? He could make an honest livin'. I didn't know you was his father. Why, with his ability and yore crooked brain, he should get hung early in life."

"Not with my brains behind him. I'll take care of that, King Colt. I owe you somethin' for this smashed hip—and I'll pay yuh. I'll break yuh and send yuh back where yuh belong."

"Now, Gila," King Colt said, smiling, "yo're all worked up again."

"Worked up? I ain't walked for twenty years. I've had plenty time to work-up a hate for you."

"A feller ort to work up a pretty good-sized hate in twenty years," said King Colt. "But you ain't the only one that suffered."

"*You* got what was comin' to yuh, King Colt. Lost yore wife and kids—"

King Colt was on his feet, towering over the wizened cripple, his huge paw-like fists doubled on the table-top. He said hoarsely: "Gila, do you know where they are?"

"How would I know? They left Cheyenne, didn't they? That was twenty-two, twenty-three years ago."

"If I thought you knew, Gila, I'd squeeze the last drop of blood from yore carcass to make yuh tell."

Gila laughed at him. "Yuh don't suppose they'd want to see you, do yuh? Yore wife was a pretty woman, as I remember her. Hair like gold, blue eyes and—"

"Shut up, you crippled rattler!" snarled King Colt.

"And there was two little kids—a boy and a girl. I 'member that the boy had curly, yaller hair, and the girl—"

Like a grizzly charging, King Colt came across the table, his hands grasping the faded shirt on the cripple's chest. He shoved his face close to the other man's.

"Gila, if you say one more word, I'll kill yuh."

For several moments they were motionless, their eyes locked. Then King Colt slowly drew back.

"All right," said the cripple. "Send for that puncher to wheel me out of yore wolf cave. But before yuh do—have yuh ever heard from Tex Rayburn?"

King Colt's eyes hardened, but he said, "Rayburn? Tex Rayburn?"

Gila Jim laughed quietly. "Yore pardner, Colt—the one they didn't get. And the one they say *got all the money.*"

"They was wrong," said King Colt. "He wasn't my pardner."

"All right—send for that puncher. This place stinks."

King Colt summoned the cowboy, who was waiting outside the door, and he wheeled Gila Jim through the saloon. King Colt motioned to one of his gamblers, and the man came into the office, closing the door.

Colt sat down in his chair and lighted a cigar. Then he said:

"Tell the boys to let Jack Tallant alone."

The gambler nodded and went out.

After a long period of contemplation, King Colt opened a drawer and took out a faded, discolored photograph. It showed a woman and two little children, posed with all the stiffness of the early pictures. After looking closely at it, he started to tear it in two, but stopped, shook his head and put it back in the drawer.

OUT IN THE saloon, standing at the long bar, was Pancho Lopez. He was twirling his tiny, black mustache as he watched a girl, who was talking with one of the gamblers. The girl was a singer known as La Mariposa, by long odds the most beautiful girl who had ever come to Wild Horse Valley. Men crowded the honkytonk to hear her voice, and after only two weeks at the Tonto, her fame had spread far and wide.

Pancho, christened Pancho Adolfo Alejo Bonifacio Guillermo Santiago Lopez, was supposed to be the boss gambler of the Tonto, but it was also said that he was boss of Agua Frio, a little town in Mexico, about fifteen miles south of Tonto City. He was taller than most Mexicans, good-looking and extraordinarily vain.

"I tell you sometheeng, *amigo*," he remarked to the bartender, smiling at his own reflection in the back-bar mirror. "She ees pitch."

The bartender stopped polishing a glass and looked at Pancho. "Pitch?" he queried.

"Sure theeng," said Pancho and smiled.

"You mean—to throw something, Pancho?"

"No! Grow on a tree. Half-brodder from a pear."

"Oh—a peach. You mean La Mariposa?"

"Sure. La Mariposa—the Botterfly. You know where she come from?"

"Nope. She came in on the stage from Scorpion Bend, asked King for a job, and got it. She don't mix much. Got a room to herself upstairs. Never takes a drink, and don't smoke."

"Hm-m-m-m-m," mused Pancho over his cigarette. "Every time I look at this girl, I get beeg ideas. She draw lots of folks here."

"That's right, Pancho; they shore flock in to hear her sing. I seen the sheriff and that old deputy in here last night, when she was singin' *My Old Kentucky Home,* and they had tears in their eyes. And I'll bet neither of'em ever seen Kentucky, except on a map."

A man came up to Pancho and said: "King wants to see yuh."

"*Gracias.*" Pancho went to the office. King Colt was sprawled in his chair, hat over one eye. He merely lifted his head, looked at Pancho and subsided again.

"'Allo, Boss," said Pancho. "You want to see me?"

"Yeah. How long have you known Gila Jim Tallant?"

"Oh, that poor devil on wheels? Maybe t'ree year."

"He came to see me today, Pancho. First time he's been in Tonto since I came here. I knowed him over twenty years ago."

"So? That ees eenteresting. He ees fadder from Jack Tallant?"

"Yeah—so he said. It was my bullet that crippled him."

"Por Dios—no!"

"Yeah, it's true. I was a special deputy."

"Why don't you shoot higher, Keeng?"

"My intentions was good."

"He ees still mad at you, eh?"

"That's what I want to see you about. Gila Tallant is smart, Pancho; and he'll give us trouble. He's the brains behind Jack Tallant, and that kid is runnin' horses and beef across the Border. We've got to stop him."

"Sure," smiled Pancho. "That ees not so hard. One leetle bullet—"

"No! I don't want him killed, Pancho."

"Dios mio, are you getting cheeken-hearted, *amigo?"*

"That's an order, Pancho."

"All right, *amigo.* I like this new seenger."

"Never mind the new singer."

"Were she come from, Keeng?"

"Never mind that. All you think about is a pretty face."

"Love," corrected Pancho, smiling broadly.

"Yeah? Well, some day love will get yuh a knife between yore damn ribs."

"You 'av never been in love, Keeng?"

"Me!" snorted King. "Me in—" He hesitated and drew a deep breath.

"I was married once, Pancho," he said huskily. "I married the best damn woman on earth. We had two little kids—a girl and a boy. Then the law got me on a shootin' and rustlin' charge, and I went up for twenty years. I served every day of it, too. And when I came out, they were gone. I dunno why, but I didn't think they'd be gone. Nobody knew where they went.

"Oh, sure, I tried to find 'em. I allus was good with a rope and a gun; so I got some money together. I didn't care much if they did send me back, but I was luckier this time. Finally I drifted down here. I've never told anybody about this, Pancho, but seein' Gila Jim kinda stirred things up again. He knew my wife, but he don't know where she went."

Pancho grimaced and shrugged his shoulders. "Women never make a fool from me, *amigo*."

"That woman never made a fool of me either!" snapped King.

"In Spanish," explained Pancho, "we say *idiota*."

"Do I look like an idiot?" demanded King.

"Well, you mus' remember that was twenty year' ago, Keeng."

"Sure, that's right. But you keep away from that girl. She's hired to sing songs—nothin' else. I hope yuh understand."

"Me?" Pancho smiled widely. "I am mos' perfec' gentleman, myself, personally. *Buenas tardes, amigo*."

2

TROUBLE FOR HENRY

FOR MANY YEARS Wild Horse Valley had been strictly a cattle and horse country. It was only a rangeland when Henry Harrison Conroy came, but some rich discoveries of gold ore quickly brought it to the front as a mining district. Because of this new activity the railroad built a branch line from Scorpion Bend, but did not haul passengers nor mail; so the stage line continued to operate as usual. Fifteen miles to the south of Tonto City was the Mexican Border, reached by a rough road. Just south of the Border was the little town of Agua Frio, isolated on that long stretch of Border, and reputed to be a smuggler's headquarters. Recently there had been complaints of missing cattle and horses, presumably taken into Mexico. There was much talk of another revolution, and the rebels were believed to be secretly buying up horses and laying in a supply of good American beef.

Just how to stop this practice was a problem for Henry Harrison Conroy. The Commissioners felt that Henry was negligent. The *Clarion* at Scorpion Bend shot its weekly shafts of criticism at the sheriff of Tonto and his assistants, accusing them of being inebriated clowns, who drew a monthly stipend from the county for turning the sheriff's duties into a vaudeville routine.

There was no direct evidence that King Colt was a law-breaker. Because the Tonto was the biggest place of its kind in the county, it naturally drew the most patrons. Henry Harrison Conroy knew that Howard McRae, the hard-faced old banker, had backed King Colt in the purchase of the Tonto; and in Henry's opinion the only way that an honest man could borrow money from McRae would be to administer an anaesthetic.

Henry knew Gila Jim Tallant and his son Jack. Their little ranch was very close to the Border, and their cattle were few. The fact that Jack Tallant, a handsome, wild-riding, young cowboy, had money to gamble with interested Henry deeply. Gila Jim had never been friendly toward Henry. In fact, he was not friendly toward any one, and Jack was a laughing, devil-may-care fellow, defiant of law and order.

Henry had several problems. There was Jimmy Miller, son of Hailstorm Miller who owned the Circle M, located a few miles north of Tonto. Old Hailstorm was a fine old-time cattleman, rough as a wood-rasp, and unquestionably honest. But as Judge said, "Jimmy goes around with a sack of wild oats on his shoulder, the draw-string busted."

The Tonto City Bank owned a ten-thousand-dollar mortgage on the Circle M, and had foreclosed a year ago. But during the extra year of grace allowed by law, it was rumored that Hailstorm Miller was raising the money to pay off the mortgage.

All of which had a bearing on the events of one sultry summer day. Oscar Johnson had just finished his mid-day siesta on the office cot. The springs creaked complainingly as he sat up and blinked at Henry and Judge. Oscar yawned cavernously, stretched his powerful arms and remarked that he had dozed off for a moment.

"Sloth!" exclaimed Judge. "You have slept two solid hours."

"Yudge," said Oscar, "var is de difference between a solid hour and a soft von?"

"I like you better asleep," replied Judge. "By the way, didn't I see a big Swede working at the livery stable yesterday?"

"He is not a Svede—he is Norvegian."

"Rather a big, handsome Viking, too," said Henry.

"Handsome Wiking!" snorted Oscar. "He is yust a knotheaded Norvegian, named Yulius Sorensen. He has yust got brains enough to vater a hurse."

"After all," remarked Henry, "one does not need an Oxford degree to work in a livery stable. He seems a perfect gentleman."

"Yentleman!" exploded Oscar.

"Come, come," chided Judge. "Who are you to say that Julius is not a gentleman."

"Ay am Oscar Yohnson, yailer; and I say he's no yentleman."

"Has he been casting sheep's-eyes at Josephine?" asked Judge.

Josephine Swenson, Oscar's light o' love, was a waitress at the Tonto Hotel. She was about thirty-six, tall, raw-boned, muscular, with a huge mop of taffy-colored hair, long, lean face and a large nose. Life had taught Josephine a lot about left hooks and straight rights, and she could land both with telling effect.

"Ship-eyes?" queried Oscar.

"In other words, is he in love with Josephine?"

"By Yudas!" exclaimed Oscar quietly. After pondering a few moments he said, "Ay vill ask him."

"You are not a man to beat around the bush, Oscar."

"Ay will beat around a Norvegian, you bat you."

Oscar went heavily out of the office, and Henry looked reprovingly at Judge.

"You *would* stir up that Swede, Judge," he said.

"That Swede," retorted Judge, "has been stirred all his life. In fact, I believe he was born stirred."

A CLATTER OF hoofs outside caused Judge to step to the doorway. "Those harbingers of bad English," he said. "Still riding one horse."

Thunder and Lightning came through the doorway, like a team.

"W'ere ees everybodee?" queried Lightning excitedly.

"Calm down," advised Henry. "We are all here. What is it?"

"A man ees as dead as las'-year doorknob, and that ees all I hope!"

"Untangle that one," said Judge.

"Take it easy," said Henry. "Now go all over it again, Lightning."

"Leesten!" exclaimed Thunder. "He steek up, jus' like he order *cinco cerveza*."

"Five beer," translated Lightning proudly. "And that ees as true as I cross hees heart, I hope you die."

"I pass," groaned Judge.

"Can't h'open the pot, eh?" smiled Lightning.

"Never mind the five beers," said Henry. "Stick to the dead man. Where is he and who is he?"

"*Quien sabe?*" replied Lightning.

"You mean to say you do not know *where* he is?" roared Judge.

"No," replied Lightning, "we don't know who."

"Where?" yelled Henry.

"The man die from fire."

"In the brush?"

"No, I theenk he burn in the stable, because he ees among the stable, which ees not a stable."

"Keep stirring, Henry," groaned Judge.

"Where," propounded Henry, "is that burned stable?"

"Oh, of course," said Thunder and grinned. "It ees the estable from the Circle M rancho."

"What?" Henry stood up hurriedly. "The Circle M stable? You mean to say that the Circle M stable burned— and a man burned in it?"

"He has the h'ash all around heem. I theenk he mus' have been there biffore the estable burn down on heem."

"My God!" exclaimed Henry. "Judge, notify Doc Bogart, while I saddle the horses. Can it be that something has happened to Hailstorm Miller?"

"That ees one," said Lightning blandly.

"One what?" asked Henry, trying to fasten a spur buckle.

"One dead man."

Henry dropped the spur and looked closely at Lightning.

"By any chance, do you mean that there is more than one dead man, Lightning?"

"Jus' more than one," agreed Lightning.

"He ees jus' as dead as both of them," declared Thunder.

"My goodness!" exclaimed Henry, sitting down heavily. "Lightning, do you actually mean that you found two dead men?"

"No," replied Lightning. "Firs', we only find one."

"And secondly," said Judge, "you found one more."

"Not the same one," replied Lightning. "There ees deeference."

"Naturally," sighed Henry, mopping his forehead. "But you actually found two dead men."

"Not togedder," said Lightning.

"T'ree, four mile from togedder," explained Thunder.

"Where is this last one?" asked Judge weakly.

" 'Bout two mile from this."

"I'll get the doctor," choked Judge. "I—I need him myself."

"Do you know either of the dead men, Lightning?" asked Henry.

"The odder one from the firs' one ees Ed Clay."

"The stage-driver!" exploded Judge. "Why, I spoke to him as he drove away this morning!"

"He ees not dead then?" asked Thunder blandly.

"Of course, he is not dead then. How could he—Henry, I am about to steep my soul in sin. Unless I suffer a complete change of heart, I feel that I must kill a Mexican before I put on my boots."

"I—I believe I would exonerate you, sir," panted Henry, fastening his spurs. "Lightning, stop grinning. Do you not realize that two men are dead?"

"W'at ees the reward?" asked Lightning.

"Reward? Reward for finding two dead men? There is no reward."

"I theenk," remarked Lightning, "that we go like hell for notheeng, my leetle brodder. Nobody ees pay for plain dead men."

"Oh, well," said the philosophical Thunder, "we don' have to bury heem."

"Get out of here, before I bury both of you," ordered Henry. "Go out and saddle our two horses—and put the saddles on so that the horn of the saddle is in front. Do something."

"The horn from the saddle ees always in front," informed Lightning.

Henry reached for a bootjack, and the two Mexicans beat a hasty retreat to the stable behind the jail. The word quickly spread, and it was a sizeable cavalcade which rode out of Tonto City. Less than two miles from town, Lightning led the way off the road, following the iron-shod tracks of the stage, and a short distance away they discovered the body of Ed Clay, the stage-driver. Near him, tossed into the bush, was the iron box, in which the stage carried valuables. It had been broken open, and was empty.

SOME OF THE men followed the tracks and found the stage and team near the rim of Mummy Cañon. They brought it back intact, and the body, after examination, was placed inside the stage and sent back to town, while most of the crowd rode on to the Circle M ranch. No one seemed to know where Jimmy Miller was.

The Circle M stable was a mass of ashes, with a few charred sticks of lumber left, and in the center of the debris, sticking out of the ashes, was the burned arm of a man, his five fingers spread wide.

"*Cinco cerveza,*" whispered Lightning to Henry.

"That poor devil!" exclaimed Henry.

Using pieces of board as paddles, Henry and the coroner beat aside the ashes and carefully removed the corpse, which had been burned almost beyond recognition. Doctor Bogart, white-faced from the tragedy, examined the body carefully, and declared at length that it was the remains of Uncle Hailstorm Miller.

The old man had been well known to all of them, and well liked. Henry secured a blanket, on which they carefully placed the corpse and carried it to the house. There was no way to take it to town.

"It seems rather queer that he should burn to death in that stable," remarked Henry, as the men gathered around the porch. "As a matter of fact, today is the last day in which Miller could have paid off the mortgage on his ranch; and I understand that he had collected the full amount, following his last sale of cattle. Doc, is there any indication of foul play visible on that body?"

"My examination was too brief for that," replied Doctor Bogart. "I shall determine that later, as soon as we can bring the body to my place. I'll send out for it as soon as we get back to town. We should find Jimmy Miller as soon as possible and tell him what happened."

They closed the house and rode back to Tonto City, where Howard McRae, the banker met them. "That treasure-box contained six hundred and fifty ounces of raw gold, shipped by the Shoshone Chief Mine," he told them. "It was worth approximately thirteen thousand dollars."

"My goodness!" exclaimed Henry. "A fortune! Except for you, Mr. McRae, who knew that the gold was sent on that stage?"

"Well, my son, who works with me at the bank—and, well, of course, some of the mine officials. The stage-driver knew nothing, except that the box was heavy. It weighed over fifty-five pounds, you know. Damn it, something must be done, Sheriff."

Henry rubbed his red nose thoughtfully. "Yes, of course," he admitted.

"Are you sure that body belonged to Hailstorm Miller?"

"No question," replied the doctor.

"Accidental, of course."

"That is to be determined later."

As Henry and Judge walked to the office, a cowboy accosted them. He was Harry Levis, who had driven the stage team back to Tonto City. He handed Henry a worn gauntlet.

"That was kinda tucked under the cushion of the stage seat," he told them. "I thought I'd better give it to yuh, Sheriff."

"Well, thank you," murmured Henry. "I suppose it belongs—"

Henry had turned it in his hands. On the back, worked in colored beads, were the initials *J.M.* Henry slowly folded up the gauntlet. "Thank you, Harry," he said. "I'll take care of it."

THEY WENT INTO the office and closed the door. "There you are, sir," declared Judge. "Jimmy Miller—"

"Wait a moment, Judge," interrupted Henry. "It doesn't prove anything. That may not be Jimmy's glove. If it is, he might have traded or sold it to Ed Clay. I must admit that—er—another thing, Judge, that bit of evidence may have been left there—to be found."

"Yes, that is possible. But I am more interested in the tragedy at the Circle M. Henry, do you suppose that it was foul play? Hailstorm Miller was not a drinking man, nor was he in poor health. I do not see how he could be trapped in a burning stable."

Henry shook his head sadly, "We better wait for Doc's report. Will you find Oscar and send him out with the doctor to get that body?"

After Judge had left the office, Howard McRae, the elderly banker, came down there. He seemed upset over the happenings of the day.

"Of course, you knew that Hailstorm Miller owed the bank ten thousand dollars," he said. "Miller assured me that the mortgage would be paid in full, before the expiration date, Henry. Today is that date. Unless Jimmy Miller knows where that money can be found, we must take over the Circle M. Of course, if Jimmy knows where to get the money, we won't hold him strictly to this date."

"The question is—where is Jimmy Miller?" remarked Henry. "I cannot find anyone who has seen him lately. More than that, I feel sure that Hailstorm Miller would not entrust that money to Jimmy."

"No, I don't believe he would. But that leaves us with the ranch on our hands."

"Not exactly unexpected, was it?" queried Henry.

"We did expect it for a long time, until Miller assured me that the money would be forthcoming. Yes, we planned on taking over the ranch. In fact, I had tentatively hired

Tuck Darnell to run the place. My son, Steve, wanted to run it, but I felt that he was too inexperienced, Anyway, I need him in the bank."

It was late that evening when Doctor Bogart finished his work. He came to the office and made his verbal report to Henry.

"In my opinion, Henry," he said, "Hailstorm Miller was killed by a blow on the head, inflicted possibly with a gun-barrel. The wound is too deep to have been done by falling timbers; and in my opinion the man was dead quite a while before the fire was started."

The doctor was about to leave, when Jimmy Miller came in. Jimmy was about twenty-five, rather small, slender and hard-faced. Just now he looked whipped as he leaned against the door-frame.

"Jimmy, I'm sorry," said Henry.

"Yeah, I know," said Jimmy huskily. "I've been out there. I've pulled the house apart, tryin' to find that money. I dunno where Dad left it, and this is the last day. Right now that bank owns the Circle M, and I can't stop 'em. Doc," he turned to Doctor Bogart, "you've examined Dad's body. Was—was it an accident, Doc?"

"Jimmy, I don't believe it was an accident."

"Neither do I. Somebody killed Dad for that money. I'll find out who killed him."

"We'll try, too, Jimmy," assured Henry. "Tell me this: do you own a pair of leather gauntlets, with *J.M.* beaded on the backs?"

"Why, I shore do, Sheriff. What about 'em?"

"You heard about the robbery and murder at the stage, Jimmy?"

"Yeah, I heard about it."

"One of your gauntlets was tucked under the driver's seat."

"One of my—wait a minute! You say that one of my—"

"Here it is," interrupted Henry, taking the glove from a drawer and placing it on the desk-top. Jimmy stared at it.

"That's mine," he said quietly: "That's one of my gauntlets. But I don't see—"

He suddenly leaped back, whipping a gun from his holster, and moved quickly to the doorway.

"No, yuh don't," he told them hoarsely. "Yuh can't put the dead wood on me like that, Sheriff. I never stuck up no stage—and I'm not goin' to jail for somethin' I never done. Stay where yuh are."

Swiftly he faded away in the darkness. Henry sighed and looked at Doctor Bogart. Then he put the glove into his desk-drawer, rubbed his red nose and leaned back in his chair.

"Impetuous youth, Doc," he said.

"Why, that fool kid might have shot both of us, Henry!"

"Well, Doc," replied Henry, "you must admit that he could not have found a nicer night for it."

"Sometimes, Henry," sighed the doctor, "I wonder whether you are as brave as a lion, or as crazy as a loon."

"If you decide—let me know, Doctor; I still have enough brains to be curious about myself."

3

OSCAR VS. NORWAY

JIMMY MILLER WENT straight to the Tonto Saloon. Ignoring everyone in the big place, he strode back to the office, kicked open the door and walked in. King Colt, seated behind his desk, swung around, scowling at the intruder. For several moments they looked squarely at each other, and then Jimmy said:

"Colt, I'm lookin' for the man who killed my father."

Slowly the big gambler removed his cigar, his eyes watching Jimmy closely. King Colt knew that this hard-faced kid was dangerous.

"Sure," he said, nodding, "I hope yuh find him, Jimmy."

"No, yuh don't either, Colt; yo're bluffin'. I know yore gang. Somebody murdered my father, burned his body in a stable fire, and took the ten thousand dollar he had collected to pay off his mortgage."

"Ten thousand, eh?" said Colt slowly. "I heard about yore father, but I didn't hear about the money."

"Then you better check up on yore gang, Colt; they're holdin' out on yuh."

The big man shook his head. "Yo're wrong, Jimmy. None of my boys got him."

"No? I suppose they all denied it and you believe 'em.

28

Well, I'm tellin' yuh, Colt, I'm goin' to get that killer. I want the man who killed my father and ruined my chance of ever owning the Circle M. Right now, it belongs to the bank. That ten thousand would have saved it. Somebody wanted that money—and they killed to get it."

"I'm sorry about yore father, Jimmy. Calm down. I'm not lyin' to you, when I say that I don't know anythin' about it."

"All right—what about that stage robbery?"

"I don't know who done that job."

"That was a dirty murder, too," said Jimmy coldly. "And the skunk who murdered Ed Clay and took that gold, tucked one of my gloves under the seat cushion."

King Colt twisted the cigar between his teeth. "I heard that," he mid. "Had yore initials on the back, worked in beads. That sure made it look bad for you, Jimmy. Have yuh seen the sheriff?"

"I just came from there. He told me about it, and I backed out with a gun in my hand. I reckon they're lookin' for me now. But I won't give myself up. Once they get me in jail, I can't never find the man I'm lookin' for. Any jury in this valley would convict me on the evidence of that glove. No, I dunno where they got the glove. I ain't worn it for weeks, months. Somebody picked it up at my place."

King Colt nodded thoughtfully. "Ten thousand from yore place, and thirteen thousand from the stage. That's big money, Jimmy."

"Damn you, I didn't get any of it, Colt!"

"I didn't say yuh did—but it's still big money."

"And two men murdered," added Jimmy. "Don't forget that, Colt; it's a hangin' job, unless I find 'em first."

Colt nodded. "I know how yuh feel, Jimmy. Do yuh think the sheriff is after yuh?"

"Who knows what Conroy will do?" countered Jimmy.

"One thing he will do—he'll rub his nose," remarked Colt. "Of all the crazy things ever done in this valley, his election was the worst."

"I know," said Jimmy. "But don't forget that he's done things. He's no fool, even if he don't fit into this country. Just about the time you think you've pulled the wool over his eyes—he'll get yuh."

"Are you warnin' me?" queried Colt.

"Take it or leave it," replied Jimmy. "You better warn yore gang that I'm lookin' for the man who killed my father."

"Yeah, I'll tell 'em. Another thing, Jimmy—I wouldn't go back through the saloon. No, I wouldn't do that. A lot of people seen yuh come in here. I'll open a window, and yuh can go out the back way."

"Thank yuh, Colt, but I'll be goin' out backwards."

"You can trust me, Jimmy."

"I trust nobody, Colt. I may thank yuh, but I'll never trust yuh."

COLT CLOSED THE window behind Jimmy and dropped the curtain. Then he summoned Pancho Lopez, who came swaggering in, clad in a white suit, white shoes, a white silk shirt and a blazing red necktie. Pancho sat on a corner of the table, smiling at King Colt, who lighted a fresh cigar and studied his resplendent henchman.

"Damn Christmas tree!" he snorted.

"You like theese suits?" asked Pancho. "Ver' nice. I sheep heem all the way from Mejico Ceety. Cost plenty *dinero*— but look so nice."

"Damn dude! But I didn't call yuh in here to talk suits. Pancho, what do you know about the killin' of Hailstorm Miller?"

Pancho shrugged his shoulders. "Notheeng. I hear he ees dead—burned in hees stable."

"The man who killed him got ten thousand dollars from him, before he made the kill."

"*Madre de Dios!* I never hear that."

"It's a fact. And the man who killed Ed Clay got thirteen thousand dollars from that treasure box. That's twenty-three thousand dollars. I want to find out who got that money."

"That ees beeg job, I am afraid, Keeng."

"I want to know. You'll get yore share."

"That ees a hanging job, Keeng—and murderers do not talk."

"I'm not in the hangin' business, Pancho. All I want is the money."

"You theenk some of our boys—"

"Who else?" interrupted King Colt harshly. "And yuh might tell 'em that Jimmy Miller is on the warpath."

"The boys can tak' care of heem," said Pancho.

"All right—but no killin'. He'd make a good man for us, Pancho. You see what you can find out."

"Sure, I do my best, Keeng."

"One more thing—keep away from that singer. I've been watchin' yuh. Twice today you dogged her from the honkytonk to the bottom of the stairs, tryin' to talk with her. Let her alone, or I'll wring yore neck."

"*Por Dios,* all I do ees spik weeth her, Keeng."

"I know all about that. You tried to take her down to

Agua Frio. I should knock yore ears off for that. Keep away from her, and that's an order, Pancho."

"Well," sighed Pancho, "I suppose theese borning love of mine mus' cool off. She won't spik weeth me, and you say you knock off my ear, eef I spik to her. La Mariposa, the Botterfly. Life ees very unkind to Pancho Lopez—he might lose hees ears for spik to a bog."

"A butterfly ain't no bug."

"Biffore hees get weengs, he's a bog."

"Forget the bugs and do a little listenin'."

"Sure. Leesten!"

From the honkytonk stage came the voice of La Mariposa, singing an Old Spanish love song, accompanied by the wailing notes of a violin. Pancho drew a deep breath and expelled it slowly, his brown eyes pensive.

"What the hell are you thinkin' about?"

"I am jus' wondering w'at a man can hear weethout ears."

"You better take a half-hitch in yourself, or you'll find out."

HENRY AND JUDGE were awakened next morning by Tommy Roper, the stuttering cowboy, who operated the livery stable. Under stress, Tommy was quite unable to say anything. He spluttered and grimaced, while Henry held the door open, bobbing his head in sympathetic understanding. At last, Tommy managed to say:

"Oska-Oska-Oska-Oscar won't lul-lul-lul—"

"Is that so?" queried Henry. "He will not let who do what, Tommy?"

"I—I—I'll sh-sh-sh-show you."

Tommy crossed the room, opened a front window, which looked out on the main street of Tonto City, and pointed down the street toward the livery stable. Henry and Judge craned their respective necks. Down in front of the livery stable, seated on one end of the watering trough, was Oscar Johnson.

"It has to do with Julius Sorensen, I presume," said Henry.

"Uh-huh, uh-huh, uh-huh!" nodded Tommy. "He— he—"

"I know, Tommy. We shall be right down."

Tommy waited for them to dress, and they all went to the stable together. Oscar looked them over indifferently. Oscar had a sizable lump just over his right ear.

"Are you waiting for someone, Oscar?" asked Henry pleasantly.

"Ay am vaiting," replied Oscar defiantly.

"Waiting for Tommy's Swede?"

"He is not a Svede—he is Norvegian."

"I see. So you are looking for trouble, eh?"

"Ay am vaiting—not look-king."

"Of course, there is a difference. But why wait for Julius?"

"Va'al," explained Oscar, "Ay asked Yosephine if dis h'ar Norvegian vars in lofe with her, and she said for me to ask Yulius himself."

"So that is the reason. But do you have to sit here? Why not go into the stable and ask him?"

"Ay will not," declared Oscar. "Ay need room for fight-ing."

"Where did you get that knot on your head?" asked Judge. Oscar grinned foolishly and felt of the swelling.

"Va'al, Yudge, Ay vent over to de stable and Ay yalled, 'Ay can vip any Norvegian in de vorld.' Yust like dat.

Yulius climbed oop in de hayloft, and ven Ay storted up de ladder after him, Yudas Priest, he hit me on de head vit a hurse-collar, und knock me silly."

"That statement is easily corrected," said Judge. "He merely hit you on the head with a horse-collar. I suppose you went into the hayloft and beat the poor devil half to death."

"Ay did not, Yudge—he had anodder hurse-collar. So Ay vent out and sat here on de hurse-trough. Out ha'ar Ay can soak my sore head and vatch for him all de same time. His yob is to vater hurses."

"You are acting like a love-sick kid," declared Henry, "Get up from there and go back to the office where you belong. Even if Julius does love Josephine—what of it? A punch in the nose will not cause him to love her less, Oscar."

"If Ay hit him in de nose, he vill forget her for a vile, you bat you."

"All right. Now go back to the office and forget Julius."

"Ay am yust like elephant," declared Oscar, getting up. "Ay never forget. Ay vill go back to de office now, but Ay vill yump that Norvegian, yust as sure as ha'al, de first chance Ay get."

They watched the giant Swede striding back toward the office, and Judge said:

"Henry, if I were you, I'd kick that Swede all the way back to the JHC."

"Judge," replied Henry soberly, "the days of such a miracle ended when David sling-shotted Goliath. I see Johnny Harper coming down the street, and I feel that he is coming to see us."

THEY CROSSED THE street and joined John Harper, the prosecuting attorney, who was anxious to know about Jimmy Miller. Someone had told him they had seen Miller kick open the door of King Colt's private office but had not seen him come out again.

"Quite interesting," agreed Henry. "He drew a gun on Doctor Bogart and me in the office last night, when I quizzed him about that gauntlet; and apparently he went straight to the Tonto Saloon to see King Colt."

"I talked with King Colt last evening," said the lawyer. "It must have been after the Jimmy Miller incident. But Miller was not in the office. After I came out I met the party who told me he had seen Jimmy Miller kick open the office door, and he said that Miller did not come out."

"I wouldn't trust King Colt as far as I could throw a locomotive," declared Judge. "I believe that Jimmy Miller blamed King Colt for his father's death, and that—well, as you say, he kicked the door open."

"I also had a talk with Howard McRae and with Tom Page, superintendent of the Shoshone Chief," said the lawyer. "So few knew of that shipment of gold that I am inclined to believe some enemy of Ed Clay killed him, not realizing that the loot was so valuable, until they smashed the lock on that treasure-box."

"One guess seems to be as good as another," replied Henry.

"McRae is taking over the Circle M," said Harper. "Tuck Darnell will run the ranch. A very good man, too, I believe."

"A good single-handed drinker, and not too dumb regarding the value of two pair," said Judge. "In the meantime, who killed Hailstorm Miller and stole the ten thousand dollars?"

"Perhaps it was an accident," said the lawyer. "In that event, the money may have been on Millers person, and was burned."

"Doc Bogart doesn't think it was accidental, John. In fact, he declares that at the inquest he will prove it a murder."

"I think," remarked Henry, "we should find out what became of Jimmy Miller."

Jimmy Miller came back to Tonto City that evening, along with Jack Tallant, a handsome cowboy, addicted to black and silver. He was about six feet in height, lithe as a panther. He wore a black silk shirt, black pants, black, bat-wing chaps, glistening with huge silver conchas, and a black sombrero, surmounted with a silver-studded, black leather hatband. His scarlet neckerchief was the only bit of color in his raiment. Swung low on his thigh, encased in a black, silver-studded holster, was a Colt .45.

A fancy cowboy, indeed, but as hard as the desert hills, in spite of his youth. He knew he was not wanted in the Tonto Saloon, but he did not hesitate to enter, followed closely by Jimmy Miller. They went to the bar, ignoring everyone, and slaked their thirst.

Henry Harrison Conroy saw them ride into town, and followed them into the Tonto. Jimmy Miller saw Henry, nodded coldly and turned back to the bar. Pancho Lopez sauntered in from the honkytonk, saw the two men at the bar, and became very serious.

4

BUTTERFLY THAT SINGS

THE ORCHESTRA BEGAN playing softly in the honky-tonk, and the voice of La Mariposa filled the room. Men ceased gambling, ceased talking, until the song was finished. Then a terrific burst of applause, during which the girl came off the stage, and started for the stairs.

Jack Tallant shoved his way between tables, moving swiftly toward the foot of the stairs. Pancho Lopez stepped in front of him but he knocked Pancho back against a table, and met the singer. She stopped short, one hand on the stair railing, and looked at him.

She was clad in shimmering black, a black and red lace mantilla across one shoulder. A huge black comb studded with glistening stones, sparkled in her hair.

"Well?" she asked, puzzled.

"So you are La Mariposa, eh? The Butterfly. I heard you sing. Why didn't they name you El Sensontle, the Mocking-Bird? Butterflies do not sing."

"Thank you for your interest," said the girl soberly. "I must go to my room now."

"Don't hurry. My name's Jack Tallant."

"Jack Tallant?"

"Yeah," smiled Jack. "You've prob'ly heard that I'm a bad

man, and—well, yore boss don't want me to come here. They've told you that I'm dangerous, eh?"

"Dangerous to be with." She smiled.

"When do yuh sing again?" he asked.

"In about an hour. Please stand aside and let me go to my room. And if you will take my advice, Mr. Tallant—be careful."

"Careful?" laughed Tallant. "If you say so—sure. I want to live to hear you sing a lot of times."

"Thank you," she said, and he stepped aside to let her go up the stairs.

Henry had been watching it all. He saw Pancho recover his balance and stand against a table, scowling at Jack's back. In the doorway of the office stood King Colt, watching Jack Tallant and La Mariposa, while at the bar, Jimmy Miller stood with his right hand close to the butt of his holstered gun.

Jack Tallant turned back toward the bar, ignoring Pancho. He saw King Colt, and called to him: "Hyah King."

The big owner of the Tonto came forward and met Jack. "You don't show much sense, Tallant," he growled. "I beat hell out of a gambler today for botherin' that girl."

"Good!" exclaimed Jack. "I don't blame yuh, King."

"You don't seem to know what I'm talkin' about."

Jack's eyes narrow, as he looked at the big man. "I know what yo're talkin' about," he said coldly. "Mebbe yuh can beat up a gambler, but yuh can't beat me, King Colt. You've got a gun on yuh and so have I. Go ahead and fill yore hand."

Pancho Lopez, close behind Jack, stepped hastily aside,

getting out of the line of fire. A man, drinking at a table, got up quickly and forgot to take his glass along. Neither man had a hand near his gun. Jack's hands were above his waist, the fingers of his right hand were scratching the back of his left. King's right hand was above his paunchy waist, a thumb hooked between his vest-buttons.

For a space of possibly ten second they watched each other's eyes. Slowly a grin crossed the big face of King Colt, and he relaxed.

"Only damn fools commit suicide," he said slowly.

"Scared, eh?"

"Oh, don't say that, Jack. Why not come back to the office and talk things over with me."

Jack Tallant laughed shortly. "Yeah, that would be fine. King Colt, I don't trust you nor yore gang."

King Colt looked sharply at Jimmy Miller and said to Jack: "You ain't teamed up with Miller, have yuh?"

"Jimmy's lookin' for the man who killed his father."

King Colt smiled thoughtfully. "I heard that the sheriff was after him—and that sheriff is settin' right there, watchin' all of us. You better come back into my office. You young fool, do yuh think we'd harm yuh, with the sheriff lookin' on?"

"All right, but yuh better talk straight and fast, King."

AS KING COLT closed the door behind them Jimmy Miller turned from the bar and went over to Henry, who nodded and spoke pleasantly. Jimmy sat down across the table from Henry.

"Are you lookin' for me, Sheriff?" he asked quietly.

"The inquest will be held in the morning, Jimmy," he

replied. "Until that jury decides—no, I am not looking for you."

"I went to Tallant's ranch last night," said Jimmy. "But first I went home and made another search for that money. I don't believe it was cached; I believe Dad had it in his pocket."

"I am afraid he did, Jimmy. Are you going to stay with Tallant?"

"It's as good as any place," replied Jimmy. "Jack said he'd help me find the man who killed my father."

"I see. You will be at the inquest tomorrow?"

"What do you think? Should I be there?"

"I should be the last one to advise against it, Jimmy."

"I reckon I understand yuh, Sheriff—and thanks."

"If I should want you," said Henry quietly, "it would be impossible for me to go across the Border into Mexico."

Jimmy leaned across the table, speaking in a half-whisper: "Sheriff, I didn't rob that stage—I swear it to you. Even if I have to stay in Mexico, I won't forget yuh—and when I find that certain man, I'll bring yuh his ears."

"My goodness!" exclaimed Henry. "I—I don't believe I would care for them, Jimmy; but I wish you success."

Henry got up and walked out of the saloon, while Jimmy waited for Jack Tallant, who was facing King Colt in the back room.

"I reckon yore father has told yuh about me," said King.

"Yeah, about you makin' him a cripple for life."

"I'm sorry about that bullet, Jack."

"Yeah, I know; sorry it wasn't higher."

"We'll pass that," said King. "Yuh know, I kinda like you,

Jack, and I'd like to be friends with yuh. I had a son—once. He'd be about yore age. Mebbe he'd be like you, I dunno."

"I don't want yore friendship," replied Jack. "In fact, I don't believe yuh. You may think yo're runnin' this valley, but yo're not runnin' me. Only a few days ago yuh passed the word to yore gunmen that I was in yore way. And now yuh offer friendship."

"You make it kinda hard for me, Jack," sighed the big man. "I'm runnin' things—kinda. I won't let anybody get in my way. I offer yuh my friendship and yuh laugh at me. Hell, I didn't need to offer yuh a chance to stay alive. Mebbe I'm gettin' soft, I dunno."

"So I'm in yore way, am I?" said Jack. "All right, I'm goin' to stay in yore way. I think I read yore signs tonight, didn't I?"

"My signs? I dunno what yuh mean, Jack."

"Don't yuh? I'll tell yuh then."

Jack sagged forward, drawing his gun swiftly, its muzzle centering on the big body of the man behind the table. Slowly he got to his feet, the unwavering gun in his hand.

"When I came in here with yuh, King," he said, "I seen yuh flash a signal to Pancho Lopez. Anyway, it looked like a signal to me. Right now, I'm bettin' that some of yore men are at the hitch-rack. Don't even move yore head—I'm goin' through the window."

Swiftly he tore the curtain aside, opened the window and stepped over the sill.

"Adios, mofeta," he called.

FOR SEVERAL MOMENTS King Colt sat perfectly still, chewing on his cigar. Then he turned, closed the window and fixed the curtain.

"*Mofeta*, eh?" he muttered. "Skunk, eh? Well, tomorrow is another day."

He turned down the lamp and walked into the saloon, where Pancho Lopez met him.

"Sometheeng ees wrong?" asked Pancho. "He ees not coming out?"

"He ain't comin' out," replied King.

"*Por Dios!* You—you keel him, Keeng?"

"Not unless he died laughin'. He read the signs and went through the window. Tell the boys to come in and have a drink on the house. Where is Jimmy Miller? Did he go with the sheriff?"

"No, the sheriff go alone. In leetle while Jimmy Meeler go out."

"It's all right, Pancho," said King Colt. As Pancho turned away King Colt stopped him.

"Did you hear what Jack Tallant said to La Mariposa?" he asked.

"Me? I am too damn mad to leesten."

"Jealous, eh?"

"No man like to be poosh around biffore the girl he lofe."

"You forget that love idea, Pancho. I won't stand for it, and I've warned yuh."

Pancho turned and went slowly toward the front doorway. King scowled after him, but turned his head toward the stairs, where La Mariposa was slowly descending. King smiled and moved over to her.

"Yuh shore look awful nice tonight."

"Thank you, Mr. Colt."

"You like to sing here?"

"Yes, I enjoy it—most of it."

"Most of it? Oh, yeah! Pancho's been botherin' yuh, eh?"

"Pancho is rather persistent, Mr. Colt. What sort of a place does he own in Agua Frio?"

"Well, it ain't—wait a minute! Has he tried to get yuh to go to Agua Frio?"

"Well, yes, he—that is, he wanted me to consider it. He said he could pay me more than I get here. But I wouldn't consider it."

"Uh-huh—I see. No, I wouldn't go to Agua Frio, if I was you. They're a bad bunch down there. Border men ain't so nice, especially on the other side of the Border. I'll speak to Pancho."

La Mariposa went on to the honkytonk. After a while Pancho came back sauntering from table to table. He came to King Colt, who motioned him back to the office. Glowering a little, Pancho obeyed. The instant the door closed after them King Colt whirled and shoved the muzzle of a heavy six-shooter into the midriff of the Mexican gambler.

"Take that gun out of yore sleeve, Pancho!" snapped King. Pancho started to protest, but finally removed the short-barrel, sleeve-gun and placed it on the desk. King Colt relaxed and holstered his own gun.

"I told yuh to keep away from La Mariposa," said King. "I found out that you've tried to get her to go to Agua Frio."

Pancho's eyes narrowed. "W'y you so concern 'bout thees girl?" he asked coldly.

"If yuh want to know—I like her myself."

"But you are too old for her, Keeng."

"I'm not old, damn yuh!"

"Well, maybe you are not so old, but you are not spreeng-cheeken."

"All right. But from now on, it's hands off that girl, Pancho. Yuh better take that suicide gun and throw it in the brush. The next time I see yuh feelin' for a gun in yore sleeve, I'll tie a string on the trigger and make yuh swaller the whole damn works. And then I'll yank the string. I hope yuh know what I'm talkin' about."

"Sure," said Pancho. "I get me sharp pain enside."

5

THE KING AND THE BUTTERFLY

THE DOUBLE INQUEST drew such a big crowd to Tonto City that they were obliged to use the dance hall, where a sufficient number of chairs were placed to seat about half of the audience. Several men from the Shoshone Chief Mine, including Tom Page, the superintendent, were there. King Colt and Pancho Lopez secured front seats. Jack Tallant was there, watching, listening, but talking to no one.

A jury of six was quickly drawn. No one had witnessed either murder, so there was no direct evidence. The inquest over Hailstorm Miller came first. Doctor Bogart, the coroner, testified on the condition of the body, and Howard McRae, the banker, giving evidence in regard to the mortgage, said that he had been informed that Miller had collected the ten thousand dollars.

"In my opinion Hailstorm Miller was murdered," stated the coroner. "His skull had been smashed and there were unburned hairs in the brain. Moreover, there was no evidence of smoke in the lungs. My opinion is that Miller was killed by a vicious blow on the head, and later burned in the stable. The fire was very likely of incendiary origin."

The jury immediately brought in the usual verdict of death at the hands of a party or parties unknown.

Thunder and Lightning Mendoza wanted to testify as
to how they had discovered the bodies, but Doctor Bogart
deleted that part. In the inquest of Ed Clay, the coroner
was also chief witness. Tom Page said that he had taken
six hundred and fifty ounces of raw gold to the bank, from
where it was loaded on the stage. He saw the money put
into the treasure-box and locked tight.

"When did you decide to ship that money by stage?"
asked Henry.

"The night before," replied the mining man. "I saw Mr.
McRae on the street, and told him I would bring in a shipment for the morning stage."

"Who else knew of this shipment?"

"My assayer. He didn't want to keep that much in the
safe, but we only made the decision late that afternoon. He
is an honest old man, with no bad habits and few acquain-
tances. You can count him out, Sheriff."

Henry nodded. "Did anyone hear you tell Mr, McRae?"

"We were alone, when I told him."

They called Steve McRae, the banker's son, to the stand.
Steve was a blond-haired, colorless sort of young man, who
had often admitted that he did not like to work in a bank.

"You knew about this shipment of gold, Steve?" queried
Henry.

"Certainly," replied the witness. "My father came home
for supper that night and told me we'd have to get to the
bank a little earlier, because of that shipment of gold. It
takes a little time to seal up the stuff properly."

"You were at the bank when the stage left town, I
presume?"

"Yes, I was at the bank at that time, sir."

*Frijole took care of the
rope-work; Oscar was
to provide the mayhem*

"Thank you, Steve. That is all."

They called Harry Levis to the stand, handed him the gauntlet, and he testified that it was the gauntlet he had found tucked under the seat cushion of the stage, when he drove the vehicle back to Tonto City. Henry gave the gauntlet to the jury for examination.

"Jimmy Miller," explained Henry, "admitted that it was his gauntlet. He said he had not seen it or worn it for weeks."

After a whispered consultation of several moments, the foreman of the jury got to his feet and said:

"It seems to us that the natural thing for a feller to do would be to tuck a glove under the cushion. We ask that the sheriff arrest and hold Jimmy Miller on suspicion of murderin' Ed Clay and stealin' that gold from the stage."

John Harper, the prosecutor, grimaced sourly, but said nothing.

"That is a mighty serious charge, gentlemen," said Henry. "That gauntlet may have been left there to incriminate

Jimmy Miller; and it may be that Jimmy Miller can prove where he was at that time."

"The gauntlet is good enough for us," replied Tuck Darnell, who was acting as foreman. "Let him prove where he was at that time."

Henry nodded grimly and sat down.

Someone in the back of the room said:

"There's a job for yuh, *nariz rojo*."

"My nose," retorted Henry, "is habitually red because I blush for the manners of such as you, my friend."

The crowd roared with laughter as they filed outside.

Harper came to Henry and they discussed Jimmy Miller. From where they stood they could look through a window into the main street. They saw Jack Tallant mounting his horse at a hitch-rack, and saw him ride away.

"Do you know where to find Jimmy Miller?" asked the lawyer.

"An hour from now, I believe he will be in Agua Frio, John."

"Jack Tallant carries the verdict, eh?"

"I hope."

"So do I," sighed the lawyer. "I should hate to chance a conviction on such evidence. A jury, my dear Henry, does queer things."

"Yes, sir, I believe you are right," nodded Henry thoughtfully. "The more I see of juries, the more I wonder why justice doesn't take off that blindfold and look at what she has done."

LA MARIPOSA WAS becoming more and more of an enigma to King Colt. She never spoke to him, unless he spoke first, never seemed to pay any attention to the life about her, and did not mix with the rest of the honkytonk girls. King Colt called one of these into the office and questioned her. She was a hard-eyed, bleached blonde, who had been in Tonto City a long time.

"She's a queer one, King," admitted the blonde. "She sings her songs, and she sure brings a lot of men to this place, but she don't have a thing to do with anybody."

"Stuck up?" queried King.

"No, she ain't; it's just her way. She's a damn nice kid, and she don't fit into this place. Men are crazy about her, but she don't pay any attention to 'em. And her voice makes it pretty bad for the rest of us. I used to think I could sing, too."

King Colt mulled over this scanty information. It was true, La Mariposa did not belong in a honkytonk. And with her singing ability, he wondered why she ever came to Tonto City, to work for twenty-five dollars a week and a place to sleep.

Her sleeping quarters were directly above his office, and she spent much of her time in her room. Occasionally she received mail, but the letters were addressed to La Mariposa, which King Colt knew, of course, was not her name.

When King Colt had wondered long enough about anything, he usually investigated. At nine o'clock at night, La Mariposa sang a song, together with at least one encore. He watched her come down the stairs just before nine that evening, and went directly to her room, using a passkey. There were two windows to the room, covered with curtains.

King lighted a lamp and looked around. For lack of a closet, her clothes hung on nails driven into the wooden walls. An old dresser intrigued him, so he carried the lamp over there and started to open a drawer. Suddenly his hand jerked back.

On the dresser, propped against the mirror, was a photograph. Staring at it in amazement, he slowly reached out and picked it up. The face of a gray-haired woman smiled out at him. King Colt's hands trembled as he held the picture to the light. From far away he could hear the voice of La Mariposa, singing. Slowly he replaced the picture, wiped his brow and started toward the door. But he stopped and came back.

He yanked open a dresser drawer and searched swiftly. He found several letters, all postmarked from Chicago, addressed to La Mariposa. Feverishly he opened one of them and began reading the small, careful script, his heavy lips moving as he spelled out the words.

With a blunt pencil he noted down the address in the letter, replaced everything, and was about to extinguish the lamp when a handful of pebbles rattled against the window. He turned the lamp low and went over to the window and carefully opened it. A voice from below said quietly:

"Leesten, *señorita;* I mus' speak weeth you. I 'ave long ladder, and eef you weel let me—it ees important. Eef it ees all right, blow out the lamp."

King Colt blew out the lamp and stepped back to the window. He heard the thump of the ladder as Pancho Lopez placed it against the wall. La Mariposa was singing her encore. The ladder-rungs creaked, and then in the darkness King Colt could see Pancho's head just below the window.

"*Señorita,*" panted the Mexican, "you are ver' sweet to

let me talk weeth you. Because of this damn Keeng Colt I never have chance to tell you that you are the mos' beautiful—"

Whap! King Colt estimated the distance perfectly, and his huge, right fist struck the amorous gambler square in the face. The long ladder swayed away from the wall, clattered back and teetered sideways. There was the sudden thud of a body striking the ground, followed by the crash of the ladder.

King Colt closed the window, locked the door behind him and went down the stairs. He had barely reached the bottom when La Mariposa, flushed from her reception, hurried past him, up to her room. He sauntered around the gambling tables for a while before going to his office. There he locked the door and sat down to light a fresh cigar.

He drew out the address he had penciled and stared at it, shaking his huge head. "Mrs. Alice McLean," he muttered aloud. "My wife." And La Mariposa's name, he knew now, was June McLean. She was his own child, singing here in the honkytonk, and she could not know that she was working for her own father.

He had recognized the photograph immediately. And from the letter he had learned the truth about La Mariposa; she was working here to support her mother. He had learned, too, that Alice McLean, his wife, was ill, in desperate need of five thousand dollars for some sort of operation.

Someone knocked on the door. King Colt jerked around and quickly unlocked it. It was Joe Hake, one of his cowboys.

"What do yuh want?" King Colt demanded.

"Well, I'll tell yuh, King. I tied my horse to that old

corral fence out back a little while ago, and I found Pancho
Lopez tryin' to crawl under the lower rail. Said he was tryin'
to find a place to sleep. He acted so damn queer that I lit
a match and looked at him. Man, he'd been hit square in
the nose and knocked silly. I asked him what happened to
him, and he mumbled somethin' about you keepin' a mule
upstairs. It didn't make sense."

"Where did he go?" asked King Colt soberly.

"I dunno. Last I seen, he was crossin' the street toward
the hotel, and he was limpin' kinda bad."

King smoked thoughtfully for several moments.

"Queer idea he had—about you keepin' a mule upstairs,"
remarked Hake.

"Mexicans get queer ideas," said King. "Forget it, Hake."

6

THE TIPPLING ROOSTER

HENRY AND JUDGE rode down to the Tallant ranch, ostensibly to look for Jimmy Miller, but knowing well that he would not be there. From his home-made wheelchair on the rickety porch of the ranch house, Gila Jim Tallant scowled at them. Gila Jim hated the law and so now he sneered at Henry:

"Well, what's the idea of you two damn fools comin' down here?" he asked.

"Oh, we are just looking around," Henry answered.

"Lookin' around for Jimmy Miller, eh? Well, damn yuh, he's in Mexico."

"It seems to me," remarked Judge, "that nature did not put rattles on all the rattlers, Henry."

"Meanin' me, eh?" snarled the cripple. "All right. I don't know why I should chuck you two under the chins and lie about my feelin's toward yuh. At least, I'm honest. Of all the damn-fool officers of the law I've ever seen, yo're the worst. You," pointing at Henry, "you, red-nosed, fat-headed specimen! Sheriff! Hell!"

"Sorry," murmured Henry.

"Sorry? You? Wild Horse Valley should be the one that's sorry."

"Oh, they are," assured Henry. "But it is their own fault, Mr. Tallant."

"Well, I reckon that's true, too. So yo're lookin' for Jimmy Miller, are yuh? Want him for robbin' that stage and killin' the driver. Why don'tcha find the guilty parties? Go find the man who killed Jimmy's father and stole that ten thousand dollars. Fine sheriff you are!"

"Well, have you any ideas on the subject?" asked Henry quietly.

"Me? Settin' here in a wheelchair? How would I know anythin'?"

"Well, you might have an idea on the subject," said Judge.

"Yeah, I might, at that. Why don'tcha talk with King Colt? If anybody in this valley knows who pulled them jobs, he does."

Henry squinted thoughtfully at Gila Jim Tallant. "Just what do you know about King Colt?" he asked.

"What do I—not a damn thing! How would I know anythin'?"

"Then how would you know that King Colt might know something?"

Gila Jim shut his thin lips tightly, and his eyes narrowed as he looked off across the heat-hazed hills. "I know when to quit talkin'," he said. "Forget King Colt."

"You knew King Colt, before either of you came here," said Henry.

"Did I?" Gila Jim laughed shortly. "You know more'n I do, I reckon. Jack tells me about him. He's a bad boy."

"Who—Jack?" asked Judge.

Gila Jim snapped back: "No! I'm talkin' about King Colt."

"As a matter of fact," said Henry, "I have never spoken to Jack about the rumors that he is sending horses and cattle into Mexico—horses which he has not paid for. You might caution him, Mr. Tallant. Jack is a nice boy, and I would hate to see him jailed as a rustler."

"So that's it, eh?" said Gila Jim. "Accusin' an innocent boy! That's like you. Yuh hear a lie and yuh believe it. Jack's an honest boy, and—who started a thing like that?"

"Like you," smiled Henry, "I know when to stop talking."

"Oh, yuh do, eh? Well, you've got all out of me that yo're goin' to get, Yuh can shut the gate as yuh go out—and if yuh hear any more lies about Jack, yuh can believe 'em or not—we don't give a damn. Good afternoon to both of yuh."

"I told you that all the information you could get from that old devil, you could put on the sharp end of a needle," said Judge as they rode back toward the JHC. "Torturing my old, rheumatic legs by forcing me to ride a horse down here in all this heat."

"We learned something, sir," replied Henry. "Gila Jim Tallant has been here several years, while King Colt has only been here about a year. I learned that Gila Jim and King Colt knew each other previous to their meeting in the Tonto Saloon a few days ago. I also learned that Gila Jim hates King Colt."

"He also hates us," added Judge.

"True, but only on general principles, sir. We are the law."

"Sometimes I wonder, Henry. The *Clarion* doesn't think so."

"That editor was suckled by a rattler and raised on

skunk-cabbage," declared Henry. "In other words, I do not like him one little bit, Judge."

"I tremble at thought of the castigation we shall receive in the next issue," said Judge. "His vials of wrath must be overflowing by this time. However, the man has a certain flair for words. In the last issue he intimates that our actions keep the people so amused that they almost forget their misery. He said that the voters, most of whom must have been color-blind, voted for you, in spite of the blob—and I love that word—of red, which shines in the center of your moon-like countenance. He cites the fact that in all signals red is the warning sign."

"Must you recite word for word, sir?" demanded Henry. "Do you forget the fact that I have read all his editorials? Or is it your idea of humor to rub the salt of criticism deeper into my wounds? I assure you, Judge, I have winced so often that some believe I have a touch of St. Vitus Dance. However, no matter, sir; we must hew our own pathway."

"But with added dignity and decorum, sir."

"I believe," said Henry, "that we will go to the JHC, before returning to Tonto City."

Judge groaned, for that it would require about two more miles of riding. "That last batch of prune whisky was damnable," he remarked a moment later.

"I realize that," agreed Henry, "but a genius like Frijole Bill Cullison must have a certain latitude. The man is an experimenter. He is trying to create a super-whisky—and he nearly had it."

"He nearly had something," agreed Judge. "That last batch boiled at ninety in the shade. We spilled a bit on the wicker covering of that demijohn, and it burned the wicker so badly that it all fell off."

THEY RODE IN at the JHC and tied their horses at the front porch. Frijole, Thunder and Lightning were asleep in the patio. Near them was a gallon jug, the cork lying on the flag-stones.

Frijole Bill Cullison, the little cook of the JHC, opened one eye and looked at them. Frijole was past sixty, wizened, thin-faced, and with a mustache that belonged on a giant.

"Hyah, Law," he said sleepily. "Set down and have a snort. Where's that danged jug? Oh, there it is. Help yourself. How are yuh, Judge?"

Henry sniffed at the jug, shook it violently and put it down.

"The jug is empty," he said.

"That danged stuff evaporates awful fast," declared Frijole. "I dunno what's in it that makes it thataway. Can't hardly keep it corked. By golly, yuh should have seen William Shakespeare on that last batch of mash! Whooee-e-e-e! Why, that danged rooster—"

"Wait a minute," begged Judge. "I have no liking for lies, Frijole."

"Lies? Oh, Judge, you hurt me. But you never believed in Shakespeare."

"I know you have a rooster by that name," replied Judge soberly, "but I never have believed any of the lies you have told about him."

"What happened to Bill Shakespeare, when he ate the mash?" asked Henry.

"Well, sir, that was shore a feat. I dumped that mash out yesterday and Ol' Bill tuck right to it. I warned him to go easy, but he jist cocked one eye at me as much as to say, 'Who's eatin' this mash?'

"Well, I'm kinda gittin' ahead of m' story. About a week ago Bill fell hard for a female road-runner. Since then he ain't given a hen one look. Every mornin' early he's out in the hills, keepin' a date with that speckled road-runnin' vampire. Well, it wasn't none of my business if Bill wants to pick hisself a pardner, and mebbe the hens was kinda relieved, 'cause when Bill got full of mash he got astigmatism. 'S a fact. He'd whip hell out of a hen as quick as he would a rooster.

"Well, I kinda felt sorry for Bill Shakespeare, runnin' around in the hills, 'cause of lions, wildcats, coyotes and once in a while we see a lobo. All them varmints are partial to chicken, Anyway, yesterday afternoon I'm out along the cañon, seven, eight miles from here, and what do I see but Ol' Shakespeare and his light-o'-love pickin' a fight with a rattler out there in a cactus patch.

"Well, it wasn't none of my business. Anyway, Bill has handled a lot of rattlers bigger 'n this'n; so I didn't worry. But I'm halfway home, with the sun gone down, when I heard a pack of coyotes runnin' on a track, 'way out yonder. Suddenlike it strikes me that they're after Bill Shakespeare.

" 'Well,' I says to myself, 'Goodbye, Bill; take care of yourself,' and I comes on home. He wasn't in the hen house that night, 'cause I took a look. This mornin' I kinda felt bad about it. Ol' Bill's almost human, and he's shore good company, even if he will fight yuh when he's drunk.

"I got up this mornin', started a fire, and went out back to get some wood, and there's Bill Shakespeare, settin' on the back porch, shy a few feathers, but still hale and hearty and layin' beside him was three coyote ears, all off different coyotes. That old son-of-a-rooster had whipped that pack of coyotes and brought back three scalps."

"I do not believe a word of it, sir," declared Judge.

"But what became of the female road-runner?" asked Henry.

"Well, sir, I dunno," sighed Frijole, "but I'm scared she's a goner. Tell yuh what makes me think so. Old Bill Shakespeare has allus been kinda choosy of his drinks. I watched him through the winder for quite a spell, and he seemed to be workin' up a mad about somethin'. Then he kicked them three ears off the porch, jumped up and down on 'em for a spell, and finally went down to the stable. I went down there, peeked inside, and there's Old Bill, drinkin' some old horse-liniment out of a cup, where it's been since I put some into that last batch of prune whisky to flavor it. Yessir, he was so despondent that he was willin' to drink horse-liniment. I reckon Ol' Bill's heart is busted."

"Frijole," said Judge, "of all the damn liars on earth, you take the first prize."

"I can prove every word of it, Judge," declared Frijole.

"How can you prove such a thing, sir?"

"Well, there's old Bill, settin' on the corral fence, all tired out, and if yuh look in that old horse-liniment cup you'll find it empty."

"Behold the walrus-tooth," quoted Judge soberly.

"What didja say?" asked Frijole.

"Nothing."

"I'VE SAVED A jug of my latest manufacture, Henry," said Frijole. "I think she's jist about the best I ever made, too.

She's about twenty hours old now, as tawny as a lion's eye. I'm right proud of her."

"Personally," replied Henry, "I am getting afraid of your distillations. As long as you stuck to prunes, it was excellent, but your experiments are dangerous. Prunes, corn, rice, raisins, apples, potatoes and horse-liniment in varying quantities, soured to the bursting point."

"The last batch had a little sody, too," added Frijole.

"Did that help it any?" asked Judge.

"Jist sort of a safety-valve," replied Frijole. "It blowed out my upper plate twice, before I got smarted-up and went around with m' mouth open, until the power died down."

"And you ask us to drink that dynamite?" asked Judge.

"It's all right if yuh don't try to confine it, Judge. Man, yuh can jist hear it crackle when yuh pour it, and she's shore aromatic. As a sedative, as the doctors say, she can't be beat."

"We will be glad to take a jug with us," said Henry. "In these days of storm and strife, a sedative might help us out, Frijole."

"Storm and strife? Oh, yuh mean two dead men? Well, yeah, that does kinda give yuh somethin' to ponder about. Oscar was out this mornin'. He took a couple quarts back with him. What's wrong with that knot-headed Swede, anyway? Him and Josephine had a fight? I noticed a lump on his head."

"Julius smacked him with a horse-collar," said Judge.

"Oh, that Norwegian stable-hand, eh? Oscar did mention him. Said somethin' about him and Julius figurin' on a duel—the winner to get the gal. Anvils at sixty yards, or somethin' like that."

"The law," declared Judge, "will not countenance duels."

"Nor murders," chuckled Frijole. "But we still have 'em, Judge."

"The law," sighed Henry, "doesn't seem to have much choice in the matter. Murder should be licensed. Then we could refuse a license to anyone—unless they were going to kill one of our enemies. I do not favor dueling, but I believe that the one Oscar contemplates might be worth seeing. Or we might make it a contest of skill."

"What sort of skill?" asked Judge.

"See who could throw the most ringers on each other with horse-collars. It has possibilities. Frijole, if you can confine that liquid dynamite in a jug, we will be going back to town."

"Well, I'll tell yuh what," said Frijole. "I'll fasten the cork with rubber bands. Then if she wants to *squee* a little on the way in, she can do it instead of bustin' somethin'."

"By the gods of my fathers," sighed Judge. "To think that a Van Treece would sink so low as to quaff willingly a liquor so wild and so vile that it requires a rubber safety-valve to cry *Squee,* crackles in the pouring, and blows out upper plates."

"The Conroys, sir," declared Henry loftily, "had their place in the sun, until I came along. I—I suppose I can not stand the heat. When my beloved uncle died here in Tonto City, I became the last of our race. In me, Judge, you see the last of the Conroy strain."

"It has been quite a strain," said Judge.

"Thank you very much, sir. Your sympathetic understanding touches me. Some day, when conditions are right, I shall tell you about my uncle, Horace Greeley Conroy. There was a *man*."

"So the name implies, Henry. You carry the jug, please; I am just a bit suspicious of that *squee*. I understand that rubber deteriorates quickly in this climate. Frijole, I give you good afternoon, sir."

"I'll take it, Judge. If yuh don't mind settin' in a chair to take yore liquor—you'll find it safer. I tried to jump that seven-foot corral fence. My intentions was good, but I reckon my agility busted several years ago. I'll give yore regards to Bill Shakespeare, when he wakes up. He'll be sorry to have missed yuh both. *Adios amigos.*"

IT WAS LATE that evening when Pancho Lopez rode away from Agua Frio and came across the desolate border. At times he would meet the Border Patrol along the road, but this evening they were not in evidence. A mile from the border he turned to the left, following an old dirt road, deeply rutted, but showing signs of little travel. There was enough moon to show objects distinctly, and he drew rein near a tumble-down huddle of small buildings. There was only a tiny light showing in one of them. Pancho went carefully to the front of an old stable and he entered, looking back at the tiny lighted window. After pawing around in the dark for a few moments, he lighted a match.

Two old, sway-backed gray mules twitched inquisitive ears at him from their rough stalls. Hanging on pegs were two well-worn harnesses, which Pancho quickly examined. Then he looked all around the stable. Swearing softly in Spanish, he went out of the stable and cautiously approached the little shack. He peered in.

Evidently satisfied with what he saw, he went around to the door and knocked loudly. After a few moments an old Mexican woman came to the doorway, opening it only a few inches. Pancho spoke to her in their native tongue.

"Where is Juan?" he asked her.

"Juan?" she replied. *"Madre de Dios!* The officers took him away this evening. For what, I do not know—nor did he understand. They have taken him to Tonto City, and I am alone, *señor."*

"Por Dios!" muttered Pancho. Then: *"Gracias, madre. Buenas noches."*

Pancho hurried back to his horse, returned to the main road, and headed for Tonto City. Something had certainly gone wrong. The arrest of Juan, a simple *maguey*-cutter, caused him to curse and to ride faster than usual.

He tied his horse behind the Tonto Saloon and entered by the rear door. Business was good, it seemed, but Pancho was not interested in gambling and drinking. He started toward King Colt's office door, but changed his mind and sauntered toward the bar. Sitting at one of the tables, smoking and apparently uninterested in their surroundings, were Henderson and Manley, two of the Border Patrol.

They nodded indifferently to Pancho, who smiled amiably. Pancho believed in being pleasant to the Border Patrol. A passing waiter whispered, "King wants to see yuh," and went on with his tray of glasses. La Mariposa began singing, and when the two officers turned to listen, Pancho went to the office.

King Colt was sitting behind his desk, a quart of whisky and a glass at his elbow, the room blue with cigar smoke. He looked at Pancho, grunted softly and fanned the smoke away from his eyes.

"W'at ees wrong?" asked Pancho quietly.

"That's what I'm waitin' for you to tell," replied King Colt. "Them Border officers brought Old Juan in this evenin' and put him in the jail. Now what do you know?"

"The stuff ees not there," replied Pancho angrily. "I search everywhere, but those damn sweat-pad are gone. Juan's woman, she says the officer tak' Juan to jail. That ees all."

"Them sweat-pads are gone?" rasped King Colt. "Yuh mean to set there and tell me they got 'em?"

Pancho shrugged his shoulders helplessly. *"Quien sabe? Eef not, w'y ees Juan een the jail."*

"My God!" exclaimed King Colt. "That stuff was worth—how much?"

"All of eet, Keeng. We breeng everytheeng."

"Five thousand dollars worth? Pancho." King Colt leaned across his desk, his big jaw clenched for a moment. "Pancho, how in hell *could they* know? Juan didn't even know. Nobody knew—except me and you."

"That ees true, Keeng. Nobody but me and you. And this ees only the second time we have had them sweat-pads with the stuff. Once, eet ees fine. Twice—they get heem. Why? How? Don't look at me like that! You theenk I throw away my own money?"

"Somebody in Agua Frio knew," declared King Colt.

"Por Dios, no!"

King Colt scowled heavily, trying to puzzle out who could have known how the contraband drugs were brought across the Border. Suddenly he struck the desk-top with a huge fist.

"Gila Jim Tallant!" he grunted. "He's the one, Pancho. In some way he figured it out, damn him!"

"But, no," said Pancho. "He would take the stuff heem-self. He would not tell the officer."

"He couldn't sell the stuff. All he wants to do is break me. We've lost a fortune, but them officers ain't got a thing on us. Don't say a word. Leave it to me, and I'll find out things."

7

OSCAR BY NIGHT

OVER AT THE sheriff's office, Jim Henderson, chief of that district, sat down with Henry and Judge. "We bungled the whole deal," sighed the big Border Patrolman. "We thought that this old Mexican knew about the thing and that we could make him implicate the men behind him. It was all very simple. Old Juan drives his team of mules across the Border in the mornin', cuts his load of *maguey* and hauls it to that little tequila distillery outside Agua Frio.

"While he is eatin' his meal at the distillery, somebody goes into the stable, removes the stuffin' from his sweat-pads, and fills it up with drugs, all tied up in oiled silk. Then the old man drives home, puts up his team of mules, and later somebody removes the drugs, puts back the paddin'— and get ready for another cargo."

"Old Juan was merely a cat's-paw," nodded Henry.

"That's right. You may as well turn him loose, and we'll take him home on our way back. He's scared white, 'cause he don't know a thing about it. We should have located the stuff and waited for someone to try and get it. Now they won't try that scheme again."

"I can understand all that part of it," said Judge, "but I do not understand how you gentlemen ever figured out that drugs were coming across, packed inside the sweat-pads on a pair of wornout mules."

Henderson smiled slowly and got to his feet. "Judge," he replied, "we listen to the little birdies."

Henry smiled and remarked, "It is fairly evident that the little birdie only sang part of the song."

"Maybe," replied Henderson, "the little birdie only *knew* part of the song, Henry. But, even a half-song is better than none."

THE NEXT EVENING Oscar Johnson, wearing a We Mourn Our Loss expression in his round, blue eyes, was sitting on the office cot, trying to coax a tune out of a leaky accordion, when Frijole Bill Cullison came in. Frijole was just inebriated enough to be sympathetic, and Oscar was inebriated enough to accept sympathy.

"Yo're plumb blue to the gills, feller," remarked Frijole. "Somethin' is eatin' of yore heart."

"Yah, su-ure," agreed Oscar sadly. "Ay am hort-sick, su-ure."

"Josephine?" queried Frijole.

"Yah, su-ure—Yosephine. She say she is going to Scorpion Bend vit Yulius Swensen to a dance tonight."

"Is that right? Is there a dance up there? Yeah? Man, I shore crave to shake a laig. I'm right nimble. Mebbe I'll decide to take it in."

"Ve both go," suggested Oscar. "Ay am nimple, too, you bat you."

"Good! Have yuh got any of my home-made whisky around here?"

"Ve have vorse dan two quarts. Ay vill get it. Und den

ve vill go to a dance, eh, Free-holey. Ay yust vant von poke at Yulius."

"Have one on me," suggested Frijole, "and bring a couple cups."

Frijole shuddered over his own concoction, and after each of them had drunk two cupfuls apiece, Frijole suggested that Oscar saddle his horse, while he still knew which was the front end of the animal. Oscar managed to saddle the steed, and as they were mounting, Julius drove past in a horse and buggy from the livery stable. He tied to a hitch-rack in front of the hotel and entered the building.

"Ay am goin' dere and knock ha'al out of him," declared Oscar. "He is calling for Yosephine, and Ay von't stand for it, Free-holey."

"Hook up yore cinch, feller," advised Frijole. "You start a fight in the hotel, and you'll get hell. Everybody in the place will land on yuh. I've got a better scheme. We'll ride out by the old adobe, and when they come along, I'll rope the horse, stop the ve-hickle, and you can show Josephine what a real lover can do with his fists."

"By Yudas, you are smort man, Free-holey!" exclaimed Oscar. "Come on."

They galloped out of town in the darkness, and drew up at an old adobe about a half-mile from town. Oscar dismounted and removed his coat, while Frijole, an expert with a rope, flung out his loop and prepared for a cast in the dark.

"Ay can hear de boggy coming, Free-holey," called Oscar. "You stop 'em, and Ay vill do de rest."

"I ain't missed a cast in forty years," declared Frijole.

"Don'tcha worry about me, feller—just spit on yore hands and go to work."

They could hear the rattle of buggy-wheels, the *thud, thud, thud* of a trotting horse. Frijole twisted his horse around, and as the vehicle went past him he flung a large loop. He felt the hondo snap tight around the neck of the horse, and took a quick dally around his saddle-horn.

A woman screamed, as the horse was stopped so short that it nearly went over backward. Roaring like a Viking, Oscar Johnson went into action. But the buggy horse, shocked and frightened, whirled, cramped the buggy so short that it upset, throwing its occupants out the opposite side from Oscar. Frijole realized that the horse had whirled; so he took no further chances, and slipped the rope off his saddle-horn. The horse and the upset buggy went past him, heading back for the main street of Tonto City in a cloud of dust.

"Oscar!" called Frijole. "Oscar, where are yuh? Oscar!"

There was no answer. Fearing the worst, Frijole dismounted. He could see enough to distinguish the dark figures on the ground; he stumbled over to them, just as one arose.

"Somethin' must have went wrong," said Frijole, and the next moment an iron-like fist hit him square in the nose, and Frijole's consciousness went out in a blaze of glory.

HE HAD NO idea how long he had been unconscious, but he did have an idea that his nose was twice its usual size, and that a tooth was missing from his upper plate. All was quiet at the old adobe, not even a horse around there. Frijole was starting back for town when he heard men talking, coming toward him. Quietly he stepped into the brush and let them go past. Then he hurried toward town.

There was a light in the sheriff's office, but no one there; so Frijole went in and looked at himself in the mirror.

"My Gawd!" he groaned. Someone was standing in the doorway, and he turned to see Oscar Johnson, his face bleeding from several cuts, his shirt nearly torn from his back, and his leather chaps hanging in ribbons around his legs.

"Oh, hallo dere," said Oscar in sort of chirping voice.

"What happened to you, Oscar."

"Va'al," sighed Oscar, leaning against the doorway, "Ay storted to yerk Yulius from de buggy ven de damn t'ing opset, knock me down, and de belt of my chaps caught on a spring. Ay yust vars dragged all de vay back to de livery stable. Ay am mess, Free-holey. Every yoint is bosted. What happened to your nose? You look like de shoriff."

"Julius hit me," replied Frijole. "That thun of a gun. That thun—thun—whath wrong with me? Oh, I gueth it muth be that topth."

Frijole limped over to the doorway. Men were coming toward the office; so Frijole took Oscar by the sleeve and drew him through the connecting doorway and down beside the jail-cells. Henry and Judge came in.

"Damme, if I can figure it out, Henry," declared Judge. "That man is sure that the horse was roped. But why? Robbery could not have been the motive, because no robbery was committed."

"Possibly contemplated," said Henry. "The man says that after the horse and buggy incident a man, heavily armed, possibly masked, accosted him. He says that he knocked the man down. His fist really shows wear and tear. Concern over his wife caused him to ignore his victim, and he does not know where the man went."

"Very queer," remarked Judge. "Luckily neither man nor woman was injured. What was their names, Henry?"

"Mr. and Mrs. Albert Crawford. He is half owner of the Shoshone Chief Mine, and they were on their way to the mine. Well, I do not know of anything further we can do. Tommy Roper says that the buggy is badly smashed, but the horse is unhurt. I suppose we better go back to the hotel and talk with Mr. Crawford."

"At least assure him of our good intentions," added Judge.

They went out. Quietly Frijole led Oscar out to the front, and they went out into the night.

"I reckon we better find them horthes and go to the ranch," said the little cook with the swollen nose. "Thith ith awful, Othcar."

"Yah, su-ure," agreed Oscar painfully. "Love is awful, too, Free-holey."

"None for me," declared Frijole. "I'll take peath for mine."

But Oscar did not go out to the JHC. He cleaned up and rode to Scorpion Bend. Oscar felt that Julius had done him a dirty trick, in letting someone else take that horse and buggy. In Oscar's single-track mind were no regrets for his mistake. The blame was on Julius Swensen, and he was going to teach Julius a lesson.

Henry could not find Oscar or Frijole, and deep in his mind was a suspicion that they were to blame for the smashing of that buggy. It sounded like something they might do. However, Henry had no idea just why they had done it.

"Tonto City," declared Judge, "is on the downgrade."

"True," agreed Henry. "Very true, sir."

"A damnable situation," said Judge. "Innocent people in a buggy."

"Six-shooters, masked men—a punch in the nose," mused Henry. "All very confusing. I wonder where Oscar and Frijole are."

"I believe, sir," said Judge soberly, "that you are getting warm."

IT WAS ABOUT nine o'clock next morning, when Henry received a telegram from Scorpion Bend, which read:

HORSE AND BUGGY STOLEN FROM ME LAST NIGHT AT SCORPION BEND. EQUIPAGE BELONGS TO LIVERY STABLE TONTO CITY. ADVISE IF IT HAS COME HOME.   JOHN HARPER.

"By gad, sir!" exclaimed Judge. "They even steal from the prosecuting attorney! Tonto City is on the downgrade, with—"

"True, Judge!" exclaimed Henry. "With brake-blocks busted, et cetera, et cetera. No need to add the crazy driver. We shall interview Tommy Roper at once."

Henry read the telegram to the stuttering cowboy, who blew out his thin cheeks and nodded his head violently.

"The huh-huh-houh—"

"The horse and buggy came home?" queried Henry.

"Yuh-yuh-yeah!"

"At what time. If you do not know, merely shake the head?"

Tommy shook.

"This morning—early?"

Tommy nodded. "About su-su-su—"

"Six o'clock, eh? You were asleep. Nod or shake, Tommy."

Toomy nodded.

"Was both horse and buggy in good shape?"

Tommy nodded violently.

Henry wrote a telegram to John Harper, sent Judge to the little depot to file it, and went over to the Tonto Hotel, where he found Josephine in the dining-room, clearing off a table.

"Greetings, my dear." He smiled at her. "Did you have a nice time at Scorpion Bend last night?"

"Ay did not go," she replied. "Ay vould not go vit Oscar Yohnson, and Yulius vars too scared to take me."

"Frightened of Oscar's wrath, I presume."

"Sure. Ay am going to knock ha'al out of that big bully."

"Oscar?"

"You bat you. Yulius is yentleman."

"No doubt of that. But did Oscar go to Scorpion Bend?"

"Ay t'ink he did."

"Thank you very much, my dear—and good luck to your romance."

Oscar was in the office, when Henry came back, looking owl-eyed from lack of sleep, but with it all was a triumphant gleam.

"You enjoyed the dance at Scorpion Bend, I presume," said Henry.

"Ay alvays enyoy a dance," replied Oscar.

"I suppose you danced with Josephine."

"Ay did not. Ay did not even go to de dance-hall. She vars vit Yulius."

"As a matter of fact, Oscar, Josephine and Julius did not go to the dance."

"Huh?" Oscar stared his unbelief of that statement. "You say Yosephine did not go? Va'al, Ay don't—"

"By the way, Oscar, I got a telegram from Scorpion Bend this morning from John Harper, saying that someone stole his horse and buggy. It so happens that someone left the horse and buggy at our livery stable about six o'clock this morning. Perchance, did you see anyone on the road, driving a single horse and buggy?"

"Yudas!" said Oscar quietly. "No, Ay didn't. Yohn Horper?"

"Yes, John Harper. I merely thought you might have seen the thief. By the way, what time did you arrive home, Oscar?"

"Orly. Oh, my gudness, Ay came home orly. It vars too dork to see."

"I see."

"Ay thought Yosephine and Yulius vars going."

"They didn't go. I believe that the stolen horse was the same one you usually rent."

"Yah, su-ure—de sorrel von. His name is Yoe."

"That is the one. By the way, Oscar, a Mr. and Mrs. Crawford hired a horse and buggy last evening and started for the Shoshone Chief Mine, but something or somebody upset their buggy out by the old adobe, tried to hold up the man and woman, but was frustrated. You haven't heard anything, have you?"

Oscar drew a deep breath.

"Frus—frus—what vars dat, Henry?"

"Frustrated."

"Who vars—and vat does it mean?"

"It means that the robber failed to rob them."

"Oh! Den everyt'ing is all right, eh?"

"Well, I suppose that is one way to look at it. Wasn't Frijole here with you last night?"

"Yah, su-ure, he vars here, but he vent home. He—he fell down on de sidewalk and hort his nose. Yeeminee, it vars all svelled oop."

Henry's mind dashed back to Crawford's statement that he had hit one of the bandits square in the face.

"Funny t'ings happen in Tonto," remarked Oscar. "Ve need more good people."

"That is exactly what Hell needs," replied Henry dryly.

8

ABOUT THAT GOLD...

KING COLT WAS curious to know more about the arrest and release of Old Juan, the *maguey*-cutter, but did not care to ask Henry Conroy. There was no question in his mind that there was a leak in his organization, but he was unable to figure out just where it was. Pancho Lopez had his own money invested in the deal; so there was no reason for him to have warned the Border Patrol. They had lost thousands in drugs; but there was no use crying about it.

He called La Mariposa into his office and asked her to sit down. She seemed uneasy, afraid of him; but he smiled at her and said:

"Are you happy here?"

"Why, yes, I like it all right." she replied. "Is—is anything wrong?"

"Wrong? Everything is just right, my dear. You bring a lot of trade to the Tonto."

King Colt leaned back in his chair, hooked his thumbs into the armholes of his vest and smiled expansively at her.

"I am goin' to double yore salary," he told her. "Fifty dollars a week. No, don't thank me. You are worth more."

"I am glad," she said simply. "I—I really need the money, Mr. Colt."

"You need money? You have to—" he frowned slightly. "You help support a—a husband, maybe?"

"No, I have never been married. I help support my mother."

"Your mother? Oh, of course. Yuh see, I—I never figured—well, yuh see, I never thought that maybe you had a mother. 'Course you'd have one."

"Yes, of course." She nodded.

"This extra money might help her out?"

"Oh, very much, Mr. Colt. You are very kind to me."

"Your mother—she lives near here?"

"No, she lives in Chicago. She isn't very well. She needs an operation, but we can not afford it, not just now."

"That's too bad. Maybe I can help. You know—loan you money."

The girl shook her head quickly. "No, it would require too much."

King Colt nodded thoughtfully. "You have a father?"

"No," replied the girl seriously. "My father died when I was very young."

King Colt scratched the back of his neck thoughtfully, his hat tilted to shield his face.

"That's too bad," he said. "Yuh know," he turned to look at her, "you never did tell me yore right name and address. And I'd like to have yore mother's name and address, in case—well, yuh never know what might happen."

"I have thought of that." She nodded. "My name is June McLean, and my mother's name is Mrs. Alice McLean. The address is 716 Totter Avenue, Chicago, Illinois."

King Colt wrote out the name and address on a piece of

paper, his hand shaking a little. June had not lied to him, and it was evident that she did not know he was her father.

"Please do not tell anyone my right name," she said. "I would rather have them know me as La Mariposa."

"Shucks, I won't tell anybody, Miss McLean."

LONG AFTER JUNE McLean left the office, King Colt pondered over what he was going to do. Finally he went out on the street and over to the bank. No one was there, except Steve McRae.

"I want one of them cashier checks for five thousand dollars," King said. "I've got more'n that much in here, I reckon."

"Certainly, Mr. Colt. To whom shall I draw the check?"

"Mrs. Alice McLean."

Wondering who Mrs. Alice McLean might be, Steve McRae made out the check and gave it to King Colt. King went out to the street, and there he met Henry Harrison Conroy.

"Sheriff," he said, "I wonder if you'll help me out in a little deal."

"I should be happy to be of assistance, sir," replied Henry.

"Well, it's like this, Sheriff. A long time ago I borrowed some money from a man. I reckon I wasn't very good pay. Anyway, I lost track of him, and today I heard that he had died years ago, leavin' a widder in bad circumstances. She's a pretty proud woman, and I'm kinda wonderin' if she'd accept the money—if she knowed I sent it. Yuh see," King Colt rubbed his neck violently, "if you'd kinda write a note, sayin' it was from—well, I dunno who. Mebbe you can fix it."

"Just step in the bank, where we may find a usable pen,"

suggested Henry. "I believe I know what you want done, Mr. Colt."

On the back of a deposit-slip, Henry wrote:

Years ago I borrowed some money from your husband. I just learned your address; so here is the full amount, and thank you.

Pawnee Bill.

King Colt chuckled over the note and nodded happily. "Pawnee Bill! That's fine. Sheriff, if I can ever do yuh a favor, jist ask it of me, will yuh?"

"It is of no moment, sir."

While writing the note, Henry had glimpsed the amount on that check. Five thousand dollars, and a note signed with a fictitious name. The act did not coincide with what he had heard of King Colt. Henry walked up to the post-office, where he found the old postmaster alone.

"King Colt is going to post a letter—possibly today," he told the old man. "I want the name and address on that letter."

"Official business, Sheriff?" queried the postmaster.

"Certainly."

"I'll watch for it," replied the postmaster.

But King Colt did not post the letter. He waited until the last moment and then gave it to the stage-driver to post at Scorpion Bend. Henry saw the stage-driver shove it inside his jacket, without even looking at the address, and drive away.

That afternoon Judge Van Treece came into the office, where Henry and Oscar were taking their daily siesta.

Judge carried a copy of the latest Scorpion Bend *Weekly Clarion*, which he flung on Henry's desk.

"There, sir," he bellowed, "is the latest in hide-rippers! If my rheumatism were better, I'd go to Scorpion Bend and force that scavenger to eat his press. Damme, sir, I sicken of his blather!"

Henry sighed, opened the paper to the editorial page and read the following:

OPEN TO ALL CRIMINALS

In one day, at Tonto City, two men were brutally murdered and twenty-three thousand dollars stolen. One man was shot down, while the other was killed by a blow on the head, and thrown into a burning stable. This, friends, was all done in one day—and in daylight.

If the Sheriff of Tonto has done anything toward apprehending the murderers and recovering the money, he has kept his activities a deep, dark secret. A coroner's jury demanded the arrest of James Miller for the murder of Edward Clay, the stage-driver, and theft of 650 ounces of raw gold, but the sheriff did not make any move until James Miller was safely across the Border. With the evidence against James Miller, why did the sheriff allow Miller to leave Tonto City the night before the inquest? Was he trying to play one of his well-known jokes on the State of Arizona?

How much longer will the citizens of Wild Horse Valley tolerate the comedy team of Conroy, Van Treece and Johnson? A red-nosed juggler of rubber balls, a drunken disciple of Blackstone, and an ignorant horse-wrangler.

While they rehearse their daily act, criminals plot and execute their crimes, unhampered and unafraid. Gentlemen of Wild Horse Valley, it is time to ring down the curtain on this abominable travesty of law enforcement, and put in men who can give us a regime of efficiency in the sheriff's office. In the meantime, Wild Horse Valley is an open invitation to any and all criminals—deplorable as it may seem.

Henry looked up from the paper, a quizzical expression in his eyes.

"Does this irk you, Judge?" he asked quietly.

"The truth," replied Judge, "sometimes irks, sir. But in the main, the editorial is right, sir."

"I deny nothing," said Henry. "Our sins seem to have found us out, Judge. There is only one thing left for us to do."

"What is that?" queried Judge anxiously.

"Keep right on running the office—in our own dumb way."

"Until we are thrown out bodily, I suppose."

"I suppose that is the only way we will get out, Judge."

THUNDER AND LIGHTNING Mendoza rode into Tonto City, tied their horses in front of the general store and went across the street to the Tonto Saloon, where they sat down on the sidewalk together. They paid no attention to anyone, until Pancho Lopez, in all his sartorial elegance, but still bearing marks of King Colt's fist, came along.

"Meester Lopez," said Lightning. Pancho stopped and glared at the two peons, who were far beneath his station.

"You like see sometheeng?" queried Lightning.

Pancho moved closer, his eyes curious. "See what?" he asked.

"Leetle closer," warned Lightning.

Curiosity overcame Pancho, who slid down beside them.
Inside Lightning's cupped hands was an object that caused
Pancho's eyes to snap wide. It was a cube of raw gold, on
one side of which was stamped:

SHOSHONE CHIEF

Pancho's eyes swept the surroundings. No one was near,
no one looking at them. He took it in his hands. Cupid-
ity was in his eyes, as he gazed upon that little pound of
pure gold.

"That ees gold, I theenk," said Lightning. Pancho drew
a deep breath and shrugged his shoulders.

"Maybe eet ees not pure," he said. "W'ere you get heem,
eh?"

"Not for telling," interposed Thunder. "How much
dinero, Pancho?"

"Oh, I don't know," replied Pancho. "Maybe he ees wort'
twenty dollar."

"You buy heem?" queried Lightning.

"Well, I tak' chance," replied Pancho. "You tell nobody,
eh?"

Pancho paid twenty dollars for a chunk of gold worth
about two hundred and forty dollars, knowing that it was,
beyond a doubt, part of the loot from the stage robbery.
Then the two delighted Mexicans, with money in their
pockets, debated their next move.

"I know w'at ees the bes' theeng for doing," stated Lightning. "We weel put the money in the bank."

"That ees not wort' the paper I can write on," declared
Thunder. "We buy two bottle tequila—pronto."

"Sure," sneered Lightning. "And w'en the headache ees over, we are bosted. We put half the money een the bank."

"That ees all right. How much ees half, Lightning?"

"How the hell do I know? Let the bank bost heem to halves."

Fifteen minutes later they came out of the bank, filled with their own importance, bearing a check-book, showing a deposit of ten dollars, and each of them jingling five dollars in silver. They went to the Tonto Saloon, where each of them purchased a quart of tequila, and then they went out behind the saloon, found a shady spot, where they began enjoying the fruits of their shrewd deal.

About an hour later Henry Harrison Conroy sauntered into the bank, merely on an unofficial visit. Howard McRae greeted him pleasantly. Then he said:

"Your two Mexican boys seem to have acquired a saving habit."

Henry looked blankly at him. "You mean Thunder and Lightning?"

"Yes. I was not in here, but Steve told me that they came in with a twenty-dollar bill, deposited half of it to a joint account, and divided the other ten dollars between them."

"I rather admire them for that move," said Henry. "A half saved, you know. Well, well! I must compliment them."

Henry walked over to the Tonto Saloon, puzzled as to where these two Mexicans had acquired twenty dollars. Henry only paid them ten dollars a month apiece, which was more than their actual worth, and payday was three weeks ago. This suddenly acquired wealth was worth an investigation. A discreet inquiry brought the information that the two Mexicans had purchased two quarts of tequila and had left via the back doorway.

Pancho Lopez was at the bar and heard Henry's guarded inquiry. King Colt was out somewhere, and Pancho anxiously awaited his return. Henry went out behind the saloon, where he found Lightning and Thunder, curled up in the shade, sodden with tequila. He took the bank-book from Lightning's pocket, looked it over and put it in his own pocket. Then knowing that it would be hours before their recovery, he went back to the office.

PANCHO LOPEZ WAS as anxious as Henry, although he knew where the twenty dollars came from. At first, Pancho decided to try and get all that gold for himself, but then he realized it would be best to let King Colt in on the secret.

When King Colt came back to the Tonto, Pancho followed him into the office and placed the ingot of gold on the desk. King Colt looked it over, shifted his narrowed eyes and studied Pancho Lopez.

"Where did yuh get that?" he whispered. Leaning across the desk, his voice low, Pancho told him about buying it from the two Mexicans. King Colt smiled thoughtfully.

"So them two Mexicans killed Ed Clay and took that gold, eh? Well, it works out, Pancho. They discovered the body. Maybe they killed Old Hailstorm, too. Pancho, we're goin' to get *all* that money."

"Sure," smiled Pancho. "We buy 'em out, Keeng. Twenty dollar for each chonk, like that, eh?"

"Buy 'em out? You damn fool, we don't have to buy 'em out. We can scare it out of 'em. Where are they now?"

"Behin' the saloon—dronk."

"Keep an eye on 'em. When they sober up, bring 'em to me."

"The only theeng," said Pancho quietly, "ees that the damn sheriff mus' know sometheeng. He come and ask the bartender where ees them two. He try to find out how much money they have. Then he go and look at them. I watch from back weendow, and I see him take something from one man's pocket and look at it. Then he go 'way. W'at you theenk?"

"What was it he took?"

Pancho shrugged his shoulders. *"Quien sabe?"*

"When nobody is around, search 'em. Find what the sheriff looked at."

Pancho nodded and walked out. A glance through the window showed that the coast was clear; so he sauntered out behind the saloon, knelt down beside one of the Mexicans and began going through his pockets.

"If you should find anything—I would like to see what it is," said a voice, and Pancho perked up to see Henry Harrison Conroy, leaning against the beer kegs.

Pancho got slowly to his feet, dusted off his knees.

"I really did not expect to find you picking pockets, Pancho," said Henry. "I believe that in the parlance of places like the Tonto, they call it 'rolling' the victim. Tck, tck, tck! And in daylight!"

"I was not peeking the pocket," Pancho managed to say.

"Pancho," said Henry, "if I were you I'd *stay* in Mexico. We do not need men around here, who would stoop to pick the pocket of a poor, drunken peon. I believe I shall speak to King Colt about it."

Pancho choked, turned on his heel and strode back into the saloon.

As a matter of fact, from behind a curtain in his office, King Colt has observed the tableau, and he was waiting for Pancho. He saw Henry arouse the two Mexicans, who staggered away with him. Pancho came in, burning with indignation.

"All right," said King Colt. "You got caught, eh?"

"*Madre de Dios!* That damn beeg-nose say I am peek-pocket!"

"Did you find anythin' in his pocket?"

"Notheeng."

"Uh-huh. I suppose that Lightnin' had another bar of gold, and that damn sheriff found it. No wonder he's guardin' 'em. Now, what'll we do?"

Pancho shrugged his shoulders and muttered, "Peek-pocket! Pancho Adolfo Alejo Bonifacio Guillermo Santiago Lopez—a peek-pocket!"

"And not a very good one, at that," added King Colt.

Pancho began rolling a cigarette with trembling fingers, while King Colt leaned on his desk, his brow furrowed with thought, his eyes centered on a sheet of white paper, where tiny particles of dust were gathering. More sifted down, as he watched the paper. Slowly his eyes shifted to a beam of sunlight, then upward to the ceiling, as though trying to make up his mind about what move to make.

"The sheriff took them two Mexicans away with him," said King Colt quietly. "Watch and see if they go home."

Pancho nodded and walked out, closing the door. King Colt ran a finger over the dusty paper, lighted a cigar and leaned back in his chair and looked again at the rough ceiling. There was only the bare, unpainted boards. Perhaps there was a bit wider crack between the boards near the center of the room, but it was not noticeable.

Finally he got to his feet and went into the saloon, where he leaned against the bar and drank several glasses of raw whisky. The bartender looked anxiously at him, because it was not like King Colt to drink so much whisky in such a short length of time.

9

FROM RATTLESNAKES TO RICHES

HENRY TOOK LIGHTNING and Thunder over to the office and put them to sleep in the jail. Frijole Bill rode in a little later and Henry questioned him about the two Mexicans. Frijole Bill laughed.

"They went huntin' rattlesnakes," he said. "I told 'em that rattlesnake oil was worth twenty dollars an ounce, and they went right out to git rich. Lightnin' said he knowed where there was dozens of fat ones in Red Wall Cañon."

Henry nodded thoughtfully. "Did either of them have any money?"

"Not a danged cent. I loaned 'em each four-bits yesterday."

"I see. Frijole, are you certain as to the market quotation on rattlesnake oil?"

"Shucks, no! I was jokin' 'em. I dunno what it's worth."

"How long would it take them to try out an ounce of oil from rattlesnakes?"

"Why, Henry, I don't even know how much oil a rattler has."

"I do not believe we can credit it to rattlesnake oil."

"What's that?" queried Frijole.

"I was merely thinking aloud," replied Henry. "You came in the wagon?"

"Yeah, I had some stuff to haul out to the ranch."

"When you are ready to go back, we will tie their horses to the endgate, and put Lightning and Thunder in the wagon."

"I dunno what this is all about," said Frijole, "but if yuh want me to ask 'em some questions, I'll shore do it—and get answers."

"I will handle the question and answer department, Frijole, but I thank you just the same."

Henry heard more about his two henchmen about ten o'clock that evening when he met Jim Henderson of the Border Patrol in front of the general store. They walked down to the sheriff's office together and stopped in front of it in the darkness.

"Conroy," said the big officer, "you have always given us all the assistance possible, and we believe in returning favors. You've got some big problems to solve, so I'm givin' you a tip.

"Those two Mexicans who work for you may not be as innocent and ignorant as they seem. Today they sold a pound of that missin' Shoshone Chief gold to Pancho Lopez for twenty dollars."

Henry drew a deep breath and exhaled it audibly.

"My goodness!" he exclaimed. "Lightning and Thunder?"

"That's right. I believe they was the ones to find the body of Ed Clay, wasn't they? I don't say they murdered him and stole the gold—but it looks funny."

"Well—er—thank you, Henderson, very much. I—I never suspected them."

"They may be deeper than you think," laughed Henderson. "Anyway, they will bear investigation."

"My goodnes—yes! But how on earth did you learn this?"

Henderson laughed shortly. "Remember that little birdie I spoke about the other night, when we had Old Juan here?"

"Oh, yes, I remember that. Thank you very much, Mr. Henderson, and I shall investigate those boys at once."

"I would—before someone else does."

Long after Henderson left, Henry sat in his office, trying to puzzle out things. He could not believe that Lightning and Thunder ever killed Ed Clay and stole that gold. If they did, why would they try to sell the incriminating gold in Tonto City. Surely, they knew that murder was punishable by hanging. And what did Henderson mean, when he said to investigate them—"before someone else does."

"I shall go out there the very first thing in the morning," Henry told himself. "I hope they can explain things satisfactory."

HENRY WENT TO their hotel room, where he found Judge reading a newspaper, and told him what Henderson had said. Judge fairly exploded.

"There you are, sir! The last person you would ever suspect. As for me, I have had an eye on them for a long time. Secure in their knowledge that you consider them too ignorant to commit a crime, they have pulled the wool over your eyes, sir."

"Wolves in sheep clothing, as it were, Judge. Wool-pullers."

"Exactly! Well, I am glad we have solved that mystery."

*After Thunder and Lightning
had suffered for hours, the
masked man returned*

"Solved it, Judge? How on earth did you ever become known as a keen lawyer, when you consider that one swallow makes a summer? That one bar of gold doesn't prove anything—except that they had the bar of gold."

"The murderers took the gold, Henry. Surely you realize that. As for my legal reputation—"

"We will pass all self-adulation, Judge," interrupted Henry. "The fact still remains that we haven't even the bar of gold as proof that they ever had it. My informant told me that Pancho Lopez bought it for twenty dollars. That provides the ten dollars they deposited in the bank, and the ten dollars in change that they took away with them. But it does not prove that they murdered Ed Clay."

"Well, surely you will arrest them, Henry?"

"That, sir, will depend on their explanation—proved."

"Your heart, my dear Henry, is larger than your brain."

"So is my stomach, Judge—which proves absolutely nothing."

"Facetious as usual, of course," sighed Judge. "But I do hope that we are able to prove them guilty, in order to pacify the *Weekly Clarion*. That editor craves a wholesale hanging, Henry. If something does not happen soon, public opinion, if nothing else, will force us out of office."

"My dear sir," said Henry quietly, "your dire forbodings do not frighten me in the least. Public office is a disease— and public opinion, were it strong enough to drive us from office, might be the cure. Holding a public office is worse than a floating kidney—you can have the kidney anchored."

"I believe we should go to bed," sighed Judge. "It is a waste of real intelligence to talk with you in your present frame of mind."

"I might get a job as a juggler," mused Henry. "King Colt might give me a spot on his honkytonk bill, along with La Mariposa."

"What about me?" queried Judge seriously.

"You? Oh, that is easily remedied. You could stand in the wings and toss the balls out to me, Judge."

"I believe," stated Judge, "that we should wait until we have been thrown out of office. I never was a good tosser."

HENRY AND JUDGE rode to the JHC early next morning. Frijole was cooking breakfast, but there was no sign of Thunder and Lightning.

"Too much tequila," said Frijole. "They're out in the bunk-house."

Henry went out to awaken them, but they were not in the bunk-house. Their beds seemed to have been occupied, but of the two Mexicans there was no trace. Henry reported this to Frijole, who went down to the stable, only to come back with the report that no horses were missing.

"That's danged funny," observed Frijole. "Do yuh reckon—aw shucks, they wouldn't go rattlesnake huntin' this early. Anyway, they'd have breakfast first. Well, I don't mind tellin' yuh that it ain't no big loss if they never come back. Set down and I'll fry yuh some flapjacks and eggs."

Henry and Judge ate breakfast, and stayed at the ranch for an hour, but neither of the Mexicans returned. At length they rode back to town.

Henry still appeared unworried, but his placidity might have been shaken if he had known the reason for the Mexicans' disappearance. During the night two masked men had entered the bunk-house, awakened Thunder and Lightning and sworn to cut their throats if they made any outcry. The bandits had blindfolded the two, forced them to mount one horse, and then had taken them to a cabin far back in the brushy hills. There the prisoners were tied up tightly and dumped on the floor.

Warning Thunder and Lightning to not make a sound, on pain of terrible death, the two men disappeared. By this time both Mexicans were cold sober, and not a little frightened. As far as they could determine, there was no earthly reason for all this to happen to them.

"I theenk we are been keednipped," said Thunder.

"Shut up!" exclaimed Lightning. "Theese man say eef we make noise he weel cut my neck from one of your ears to the odder one. Squissh—like those."

"W'at ees the rizzon?"

"The rizzon for wheech, my leetle brodder?"

"For tie us up like those. Who the hell he theenk I am, anyway?"

"I theenk he know pretty good, too."

"W'y you theenk?"

"He call me damn hot-head *Mejicano.*"

"Well," sighed Thunder, "I guess he know you. *Por Dios.* I geeve *mucho dinero* for dreenk tequila."

"I dreenk anytheeng," declared Lightning. "I am so dry I dreenk *agua caliente.*"

"I theenk," said Thunder, "we are in plenty hot water, weethout you want dreenk eet. W'at you theenk they do weeth us?"

"I am too scare for theenking. You know where we are?"

"Sure—togedder."

"Sometime," stated Lightning, "I theenk that eef you had all my brains divide among us, we would be half-witted—I hope."

"Sure," agreed Thunder. "But I trade my brain for one knife, biccause all the brain in your head don't cut the rope."

"You fill all right?" queried Lightning.

"Sure—I fill all right."

"Then shut up, biffore these men come back and cut some necks."

BUT THE MEN did not come back that night nor all the next long day to give the suffering Mexicans food or water. And they were a sorry pair, when about midnight several horsemen stopped at the front of the shack and came in, carrying a lantern. They were all masked.

They flashed the light in the faces of the two Mexicans, and one of the men said, "They're all right."

"All right," said one of the men and squatted down

beside Thunder and Lightning. "Do yuh know what I want to know?" he asked.

Lightning shook his head.

"Yes, yuh do—you know," denied the man harshly. "Right now yo're goin' to tell me where yuh cached all that Shoshone Chief gold that yuh stole from the stage."

"*Madre de Dios!*" gasped Lightning. "We never steal those gol'."

"Liar!" The man slapped him across the face. "You sold a piece of it to Pancho Lopez. Where's the rest of it?"

Lightning, his eyes full of tears from the slap, turned and looked at Thunder, who groaned wearily.

"I theenk we are in hell of a feex, Thonder," he said.

"All right—talk!" snapped the man. "If yuh don't tell us where the gold is cached, we'll see yuh both hung for murderin' Ed Clay."

"We never keel heem," quavered Thunder. "You bili've me?"

"I don't believe a damn word of it! But if you'll show us the gold, we won't tell anybody that you murdered the stage-driver."

"We never morder nobody," wailed Lightning. "We jus' fin' these gol', that ees all."

"Where is it?"

Lightning groaned, but finally he said:

"We show you these gol'—you let us go?"

"We shore will, Mex. All we want is the gold."

"*Buena*—we tell."

"That's the stuff, Mex; where is it?"

"We tak' you to the cabin."

"Cabin, eh? So it's in a cabin. What cabin?"

"You know where ees Rad Wall Cañon?"

"Yeah, we know where it is."

"You know the ol' cabin een the cañon?"

"Yeah, we know where that is, too. Is the gold there?"

"Onder the floor in the back end."

"That's fine, Mex. But how did you find it?"

"We look for the rattlesnake," explained Lightning. "Frijole tell us that oil from these damn snake ees wort' plenty money. We see the beeg, fat one crawl under the cabin, so we deeg heem out."

The men laughed. The explanation was a natural one, and they knew that Lightning was telling the truth. After a whispered consultation the ropes were removed from Lightning and Thunder.

"There yuh are, boys," said the leader jovially. "It's quite a walk home, but I don't reckon you'll mind it. *Buenas noches.*"

Then they rode away, taking the lantern with them. Lightning and Thunder, suffering from returning circulation in their cramped arms and legs, managed to get out of the cabin. There was enough moonlight to show them where they were.

They had been at least twenty-four hours without food or drink, and they realized that it was about ten miles back to the JHC, and over mighty rough going.

"Damn the gold!" said Thunder emphatically.

"The same to you, my leetle brodder," replied Lightning. "One day I'm hearing Henry saying to Jodge that gold ees where you find heem."

"I never look for heem any more. If I never find gol' in your whole life, I am glad—and that ees all I hope."

And they went stumbling down the rocky slope, heading for the comforts of the JHC.

ABOUT ONE O'CLOCK that morning Joe Hake, one of King Colt's most trusted cowboys, came into the Tonto Saloon, and met King Colt in the private office. Hake leaned on the desk for several moments, his thin lips shut tightly, as he looked squarely at King Colt.

"Well?" queried the big gambler.

"We follered yore orders, King," he said quietly. "We scared hell out of them two Mexicans, until they were damn glad to tell us where the gold was cached. Then we turned 'em loose."

"That's what I told yuh to do, Hake."

"Well, we done it. Then we went to the old cabin in Red Wall Cañon, took up the floor—and the gold was gone."

"Gone?"

"That's right. There was the fresh dirt, and—hell, that gold was there all right, but somebody beat us to it."

King Colt swore feelingly. "The Mexicans lied, Hake?"

The big cowboy shrugged his shoulders.

"*Quien sabe?* If they didn't, they'd done told somebody where it was, or they moved it when they took the one brick. They may not be as ignorant as they act and talk, King."

"All right. See that the boys gets some drinks. See yuh *mañana.*"

… Completely unaware of King Colt's interest in them, two sore-footed Mexicans faced Henry and Judge at the office next morning. Frijole had brought them to town, and now he told Henry what the two boys had related to him when they reached the ranch.

"Why did you not bring me the gold, instead of taking it to Pancho Lopez?" asked Henry.

"I don't theenk you want to buy heem," replied Lightning.

"Of course, I did not want to buy it. You knew it was stolen gold."

"Gold ees w'ere you find heem," quoted Lightning.

"Shall I bust him in the nose, Henry?" asked Frijole.

"Certainly not. Lightning, can you describe the men who forced you to tell where you found that gold?"

"Sure—he's got on mask."

"How many men were there in the party?"

"Theese ees no party," interposed Thunder.

"Damn such ignorance!" snorted Judge.

"Well," sighed Henry, "we lost a chance to recover that gold."

"Perhaps they did not find it," suggested Judge. "We might go out there and look. And what about Pancho Lopez? He knew that it was part of the stolen gold. Lightning, was there anything on that piece of gold?"

"Sure theeng—dirt."

"I mean, were there any markings, such as initials?"

Lightning seemed puzzled over the word.

"Letters," Judge explained.

"No letter," replied Lightning. "Not even one damn paper."

Judge made a helpless gesture and subsided. Henry asked Lightning:

"Did you tell anybody else that you had found all this gold?"

"We no tell anybody."

"What did you tell the man at the bank when you made your deposit?"

"We tell heem we want put een ten dollar, no cents."

"No sense," echoed Thunder. "We lose the book."

Henry chuckled quietly. "Did he ask you were you got all the money?"

"Sure," said Lightning. "He tell us we are pretty reech, and I tell heem that gold ees w'ere you find heem."

"I see. And what did he say to that?"

"He ees saying that this ees not gold."

"Not gold," agreed Thunder. "Eet ees jus' paper money."

"What about Pancho Lopez?" queried Judge. "We might force him to give up the gold, so that we may determine whether or not it is part of the loot from the Shoshone Chief. I believe they stamp the ingots."

Henry shook his head. "Not if I know Pancho Lopez, Judge. It is his word I against the word of these two—and they can not prove anything, except that they found what seems to have been an ingot of gold. Perhaps we might prove criminal intent, but we would have to prove first that Pancho knowingly bought stolen gold—and we cannot. Take them home, Frijole, and doctor up their foot-blisters."

10

THIRTY DAYS TO ABDICATION

THE FAILURE OF his men to find that stolen gold annoyed King Colt. It meant that another organization had beaten him to the punch; and King Colt did not like that. He told Hake to bring the men into his office that evening. When they were all gathered there he said:

"We've been overlookin' Jack Tallant and his crippled father, Gila Jim Tallant. Gila Jim hates me, and he said he'd lick me at my own game. I'm bettin' that he's behind that stage robbery. Mebbe he's behind the killin' and robbery of Hailstorm Miller. He's as dangerous as a rattler, even if he can't walk. Look out for him.

"Hake, I want you to send men to watch Tallant's ranch. I believe that they're sellin' horses across the Border. My hunch is that Jack Tallant is takin' 'em down there, and Jimmy Miller is herdin' 'em on down to a bunch of revolutionists. Stop Jack Tallant, even if yuh have to use hot lead. With him out of he way, I can deal with Gila Jim."

"I'll send a couple of the boys," agreed Hake. "But I wouldn't trust Pancho Lopez too far, King. That fancy Mexican would cut yore throat if it meant a dollar in his pocket. And he's still after La Mariposa."

"I'll handle him, Hake."

"I seen Frijole Bill and the two Mexicans over at the sheriff's office this mornin'," said Hake. "Old Red-Nose is prob'ly tryin' to find out who kidnapped 'em and where the gold went to."

"He's too dumb to know anythin'," remarked a cowboy.

"And that is just where yo're wrong, Ed," replied King Colt.

"*You* don't think he's smart, do yuh, King?" said Hake, grinning.

"In my business," replied King Colt, "all guns are loaded. The safest thing is to figure that all men are smart. Only a damn fool underrates an opponent, Hake. If you'll check back on things that happened before we came to Tonto City, you'll find that Old Red-Nose has been rated pretty smart, even if they did laugh at him."

"Well, he shore don't look like much," said Hake.

"Hake, I've knowed men that made the same mistake with a stick of dynamite—because of its looks. You send the men down to watch the Tallant ranch, and don't overlook Henry Harrison Conroy and his misfit bunch of helpers. They can hang yuh just as high as the best gun-fightin' sheriff that ever made a track in the sand."

He dismissed his men then, and as soon as they left the office, one of the gamblers came in.

"The depot agent brought a telegram to La Mariposa a while ago," he told King, "I took it up to her room."

"Well?" queried King.

"There wasn't any light in her room," continued the man. "She came to the door in the darkness and took the message. Her window was open, and the wind was blowin' out into the hall."

King Colt looked curiously at him, but said nothing. Lowering his voice, the gambler said:

"Maybe I'm wrong, King, but I believe there was somebody else in the room."

King Colt started slightly, but managed a smile as he said: "What made yuh think there was?"

The gambler shrugged his shoulders. "Oh, I suppose it was a hunch."

"Let it go at that," said King Colt. "Thanks for the information."

After the gambler had gone, King Colt sat there a long time, chewing his cigar. He glanced at his watch and noted that it was nearly time for La Mariposa to sing again. There was a light tap on the door.

"Come in," he growled. It was La Mariposa. She closed the door and came over to him.

"Good evening, my dear," he said pleasantly.

"Good evening, Mr. Colt. I—I received a telegram tonight from my mother. I thought you might be able to give me some information. Here it is."

The telegram read:

FIND OUT ABOUT MAN NAMED PAWNEE
BILL WHO SENT ME A CHECK FOR FIVE THOU-
SAND DOLLARS FROM TONTO CITY. THE BANK
MIGHT KNOW HIM.

MOTHER.

King Colt lifted his head and looked at her.

"Well, that's shore funny," he said. "Pawnee Bill was here a few days ago and told me he was headin' for San

Francisco. He didn't say anythin' about sendin' yore mother money. I don't *sabe* that."

"But who is he?" she asked.

"Oh, I dunno. Sort of a queer old jigger—allus has plenty money. Yore mother don't say why he sent the money."

"No, she doesn't say," agreed La Mariposa. "It seems so queer—that five thousand dollars."

"Yuh mean it's queer he sent it?"

"My mother needs an operation," explained the girl. "The doctors said it would cost about that much. It seems as though Heaven sent it."

"Well, that's a good way of lookin' at it," said King Colt. "But I'd tell her to spend it and not bother who sent it. Pawnee Bill can shore afford to send that much money."

"But why should he?"

King Colt shook his head. "Pawnee Bill didn't tell me. Mebbe he's payin' a debt. That kinda looks like the reason. Mebbe he's an old friend, who changed his name."

"But he sent it to my mother's address and she has only lived there three months."

King Colt squinted thoughtfully for several moments. Then:

"By golly, I plumb forgot that Pawnee Bill said he just got back from a trip east. I'll betcha he found out back there, mebbe he seen her, and she didn't know him. But, shucks, there's no use makin' guesses."

"No, I don't suppose there is, Mr. Colt. Well, it is nearly time for me to sing again. Thank you very much."

"Yo're welcome, I'm shore. Come in any time."

King Colt chuckled after she had gone.

"I dang near showed my hand that time," he told himself.

"I almost denied knowin' Pawnee Bill—the danged old spendthrift."

HENRY AND JUDGE were in the office, when Oscar Johnson came from the post office with a letter, which he handed to Henry. It bore the letterhead of the Board of Commissioners. Henry sighed and looked at Judge.

"The shooting," he said, "will take place at sunrise."

"You anticipate, sir," reminded Judge.

"And correctly, Judge. I have been expecting it, since the commissioners met yesterday."

"Read it," said Judge. "It cannot be worse than this suspense."

Slowly Henry removed the letter and smoothed it on the desk-top. It read:

Dear Sheriff:

At a meeting held today to discuss the situation existing in Wild Horse Valley, we decided to withhold any drastic action for thirty days.

Newspapers and public opinions force us to act, no matter what our private opinions may be. Please be advised that unless the crime situation is cleared up within thirty days of the above date, your resignation will be demanded. Wishing you luck, I am

Sincerely yours,

Edward Mitchell,

Chairman.

"The wolves," declared Judge, "have warned the sick calf."

"Who is a sick calf?" demanded Henry. "You? I will have you know, sir, that I am not ailing in any manner or form."

"Thirty days—then what?" asked Judge. "Abdication?"

"You were never intended for tragedy, Judge," said Henry. "Your voice squeaked on that last word. The audience would laugh. Sit down. One would think that thirty days were only thirty seconds. You are pawing mentally, sir. Be calm. After all, it is my resignation, Judge. They might appoint you."

"I am afraid," said Judge, "that Wild Horse Valley has lost its sense of humor and has begun to look facts squarely in the face."

"Then you agree with the commissioners, Judge?"

"I do not—except from their angle, of course."

"Judge," said Henry soberly, "what would you say were I to tell you that within a week we will have the murderers behind the bars, and will have recovered all the stolen money?"

"I would say that you are crazy."

"So would I," replied Henry.

"Well, but—er—do you claim such a thing, Henry?"

"I am not that crazy, Judge," replied Henry dryly.

"I have my private opinions," mumbled Judge. "Well, what is to be done? Are we to sit here waiting for the end? Thirty days goes quickly, sir. If you go, we all go. What do you say, Oscar?"

"Me?" Oscar looked up quickly. "Ay can vip him on a ship-skin."

"Who?"

"Yulius Swensen, das hurse-faced Norvegian."

"Oscar, have you any idea what we were talking about?"

"Ay have troubles of my own, Yudge; to ha'al vit anyt'ing else."

"A true philosopher, Judge," remarked Henry. "Self comes first. Please do not bother to explain it to him, it would not help the issue in any way. In fact, he might adopt the wrong attitude, and cause a vacancy or two in the commission. Let two-thirds of us worry, while one-third plans an attack against Norway."

Just then Tuck Darnell of the Circle M sauntered into the office. Tuck was tall, lean, raw-boned, lazy-eyed. He had tried his hand at being a professional gambler, but with little success, and this had been his first chance at running a cattle-ranch.

"Hailstorm Miller didn't leave much to be run," he told Henry. "If yuh ask me, I'd say that the bank got the worst of the deal. But McRae says he'll ship in a bunch of Mexican calves pretty soon, and we'll get goin' all right."

"I hear that Steve McRae wants to run the ranch," said Henry.

Darnell laughed shortly. "Steve couldn't run a ranch. He's all right there in the bank."

"Not exactly a fount of commercial and financial wisdom," remarked Judge.

"Well, he ain't so awful smart," admitted Darnell, smiling. "Have yuh heard anythin' from Jimmy Miller?"

"Not a word," replied Henry. "I suppose he is in Mexico."

"I was readin' the *Weekly Clarion*," said Darnell abruptly.

"You should spend your spare time in reading something intelligent," said Judge. "The classics, for instance."

"Yeah," replied Darnell, grinning. "King Colt said *that* was a classic."

"True," agreed Henry. "Rather bombastic and belligerent, but true."

"You don't agree with him, do yuh, Sheriff?" asked Darnell.

"Oh, absolutely."

"Yo're a queer sort of a jigger, Conroy. Nobody has ever been able to quite figure you out, don'tcha know it?"

"And when they do," said Henry seriously, "it will be too late."

"Too late for what?"

"Well, Darnell, I haven't quite figured that out myself."

"Uh-huh. Well, I've got to go to Scorpion Bend, along with Steve McRae. Some kind of a show up there tonight, and Steve wants to see it."

"Tonto City," sighed Henry, "needs a theater."

"Tonto City needs a lot of things," remarked Judge.

"We will not go into that, sir," said Henry quickly. "I believe that has been capably outlined in the *Clarion*."

11

CONROYS DON'T CRINGE

THINGS WERE LIVELY at the Tonto that night. The place was filled with miners, and all the games were going full-blast. King Colt smiled his satisfaction at the play as he lounged around the room. Suddenly Hake and two of his men came through the crowd and joined King Colt.

"We've been watchin' Tallant's ranch, King," reported Hake. "Just before dark Jimmy Miller rode in from the south and joined Jack Tallant at the ranch. They both came to Tonto City."

"You mean to say that Jimmy Miller and Jack Tallant are both in town?"

"Yeah," said Hake. "I dunno where Tallant went—but Miller's in jail."

"The sheriff got him, eh?"

"We got him, and turned him over to the sheriff, King."

"I'll be damned! But where is Jack Tallant?"

Joe Hake shrugged his shoulders. *"Quien sabe?* We lost him."

"So Jimmy Miller's in jail, eh?" mused King Colt. "Well, that should satisfy folks. Keep an eye out for Jack Tallant."

"We'll be on the lookout for him, King."

King Colt was pleased about the arrest of Jimmy Miller,

but Sheriff Henry seemed to feel very differently. Over at the sheriff's office he and Judge were conferring with John Harper, the prosecutor.

"The only thing to do is go ahead and try to build up a case against Jimmy Miller," said Harper.

"Damned meddling fools!" exploded Judge. "One would think they had been hired to hunt outlaws. I do not believe Jimmy Miller ever had anything to do with that stage robbery and murder. What is your opinion, Henry?"

"I am merely the law, sir; a hired servant of the public, sworn to combat crime in all its phases. It is not my business to pass upon the guilt or innocence of anyone. In plain English, I don't know a damn bit more about it than you do, and I felt like kicking the seat of Joe Hakes pants right up around his scrawny neck."

"Bravo!" applauded Judge. "My sentiments, exactly, sir."

"And I do not believe," added Henry. "Joe Hake's pants are in any immediate danger."

With that the conference broke up and Henry went over to the Tonto Saloon. He drifted from saloon to gambling room and over to the honkytonk, smiling, greeting friends. He was listening to La Mariposa sing an encore, when a man grasped him by the sleeve and panted in his ear:

"The bank, Sheriff! The front winders are busted. Didn't yuh feel the explosion?"

"Explosion?" gasped Henry. "No, I never heard nor felt it."

The word had spread, and Henry was at the tail-end of the procession which rushed across the street to the bank. There Judge was trying to keep the crowd back while someone went to find Howard McRae.

"I heard and felt it, Henry," said Judge. "The windows are ruined, and the bank is still full of powder smoke."

"My goodness!" exclaimed Henry. "What next?"

HOWARD MCRAE ARRIVED a moment later, and they entered the bank with the crowd at their heels. The vault door was sagging on twisted hinges, and it seemed as if everything had been taken except papers, which were strewn all over the room, flung there by the force of the explosion. The lock on the back door had been jimmied. McRae was speechless.

Henry was puttering around, examining things, when Ed Mitchell, chairman of the commissioners, and Al Cooper, another member of the board, came up to him.

"It looks very bad, Sheriff," observed Mitchell. "The loss of all that money will be a blow to Wild Horse Valley. McRae will never be able to weather the storm, I am afraid. Outside his own, there is little money invested in this bank; but there were plenty of depositors."

"My goodness!" exclaimed Henry. "Something must be done."

"Gentlemen," said Howard McRae, "I am afraid there is no use posting guards around here, because there is nothing left for anyone to steal."

Henry and Judge went back to the office, and sat down to talk things over. Oscar joined them, but said nothing. After a moment or two Henry looked at his watch thoughtfully.

"They must have timed that explosion for the moment when La Mariposa was singing," he said. "I never felt it. I suppose it was because of the confusion in the Tonto. You felt it, Oscar?"

"Yah, su-ure," replied Oscar. "Ay hord it."

"Where were you?" asked Henry.

"Ay vars in here. Ay vars back in de yail, and Ay vars yust going to find you, ven Ay hord de dynamite go off—unt Ay forgot."

"Intelligent, to say the least," remarked Judge.

"You were going to find me and then forgot," said Henry. "What were you going to find me for—and what did you forget, Oscar?"

"Va'al," explained Oscar blandly, "Ay vars back in de yail to talk vit Jimmy Miller—und he vars not in de yail; so I—"

"He was not in the jail?" yelped Judge. "What do you mean?"

"Va'al, he vars not in de yail, Yudge; he vars gone."

"What!" gasped Henry, getting to his feet. "Gone!"

They crowded down the narrow corridor to the cell, in which they had locked Jimmy Miller. The door was sagging open, and of their prisoner there was no trace. Judge leaned against the bars, staring into the empty cell.

"My God!" he exclaimed. "Even if someone brings us a criminal, we cannot keep him. Henry, that door has been unlocked! It hasn't been broken."

"Thank goodness!"

"Thank—Henry, why do you say that?"

"No repair bill, Judge."

"Of all the—Henry, I believe I can see it now! Jimmy Miller came to town with Jack Tallant. Tallant got Jimmy out of jail, and together they wrecked the bank. What a mess!"

"You may be right, sir," admitted Henry. "Let us go back where we may sit down; I feel weak in the legs."

John Harper entered the office, as they came in, and Judge blurted out the latest news to the prosecutor.

"This situation is really getting funny," said Harper. "I do not mean the fact that the bank was looted, nor that the prisoner escaped. There is no humor in that situation; but the mere fact that everything seems to happen around here."

"I would advise that we apprehend Jack Tallant and Jimmy Miller," said Judge. "No doubt they came here to rob the bank, and there is no doubt in my mind that Jack Tallant released Jimmy Miller. In my—wait a moment! that lock was not broken. Well, where on earth would Jack Tallant get a key to that jail door? Henry, I believe you were the last to—Oscar, was the front door locked, when you came here, before you discovered that the prisnner was missing?"

"The door vars not locked," declared Oscar.

"Henry, did you forget to lock the office door?"

"I forget whether I did or not, Judge. But that is beside the fact that the cell door was unlocked. Did you or Oscar forget to lock Jimmy Miller in that cell?"

"Oscar, did you forget to lock the cell door?" asked Judge.

"Ay did not lock it," stated Oscar. "Ay vars not here."

"No, that is true," nodded Judge. "I locked it myself."

"You think you did, Judge," said Henry.

"Well, he's gone, so there's no use accusing anyone," said Harper.

AFTER JOHN HARPER left the office, Oscar sauntered out to the street. Judge tilted back in his chair, deep in a study of the situation, while Henry hunched over his desk, drawing meaningless curlycues on a sheet of paper. Finally Judge said:

"Henry, I do not expect an answer to this, but by any chance, did you—"

"I did not, sir."

"You might at least wait for the question, sir. But as long as you anticipated it, I shall accept your answer."

"What did you want to know, Judge?"

"If you really locked that cell door."

"Just like a lawyer," sighed Henry. "But *you* locked that door."

"And," declared Judge, "it required human hands and a cell-door key to unlock it again. There are no miracles."

"One never knows, does one?" asked Henry quietly. "The day of miracles may be past in most places, but anything can happen in Arizona."

"You might make an effort to perform one during the next thirty days, Henry. Nothing less than a miracle can save us."

"I think," said Henry wearily, "that I shall go over to the Tonto and buy a drink. Wouldst join me?"

"Wouldst," nodded Judge. "I feel the need of several drinks."

King Colt bought them a drink and tried to find out if they had any suspicions. They did not tell him that Jimmy Miller had escaped. Colt said that he was afraid that Howard McRae's finances would not allow him to reopen the bank or pay off the losses to the depositors.

"I lose plenty money," he told them sourly. "In fact, every cent of my cash was in that bank. If anybody won heavy tonight, I'd shore be stuck, 'cause all I've got is what I've taken in today."

"You have a good play tonight," remarked Henry, looking around.

"Yeah, it's goin' pretty good. Say, did you fellers see Jack Tallant?"

They had not seen him. King Colt was thoughtful for several moments.

"He came here with Jimmy Miller," he told them. "My men brought Miller over to you, but they lost track of Jack Tallant."

"Just why were your men watching the Tallant ranch?" asked Henry.

"Why—uh—who told yuh that?" asked King Colt quickly.

"Jimmy Miller. He said that Jack told him."

King Colt finished his drink and bit the end off a fresh cigar.

"Jack Tallant must have been imaginin' things," he said. "There ain't no reason for my men watchin' him."

"When you asked about Jack Tallant," said Henry, "did you have any idea that Jack might be connected with that bank robbery, Mr. Colt?"

"Oh, no; I was merely wondering where he went."

"I see," nodded Henry. "Well, let us have another drink, before we go to bed. You will join us, Mr. Colt? Thank you, sir."

They filled their glasses, and Henry said:

"That last libation was to our good healths. Let us drink this one to the complete success of the first miracle I have ever performed."

King Colt looked curiously at Henry. "Miracle. What the devil is a miracle, Conroy?"

"In plain English, Mr. Colt, a miracle is something that cannot be done."

"That's funny. Yo're goin' to do somethin' that can't be done? What is it?"

"I can't tell you yet," said Henry. "There is one I have been practicing ever since I was elected, but I have failed dismally."

"What is the miracle you have been practicing?" asked Judge.

"Putting my two feet on the desk-top, and not upsetting my chair. Good night, Mr. Colt."

PANCHO LOPEZ JOINED King Colt, and they went back to the office. "I 'ave check up on the boys," said Pancho, "and I do not theenk any of them rob that bank. Mos' of them were here in the saloon."

King Colt nodded grimly. "Jack Tallant pulled that job," he said.

"You theenk so?"

"Sure. Old Gila Jim said he'd get even with me. Damn him, he knew that my money was in that bank. For a plugged nickel I'd go down there and fix him so that he couldn't even ride in a chair."

"Suppose we go there?" queried Pancho. "Men can be made to talk."

"Not that old sidewinder; he'd die first. Jack might, but I don't believe he would. Maybe we'll try it—later. Pancho, we've got to stop all this stuff that's goin' on. Damn it, we haven't got a cent of it! You ain't seen them two Mexicans, have yuh?"

Pancho shook his head, "I don't theenk they help us any, Keeng."

"I reckon we're kinda goin' to seed around here, Pancho. Instead of featherin' our own nest, we're losin' what feathers we've got. Go back and keep both ears open. Tell Joe Hake to take one man and go back to where he can watch that Tallant ranch. We've got to be smart."

The heavy play at the gaming tables slowed down about two o'clock in the morning. Because most of the bets were in silver and gold, the bulk of the money was moved back to King Colt's office, rather than to keep it in sight on the tables. A guard stood at the door, which was locked as an additional safety measure, and only men with the money were admitted.

King Colt had an old iron safe, standing wide open against the wall. On his desk, in more or less orderly stacks, were the gold and silver coins, which he was checking on a piece of paper before sacking them for the safe.

Suddenly he heard the sound of crashing glass behind him. He reached for a six-shooter on the desk near his right hand, but a voice drawled:

"Don't touch it! Turn around."

Slowly King Colt drew his hand back and turned his head. Coming through the window, shoving the curtain aside, were the twin muzzles of a double-barrel shotgun. The voice continued:

"Hand over that money, pardner. Sack it up and hand it over—and be damn quick about it. I'll take it, whether yo're alive or dead. That door is locked and you've got the key. I can come in, take the money and be gone, long before they can break down the door. And two dozen buckshot in yore belly won't help yuh none. Make it fast, hombre."

Cursing quietly, impotently, King Colt sacked the money. He knew that he was losing over three thousand dollars, and he also knew that the man behind that gun would not hesitate to shoot him. The muzzles were almost against his waist as he shoved the money between the curtains, but he realized that it would be foolishness on his part to try and do anything about it.

Then the shotgun was withdrawn, letting the curtain sag back into place. Someone was knocking on the door. He unlocked it to admit the dealer from the roulette wheel.

"I've got to have a couple hundred more, King," he said.

"Get it from the bartender. I've just been robbed of every damn cent we've taken in today—through that window."

"Are—are you joking, King?"

"Do I look like I was? Find Pancho Lopez and send him in to me."

"Shall we notify the sheriff, King?"

"Wait until mornin'—he can't do anythin'."

"Say, I just heard something, King. That Swede jailer told one of the boys that Jimmy Miller escaped before the bank was robbed."

"How did he escape?" asked King Colt.

"The Swede seemed to think that they forgot to lock his cell."

"Before the bank was robbed, eh? And Jack Tallant was in town. Send Pancho to me as soon as yuh can find him... That dirty old cripple!"

HENRY AND JUDGE knew nothing about the Tonto

robbery, until they were eating breakfast in the hotel next morning. Then Josephine told them.

"Ay don't know yust vat happened," she explained. "Yulius told me."

"He said that someone robbed the Tonto?" queried Henry.

"Yah. Yulius says they get about t'ree t'ousand dollars."

"And they never even awakened us," mourned Judge. "That is what they think of us, Henry."

"Anyway, they are considerate, Judge; they let us sleep."

"A fine state of affairs, when—oh, well, it doesn't matter, as far as that is concerned. Next week would have done just as well, as far as us being of any assistance is concerned. We are still the Shame of Arizona."

"You should write a piece for the paper," said Henry, helping himself to more toast, "and sign it *Vox Populi*. Or is it *Nux Vomica?* I get my Latin twisted at times."

"The latter would be more appropriate. But the news does not seem to have affected your appetite, Henry."

"You mean the fact that the Tonto was robbed? It is rather amusing, Judge. Dog eat dog, I would say. King Colt and his gamblers take the money away from the public and the robber takes the money away from King Colt. It is much the same thing, except that the robber has a smaller overhead."

"You condone crime, Henry?"

"Not at all, sir. I *am* concerned over the bank robbery, because innocent folks suffer. There is no innocence connected with the Tonto so I refuse to lose my appetite. Now, if you are sufficiently calm, we will go over and have a talk with Mr. Colt. He may have interesting news."

King Colt was still asleep in his room, so they stood at the bar and received most of the details from the bartender. He had not been on shift, but he had heard it from one of the gamblers.

"He told me," informed the bartender, "that the feller got over three thousand dollars. But King Colt is a good loser, Sheriff."

"The world has too few of them, sir," replied Henry, and they went over to the bank. There Howard McRae was trying to bring about some semblance of order.

"It is useless," he told Henry. "The vault is empty. All that is left are a few mortgages, non-negotiable bonds, and such things that were of no value to a thief. I am afraid that the Bank of Tonto is no more. The vault contained approximately twenty thousand in silver, gold and currency. Every cent is gone."

"This will be quite a loss to everyone," said Henry.

"Every cent I had was in this bank," declared McRae. "Every cent my son had, too. Not that it was any fortune, but a fairly good nest-egg for a young man."

"Where is Steve?" asked Judge.

"At Scorpion Bend, unless they have started home. He and Tuck Darnell went up there yesterday. Some show was coming to town and Steve wanted to see it."

"We need a theater in Tonto City," said Henry.

"We shall need a bank worse than a theater," said Judge.

They went down to the office, where Henry picked up a pencil and did a little simple arithmetic.

"Forty-six thousand dollars has been stolen in our bailiwick in just a few short days, Judge," he announced. "A tidy sum, indeed."

"And two men have died," added Judge sourly. "That is of more importance, Henry. I shudder in anticipation of what will be in the *Weekly Clarion*. The editor is a close friend of Al Cooper, and Cooper might give him a copy of the letter to you. These two robberies, coupled with the fact that Jimmy Miller escaped from a locked jail—Henry, I cringe inwardly."

"I never cringe in anticipation, sir," declared Henry. "The Conroys have never been cringers. We have qualms, of course. Sometimes qualms are mistaken for cringes. But if you get right down to the scientific aspect of a qualm, you will discover—"

"Henry," interrupted Judge, "you are a damn fool, sir."

"I bow to superior wisdom. Let us ride out to the ranch and see if Bill Shakespeare has brought in any more coyote ears. I feel depressed over the whole affair, and some of Frijole's distillation might serve to lift us out of the slough of despond. And it will also save us from answering embarrassing questions."

12

THAT FINE CASTILIAN HAND...

PANCHO LOPEZ STOOD in the dust of the road, holding the reins of his horse and talking with a little, wide-eyed Mexican boy, mounted on an old, gray mule. They were only about a mile from Tonto City. Pancho had a small, folded sheet of paper in his hand which he had taken from the little Mexican.

"She say," said the boy, "you tak' theese *nota* to Jack Tallant, and you not tell anybody."

"*Buena,*" said Pancho. "You are a good boy. She geeve you a dollar to tak' the *nota*—I geeve you a dollar for the note. You get two dollar, instead of one dollar. Pretty queek you be reech man."

"But the *señorita* say for me to tak'—"

"Leesten!" snapped Pancho. "You know who I am? No? I am ver' bad man. For two *centavos*, I cut off your ear. You go home and say notheeng to this *señorita*. You say notheeng to anybody. You onnerstan? You spik of me tak' the *nota*, I cut off your ear."

"I not spik," said the boy nervously.

"*Buena!* You are smart. You tell anybody—I find out— and you lose two good ear. Go home and say notheeng. Anyway, you got two dollar."

"I not spik," said the boy. Pancho motioned, and the boy went back toward Tonto City, his mule shuffling the dust in a half-trot.

Pancho looked after him, a speculative smile on his face. The boy would not tell anyone, Pancho was sure. As the boy and mule faded away in the dust-haze, Pancho read the note to Jack Tallant from La Mariposa.

Jack:

They think you robbed the bank and the Tonto. You and your father are in great danger. Take him to a safe place.

E.M.

Pancho read the note carefully several times, after which he put it in his pocket and rode back to Tonto City. He had seen La Mariposa give the note to the little Mexican boy and had decided that it was worth investigation.

Actually the note was worth many times that dollar to Pancho. It was simple as two and two now. La Mariposa, rooming directly above King Colt's office at the Tonto, was able to hear what was said down in that office. It was she who had told the Border Patrol about the drug smuggling scheme. She had heard King Colt's plans to get even with Gila Jim Tallant—this note proved it.

Just how to handle the situation, Pancho was not sure. If he told King Colt about it, that might be the end of La Mariposa's engagement at the Tonto. It might also be the end of La Mariposa's engagement at any place. King Colt knew how to deal with spies. And Pancho Lopez desired the beautiful singer.

He decided to withhold this information and handle the

girl in his own gentle way. So he went back to the Tonto, the note safely concealed in his pocket.

King Colt was at the bar and he had been drinking heavily.

"I sent for Joe Hake to come in," he told Pancho. "I'm through foolin', Pancho. There's been forty-six thousand dollars stolen in the last few days and I want to know what became of that money. Nobody talks. I'm goin' to make somebody talk!"

"You forgot to add the loss of those drugs," said Pancho quietly.

"Yeah, that's right."

Pancho laughed shortly. "I have talk weeth Old Juan. He don' know w'at it was all about, Keeng. But somebody know, eh? We go broke pretty queek."

"Some day," said King Colt darkly, "I'll find out who told the Border Patrol about them sweat-pads, and I'll cut his heart out."

"Sure," agreed Pancho. "You tak' the heart—I'll tak' the leever."

They walked back to the office. From overhead came the sound of hammering. Pancho looked curiously at the ceiling.

"W'at ees going on up there?" he asked.

"Oh, I'm fixin' up the room a little for La Mariposa," replied King Colt easily. "She's worth a little extra; so I'm havin' a man put down a extra heavy carpet in her room. It's shore a beauty, Pancho. Got a thick pad under it, and the carpet is awful thick, too. Cost me a couple hundred dollars in Scorpion Bend, but it'll be worth the money."

Pancho looked thoughtfully at King Colt, who was leaning back in his chair, smoking his cigar and gazing up at the ceiling.

"She only had a couple cheap rugs on the floor," said King Colt. "Sometimes yuh could hear her walkin' across the floor."

Pancho nodded indifferently. It was clear that King Colt knew that La Mariposa had spied on them.

"How much you lose in the bank robbery?" asked Pancho.

"All I had in there," replied King Colt. "Then I lost most all I make here. Pretty soon King Colt will have to take a shovel job in the mines, unless my luck turns."

SOMEONE TAPPED LIGHTLY on the door, and King Colt opened it, to find La Mariposa. She saw Pancho and drew back. "Oh, I thought you were alone, Mr. King," she said. "I'll come back later."

"No, no, come right in."

She entered the room, closing the door.

"How do yuh like the new fixin's for yore room?" asked King Colt.

"They are lovely. But I—I received a letter from my mother today. She is not very well, and asks me to come home. I'm sorry, but I must leave here Saturday night. You see, I didn't want to leave you until after the Saturday night show."

"Well!" exclaimed King Colt, "I'm shore sorry about that. Why, I dunno what we'll do without yuh. Would yuh—is it money trouble?"

"No, you have been very generous. But I feel that she needs me."

"Well, shore—shore. But can't yuh come back again?"

"No, I'm afraid not. Mother isn't able to travel, and I don't like to leave her alone. I am very grateful to you, Mr. King, and I wish you all the good fortune in the world."

"Well," laughed King Colt, "we won't say goodbye—not yet. You've still got a few days to play yore tunes on the fiddle. But we'll shore miss yuh."

"Thank you, Mr. King. Well, that's all, I guess."

After she left the room, King Colt smoked thoughtfully for a while.

"Mighty nice girl, Pancho," he said. "Good blood."

"W'at do you know about blood?" queried the Mexican.

"Well, I've spilled quite a lot of it. She ain't no riff-raff."

"W'at ees reef-raff?"

"Well, blood like ours—me and you."

"*Por Dios*, I am no reef-raff. You theenk I am *Mejicano?* You know w'at blood ees een me?"

"Sure; Mexican and Yaqui Injun."

"*Madre de Dios!* Yaqui! My modder was from Castile, and my fadder was from Valencia. I am pure Spanish, me— Pancho Adolfo Alejo Bonifacio Guillermo—"

"Names! They don't cost anythin'. You was born in a mud hut in Hermosillo and don't lie about it."

"Eet ees no crime for being poor, Keeng."

"Aw, hell, I'm sorry, Pancho. They didn't yank no silver spoon out of my mouth, when I made my first yelp in this world. I reckon I was thinkin' about La Mariposa leavin' here. I dunno how I'll find somebody to take her place. I reckon I'll go up to my room and take a snooze. You watch for Joe Hake, and send him to me, Pancho."

HENRY WAS AT the general store that evening, when Steve McRae and Tuck Darnell rode in from Scorpion Bend.

Steve McRae went home, but the foreman of the Circle M stopped to chat a few minutes.

"Did you enjoy the show at Scorpion Bend?" asked Henry.

"Not me," replied Darnell. "I like to laugh."

"What was the play, Tuck?"

"*East Lynn,*" replied Tuck, grimacing. "I never did like that show, but Steve wanted to see it. Too much tears t' suit me. But we don't get no shows very often; so we have to take what we get."

"We need a theater here," remarked Henry.

"Well, if yuh do," said Tuck Darnell, "get us some funny shows."

A little later Steve McRae came from the McRae home, joined Tuck Darnell, and they rode toward the Circle M ranch.

… Henry and Judge were still in bed next morning, when a commotion on the street awakened them. Judge went to a front window and drew aside the curtain, peering sleepy-eyed into the street. Then he turned and said:

"Some men are running up the street, Henry, following two men on horseback. This may mean more trouble, sir."

"Verily," yawned Henry. "Anything from a robbery to a free drink. Well, I suppose we may as well arise to face another day."

Someone knocked heavily on the door, and the unmistakable accents of Josephine Swensen followed:

"Hanry! Yoo-hoo! Yudge!"

"Yes, my dear," called Judge, tugging at a boot.

"Dere is ha'al to pay!" she yelled. "Somebody has mordered de banker."

"The banker?" exclaimed Henry.

"Yah! Ay vars told to tell you."

Then Josephine went clattering down the hall, her mission fulfilled. Henry and Judge stared at each other.

"Howard McRae!" grunted Judge. "Henry, this is terrible."

"Yes," agreed Henry quietly, "but it could have been worse."

"How could it have been worse?"

"It could have been you or me, Judge. Pardon me, but that is my coat, not your pants, which you are trying to put on your legs."

Judge cast aside the offending garment and grabbed for his pants.

"Why on earth would anybody kill Howard McRae?" he demanded.

Henry yawned and reached for his boots. "I'm very sure I do not know the answer, Judge. His rate of interest was normal, I believe. Well, if you are ready... Judge, you simply can not make a bow-tie from one of my black silk socks. I have tried it."

"Things like this make me nervous," admitted Judge. "What will that damnable editor say now, I wonder. Why, McRae is one of our most prominent men, and we can ill afford to lose—"

"No eulogies, please," begged Henry. "We must investigate."

Half the population of Tonto City was milling around the McRae home. Someone had called Doctor Bogart, and he had arrived soon enough to keep them out of the house and away from the corpse.

HOWARD MCRAE WAS lying in the middle of the main room, sprawled in his own blood, fully dressed. He had been killed by a blow on the head. Steve McRae and Tuck Darnell, who had discovered the crime, were there. They had ridden in from the ranch that morning and discovered the tragedy.

Henry examined the corpse, listening to Doctor Bogart explain the cause of death.

"It is apparent that robbery was the motive," said Judge. "You can see that everything has been searched."

"It's the same thing in every room," said Tuck Darnell huskily. "Me and Steve went all over the house. They shore upset every room."

"Looking for what?" queried Henry. Steve McRae shook his head. He was very white and seemed sick.

"Did your father keep any considerable amount of money in the house?" asked Henry. Steve laughed shortly.

"After that bank robbery? It cleaned us both out."

"Your father had something that someone wanted, I presume."

"I don't know what it could have been, Sheriff. Maybe they thought he had money. When he tried to fight them off—well—"

Henry nodded and went back to Doctor Bogart.

"I want to look over the place alone, Doctor," he said.

The doctor nodded, and Henry began a search of the rooms. Dresser drawers had been yanked out, the contents flung aside. Beds had been torn apart, and even carpets had been torn loose from the floor. Henry picked up some of the scattered papers and glanced at them. One small one happened to be a bill-of-sale for two horses, written in pen and ink by King Colt, and signed by him.

After looking things over carefully, Henry went back to the coroner, who had asked several of the men to help him carry the body down to his place.

"Any luck, Henry?" queried Judge, as they went back to town.

"Sir, I never depend on luck," replied Henry. "My observations are strictly scientific. I presume you meant to ask me if I had any worth-while ideas on the cause of the murder."

"I am willing to change my query to read as you state, Henry. Have you any worth-while ideas on the cause of the murder?"

"None at all, sir. But I will say that I have a glimmering of an idea. It is nearly as vague as the Lord's Prayer on the point of a pin, but I shall attempt to magnify it."

A little later Henry met Steve McRae on the street and tried to get some information from the young man.

"Do you know of any enemy your father may have had who would do such a thing, Steve?" he asked.

"I don't believe my father had any enemies," replied Steve.

"That would be rather remarkable, my boy. I ask you to be frank with me in this matter."

"I don't know a damn thing," declared Steve stubbornly.

"What were your father's relations with King Colt, previous to the time King Colt came to Tonto City?"

"What are you gittin' at, anyway?" asked Steve. "They didn't know each other. What made you think they did?"

"Your father financed King Colt to buy and rebuild the Tonto."

"Why not? Bankers do things like that."

"What collateral did King Colt furnish him?"

Steve's eyes narrowed, as he looked at Henry. "That was my father's business, Conroy," he said. "King Colt paid it all back."

"That is fine. I suppose it will show on the books of the bank."

"Why—er—oh, certainly. Of course, it will. But my father is gone and the bank is broke."

"Yes, I understand all that, Steve. But I still have a feeling that you could help me, if you were so inclined."

"Like I told you a while ago—I don't know a damn thing, Conroy."

"Well, thank you very much—for not knowing anything. Good day, sir."

Henry found John Harper, the prosecutor, at the office, talking with Judge. Harper was extremely upset over the murder of Howard McRae.

"This is terrible, Henry," he declared. "No clues, I suppose."

"None, John. Are the bank books still locked up in the bank?"

"Why, yes, they are, Henry. I have a key, of course."

"Good. Could those books be removed to a vault in the courthouse?"

"Why, yes, I suppose they could. But why should they? You don't suppose that the books would show—"

"John, we are grasping at straws," interrupted Henry.

The lawyer looked keenly at Henry for several moments.

"I shall have them removed at once, Henry," he said. "You may be right."

John Harper lost no time in getting some men to assist him in removing all the books from the bank. Henry saw Steve McRae on the Tonto porch, watching the operation and talking to Tuck Darnell. Later they rode away together, presumably going back to the ranch.

"Surely, you do not suspect Steve McRae," said Judge. "Why, he was devoted to his father."

"Judge," replied Henry, "I have no idea of linking Steve McRae with the murder of his father, but I do believe that Steve knows more than he is willing to tell. There may not be a thing wrong with those books. But if there is—someone is going to become worried. I believe you are familiar with that old saying, 'Whom the gods would destroy, they first make mad', or something to that effect."

Judge nodded thoughtfully. "Yes, I have heard that, Henry."

"In plain words, Judge, I am going to try and make them tip their hand, if that makes it more plain."

"Even," remarked Judge soberly, "if that tipping gets us each a load of buckshot in our vitals."

"Even so," nodded Henry, and added, "within thirty days, Judge."

THE SCORPION BEND *WEEKLY CLARION* came next day on the stage, and Judge fairly limped as he brought a copy down to the office.

"The driver," remarked Judge wearily, "said that the editor worked all night, getting out this damnable malformation of—look at it, Henry."

Across the top of the page in large, block type was:

ANOTHER MURDER IN TONTO CITY!

And under that, printed in type only a trifle smaller was this:

A LAST MOMENT DISPATCH TELLS OF THE FOUL MURDER WEDNESDAY NIGHT OF HOWARD MCRAE. BANKER AND PROMINENT CITIZEN OF TONTO CITY. BEATEN TO DEATH IN HIS OWN HOME. THE SHERIFF'S OFFICE HAS NO CLUES—AS USUAL.

"The printing," said Henry, "is atrocious."

Judge groaned and made burbling noises in his skinny throat.

"Ah, yes, the editorial," mused Henry, turning the page. "Well, well! He also prints that in large type. Badly printed, too. Let me see-e-e. He has a heading which reads:

" 'The invitation was accepted.' Not bad, Judge. He further deposes:

" 'Tonto City's open invitation to crime seems to have been accepted. Bank robbers, working under the scarlet proboscis of our estimable sheriff, wrecked the Tonto City Bank, financially and physically. They shook the city with dynamite, unheard and unfelt by the sheriff, who was at that moment listening to a fiddler at the Tonto Honky-tonk, and made away with over twenty thousand dollars.

" 'And then, while our protectors of Wild Horse Valley debated the proof of some newly and illegally made liquor, bandits held up King Colt, owner of the Tonto Gambling

Palace, and took away more than three thousand dollars. Nothing has been done about it, nothing will be done.

" 'But there is one ray of sunshine for the peace loving folks of Wild Horse Valley. The Board of Commissioners have given the present incompetent incumbent of the sheriff's office just thirty days in which to solve these crimes—or get out. In less than twenty-five days we will have a new, and we hope, competent sheriff in office.' "

Judge groaned aloud, as Henry laid down the paper. Henry looked at him thoughtfully, but returned to his paper. Then his eyes searched out a small item, tucked away in a corner of the page. Slowly he folded the paper, a queer expression in his squinty eyes.

"I have a mind to sue him," declared Judge.

"Why?" asked Henry quietly.

"For slander, damme!" roared Judge. "That scurvy rat!"

"You were not mentioned, Judge," reminded Henry. "He never said one word about you or Oscar. I, alone, was the target for his vitriol throwing this time. And as for suing him for libel—I'm afraid he can prove his words."

"Well," groaned Judge, "what are we going to do, Henry? What can we do? Neither of us would recognize a clue if it were the size of Jumbo and made a noise like a locomotive."

"I agree," replied Henry soberly, "but it would be worth seeing."

"Is it possible for you to be serious, Henry?"

"My dear Judge, right now I am the most serious person in Wild Horse Valley. Within me is a wild, consuming desire to do something—and this time," Henry lowered his voice, "it is not a thing that baking soda will alleviate. For a little while we will sit quietly, waiting, waiting—"

"Waiting for what, Henry?"

"That," replied Henry quietly, "is something I haven't worked out."

KING COLT HAD ridden away with Joe Hake and two of their men. Pancho swaggered through the Tonto barroom, immaculate in a white flannel suit, freshly barbered and perfumed. La Mariposa, erstwhile June McLean, was in the honkytonk, rehearsing a song to the accompaniment of a tinny piano. Pancho stopped at the doorway between the gambling room and the honkytonk and listened to the song.

La Mariposa finished and started for the stairway, but Pancho blocked her way, a smile on his lips.

"*Señorita,* that was beautiful," he told her.

"Thank you," she said coldly. "And now, will you let me pass?"

"Oh, so the leetle song bird ees getting toff, eh? Leesten to me. You weel seet down weeth me for a leetle talk— about your good health."

"What do you mean?" she asked anxiously.

"Over at the leetle table, w'ere no one may hear, *señorita,* eh?"

Half-frightened, the girl followed him to a small table, where they sat down. Pancho waved a waiter away, and watched La Mariposa closely, as he carefully rolled a cigarette.

"You are very beautiful," he remarked. "Very beautiful, but not so very smart."

"What is this all about?" she asked, regaining her composure.

Pancho thought it over deeply. Suddenly he flashed her a smile and asked:

"How do you like your new carpet?"

"My carpet? What about my new carpet? Have you been in my room?"

"No, *señorita*," answered Pancho. "I hear the hammering on the ceiling, and Keeng Colt he tells me about the nice theek carpet on the floor. W'en you walk on the floor now, no one can hear you. Try to leesten—you hear notheeng."

La Mariposa went just a shade white, but she tried to fight off the fear that the carpet had been placed there for a purpose. Pancho was smiling at her.

"It is a nice carpet," she said. "King Colt is very thoughtful of my comfort."

"Aud of hees safety," added Pancho.

"What do you mean?" demanded the girl.

"Leesten to me," Pancho leaned closer, lowering his voice. "You forget that I am partner weeth Keeng Colt. In some theengs, eef he loses money, Pancho lose too. And Pancho ees damn bad loser, *señorita*."

"I—I don't understand what you are talking about."

"Eet must be true—w'at I said—you are ver' beautiful, but not so smart, La Mariposa. You leesten through the floor and you hear some plans. W'at you hear cost Keeng Colt and Pancho Lopez much money. You theenk you pull the wool over Keeng Colt's eyes? Bah! He ees like a cat weeth a mouse. You theenk you ever leeve here? You theenk wrong. There ees only one man who can help you—and that ees Pancho Lopez."

"And you would doublecross your partner to help me,"

said La Mariposa. Pancho flung his cigarette aside and leaned closer.

"*Dulce amiga,* w'en Pancho loves, he would doublecross the whole damn worl'."

"You are rather amusing," said the girl. "I have heard it said that King Colt only waits for a chance to kill you, Pancho Lopez."

Pancho shrugged his well-tailored shoulders. "*Quien sabe?* But I am not eenterested een my own life. That ees sometheeng to save, w'en the time come."

"Perhaps I feel the same about my own life."

"That ees being good sport," smiled Pancho. "Well, I 'ave warn you. Eef you tak' my advice you weel not wait for Saturday. The road ees open to Scorpion Bend—yet."

With a wave of his hand, Pancho got to his feet, bowed to the girl, who hurried away, and sauntered back to the bar.

"How are yuh hittin' it off with La Mariposa?" asked the bartender.

"I theenk she like me pretty good," replied Pancho expansively.

"Yeah, mebbe she does. I seen her talkin' with yuh, and that's more than she's talked with anybody else around here."

"The weemen all like Pancho Lopez. I am gentleman, educate', refine', handsome, got the good feeger, wear the swell clothes. Pretty good eh?"

"Yeah, that's right. But I'd keep away from La Mariposa, if I was you. King Colt is kinda staked out on that claim. He's done warned every man in the place to keep away from her, and he's prob'ly warned you, too."

"Keeng Colt may be the boss of the Tonto, but he ees

not the boss of Pancho Lopez. No man ees my boss—no man can geeve me the order. W'at you theenk of that, eh?"

"I'll leave it to you to do the thinkin', Pancho. Have a drink?"

Meanwhile La Mariposa paced restlessly in her room. She was genuinely alarmed over what Pancho had said, and she knew that it would be dangerous for her to stay in Tonto City. Pancho was not in sight when she came downstairs again, carrying some sheet music. She went to the piano, where she tried out the melody of one piece on the piano, picking it out with two fingers.

Tommy Roper, the stuttering proprietor of the livery stable, came in looking for someone. He smiled bashfully at La Mariposa. Suddenly she motioned him to her.

"I want to go to Scorpion Bend tonight," she told him quietly, "and I don't want anyone to know it. Could you have a horse and buggy out behind here at half-past nine tonight?"

Tommy nodded violently.

"You will drive it?" she asked.

Tommy nodded again. The girl drew a deep breath of relief.

"Behind here is a ladder," she told him. "My window is the last one toward the back. Could you put that ladder up to my window? I will let my valises down on a rope."

Tommy grinned foolishly and nodded again. It appealed to him.

"Remember—half-past nine tonight," she said.

One of the girls saw Tommy take off his hat to La Mariposa, and smiled widely. But La Mariposa paid no attention as she sat down at the piano again. The girl sauntered

back into the barroom. Pancho came from the front doorway, passing Tommy Roper. The girl smiled at Pancho and
said:

"The song-bird must be gettin' friendly, Pancho."

"You mean La Mariposa?" he asked.

"Sure. I seen her talkin' with you a while ago, and just
now she was talkin' with Tommy Roper, back by the piano,
and was he grinnin' and noddin'!"

"Oh, I theenk maybe she get lonesome," said Pancho,
and walked on to the bar, where he ordered a drink.

"So she talked with Tommy Roper, eh?" he remarked to
himself. "That *is* interesting."

13

CANTINA OF CUTTHROATS

HENRY HARRISON CONROY spent most of the day tilted back in his desk-chair, either deep in thought or half-asleep. He either grunted in reply to Judge's questions, or ignored them entirely. Oscar Johnson and Frijole Bill came from the ranch in the buckboard, and it was evident that both of them had been sampling Frijole's prune whisky. Henry yawned and looked at Judge.

"I believe we are going to Agua Frio, Judge," he said.

"Why go to that village of vice?" queried Judge. "If it has taken you all afternoon to arrive at such a decision—why waste your time, sir?"

"I believe we will find Jimmy Miller at Agua Frio, Judge."

"Suppose we do, Henry? We have no authority to take him out of there. In fact, as officers of the law of the sovereign state of Arizona, we have no right to go down there."

"I have no designs on the person of Jimmy Miller, Judge; I merely want to ask him a question."

"What sort of a question?"

"I shall ask him to identify his father's signature."

"His father's signature? On what, if I may ask, sir?"

"Oh, on a little bank check, Judge. If you remember correctly, Hailstorm Miller closed his small bank

account just before his death. He made out a check for
the full amount. After the dynamiting of the bank vault,
I happened to find that canceled check among the ruins.
Fate, perhaps."

"And you doubt the validity of that signature, Henry?"

"Yes—but without reason. You see, Judge, I am grasping
at straws and nothing is too small to investigate."

"But you surely do not suspect that the bank—"

"The bank held that mortgage, sir."

"But Howard McRae told me himself that they would
lose money—having to take the ranch in lieu of the ten
thousand dollars."

"I heard him say that, Judge. But just remember that
both the ten thousand dollars and the ranch were lost."

"Well," sighed Judge, "I am afraid you are barking up the
wrong tree. Anyhow, Howard McRae is dead."

"True, Judge, true. But Howard McRae had something
that the killers wanted. The condition of the house plainly
indicates that. McRae's fortune was supposed to have been
wiped out in that bank robbery. If he had no money left,
what did the murderers seek in his house? Anyway, I want
to find Jimmy Miller; so we will take that buckboard and
go to Agua Frio, hoping that we will find him."

Frijole and Oscar came in, Frijole lugging a big, battered
valise, roped shut.

"Going on a trip, Frijole?" inquired Judge.

"No, I ain't goin' very far," replied Frijole. "Me and Oscar
decided to drive down to Agua Frio and shake our feet a
few times. We ain't been to a Mexican dance for a long
time."

"What is in the valise?"

"Oh, that? That's my dance clothes, Henry. The ones you gave me."

"Oh, I see—the cutaway and the striped trousers."

"What about your dance clothes, Oscar?" asked Henry. Oscar grinned widely and with a glint of triumph in his little eyes.

"Oh, Ay am all fixed oop. Ay sent avay long time ago for suit, and it coom by freight t'ree days ago. Fits like ha'al, you bat you. You vait."

"Something special?" queried Henry.

"You bat you! Ay gave de measure to faller in Scorpion Bend and he sent it avay to New York. He said de President of de United States vould yump at a suit like dat. Ay have never seen anyt'ing like it."

"Well, now I think this will work out fine, Judge," said Henry. "We will rent a spring wagon at the stable, use our team, and all four of us go to Agua Frio tonight."

"It may not be as bad as it seems—to me," replied Judge, "but right now you could easily scratch a match on the goose-pimples on my back. Frijole, you and Oscar stop drinking, Sober up, so we may drive to Agua Frio in safety."

"Ay am de best damn driver in Arizona," declared Oscar.

"That cock-eyed Swede couldn't drive a nail," declared Frijole. "Leave it to me, Henry."

"Yes, Frijole—and we will all end up in some cañon."

"I believe I shall do the driving myself," said Judge.

"Perhaps," suggested Henry, "we should draw straws to see who does the driving—and then walk down there. It might be safer."

BUSINESS WAS QUIET at the Tonto that evening. King Colt had not returned; and Pancho Lopez had not been in the place since earlier in the afternoon. There was only a handful of men in the honkytonk, when La Mariposa sang at eight o'clock, and she was too nervous to sing well. Her two suitcases were packed, and she had a length of rope with which to lower them from the window.

No one seemed to know where King Colt had gone. The air was sultry, and someone mentioned that there was a storm coming down the valley. La Mariposa went back to her room to wait for the nine o'clock show, and from her window she could see the faint glow of lightning flashes far to the north.

It was the longest hour La Mariposa had ever spent in her life, watching the lagging hands of her little clock span the short distance between eight and nine. Nervously she went down the stairs, carrying her music. There were a few more people in the place, but there was not the usual confusion, it seemed. King Colt was not there yet, nor was Pancho.

Lonny Blair, the skinny piano player, with his inevitable half-glass of stale beer on the top of the piano, a limp cigarette hanging from a corner of his lips, played jerkily. There was only a spattering of applause when La Mariposa finished her song.

"It must be the storm, kid," muttered Lonny. "No business t'night. Might's well close up. No use givin' 'em an encore."

"Thank you, Lonny."

"You're welcome. I wish Colt would git this thing tuned. Sounds like a dented dishpan. See yuh at ten, kid."

La Mariposa nodded and went back to the stairway, where she met one of the girls.

"I was out looking at the storm," said the girl. "Gee, it sure looks fierce. First I ever seen here. They say it gets pretty bad sometimes."

"I hope our rooms don't leak," said La Mariposa. "I have seen the stars through my roof."

"Same here, pardner. I think I'll stay down here, until the rain is over."

La Mariposa went swiftly up to her room and lighted the lamp. A quick glance showed that the ladder was in place. Tommy Roper had not failed her. The wind whistled through the window, as she lowered a suitcase on the end of a rope. It was quickly untied in the darkness. Then she sent the other one down, flinging the rope after it, when it had reached the bottom.

Quickly she slipped on a coat over her evening gown, flung aside her big comb, and put on a small felt hat. She put out the light and crawled over the edge of the window onto the ladder. Rain beat against her, as she went down the ladder. Into the blackness of the storm a hand caught her sleeve, guiding her, and she stumbled away to a buggy. A flash of lightning blinded her, and a crash of thunder was like the explosion of dynamite, but her groping hands found the buggy, and she managed to get in.

Then they were driving away slowly, into the teeth of the storm, with no lights visible anywhere, except the flashes of lightning, which were gone too quickly for rain-filled eyes to locate objects. La Mariposa bowed her head and let Tommy Roper do the worrying.

AGUA FRIO WAS only a huddle of buildings, mostly adobe, where the riff-raff of the Border congregated at times. Wanted men found a haven in Agua Frio, far removed from things official in Mexico. Smugglers, horse-thieves, killers and crooked gamblers predominated. In Agua Frio Pancho Lopez was the boss, although he spent most of his time in Tonto City. He owned the only cantina and dance hall in the town. At times many of the dance-hungry of Tonto came to enjoy the pleasures of Agua Frio.

Frijole and Oscar brought their dance clothes with them that evening, and were making a change, while Henry and Judge sat at one of the little tables in the old adobe dance hall, drinking sparingly of the potent tequila, and watching for Jimmy Miller. There were only a few patrons in the place, which reeked of liquor, cigarette smoke and cheap perfume.

They had made discreet inquiries about Jimmy Miller, but with no success. Agua Frio recognized Henry and Judge—and protected its own.

"Just another of your wild-goose chases, Henry," remarked Judge.

"Enjoy your tequila," replied Henry. "I find it delightful, in spite of that fact that I know they sour the *maguey* mash in bull-hide vats out in the sun, where scorpions, tarantulas, red ants and tumble-bugs sniff of the perfume and fall into the mash, adding zest to this devil's mulligan."

Judge shuddered visibly. "My soul revolts," he said soberly, "but my stomach remains a true Van Treece."

A waiter, who greatly resembled Pancho Villa, came to their table and filled their glasses from a jug.

"Look like damn rain," he told them.

"Mixed with carbolic acid," added Judge.

The waiter nodded and went on. Someone called Henry by name, and they turned to see Jimmy Miller beside them.

Jimmy looked older, hard-eyed, as he sat down at their table.

"Has Arizona annexed Mexico?" he asked quietly, "or have you gents forgotten that there's a line between the two places?"

"We are not acting officially, Jimmy," replied Henry.

"I just wondered. The boys was kinda upset—you bein' here. Were yuh lookin' for me?"

"In a way, Jimmy. Frijole and Oscar wanted to come down here and dance a while, so we came along. Jimmy, would you know your father's signature?"

Jimmy looked keenly at Henry for several moments. "I sure would," he replied quietly.

Henry produced a soiled, canceled check and handed it to Jimmy. It was the check that closed Hailstorm Miller's small account at the Tonto bank, drawn the day before he died. Jimmy examined it closely, jerked up his head and looked at Henry.

"Where did you get this?" he asked huskily.

Henry explained about finding it after the explosion.

"Dad never signed that check, Henry," declared Jimmy. "That ain't even a good forgery. And Dad wasn't in Tonto City the day that check is dated. He was in Scorpion Bend for two days, sellin' cows. Henry, what does it mean?"

Henry shook his head slowly. "I do not know, Jimmy, except that it seems the bank closed out his account—without his knowing anything about it."

"You heard about Howard McRae being murdered, Jimmy?" asked Judge.

"Yeah, we heard that down here. Henry, do you think

that McRae had anythin' to do with the murder of my father?"

"Jimmy, if that signature is a forgery, the forger knew that your father would not live to prove it."

"I see." Jimmy nodded grimly.

The room was filling up rapidly. Suddenly Henry leaned forward, looking across the smoke-filled room toward the doorway. Josephine Swensen and Julius Sorenson were entering the place. Julius' huge figure was encased in a wrinkled, black suit, a stiff-bosom white shirt, sans collar or tie, while Josephine was clad in a yellow and black dress. On the exact top of her once-blond mop of hair sat a small, multi-colored hat, from which a single black and white feather reached almost to the ceiling.

"My goodness!" whispered Henry. "The senior member of the Cherry Sisters!"

"Look!" gasped Judge. "Over there. Henry—the cantina doorway!"

14

OSCAR ON PARADE

HENRY SWUNG AROUND in his chair. Standing just inside the doorway to the cantina were Oscar Johnson and Frijole Bill Cullison. Frijole Bill, only a half-pint in size, was wearing a pair of Henry's striped trousers, at least twelve inches too large around the waist, while draped on his narrow shoulders was a cutaway coat, the sleeves of which came just past the ends of his fingers. He wore a yellow, silk shirt, surmounted by a scarlet muffler, and on his head was his shapeless old sombrero. The bottoms of the ruffled trousers completely covered Frijole's boots.

But it was Oscar Johnson who scintillated sartorially. His new suit of billiard-cloth green fit him so tightly that any sudden movement might end in disaster. The sleeves were too short, as were his skin-tight trousers, disclosing inches of wrinkled sock and a pair of bright orange button-shoes. Oscar's shirt was a mixture of red, blue and orange, and his necktie was lavender. Balanced on his head was one of Henry's discarded gray derby hats.

Henry gasped, choked back his tears and made a desperate grab for his glass of tequila. Judge seemed transfixed, blinking painfully.

"The figure at the right, gentlemen," whispered Henry,

"shows the evil effect of alcohol on the human system. Observe the gangrene."

"And they are both as drunk as lords!" gasped Judge. "Henry, I see it all now. Julius brought Josephine—look! She sees Oscar."

"My goodness!" exclaimed Henry. "He ignores her."

After a false start or two, Oscar and Frijole came over to their table.

"Oh, hallo dere, Yimmy," said Oscar, grinning owlishly. "Velcome home."

"How are yuh, Oscar," replied Jimmy. "Yo're sure all duded up tonight."

"Ay am properly dressed," corrected Oscar. "Ay am yust as tight as Ay can be."

"Tight!" snorted Frijole. "I had t' throw him, to button up them pants. I'm through, y'betcha. He can peel himself, after the dance is over."

"I see that Julius and Josephine are here tonight," remarked Judge.

Oscar turned his head and looked at them, a tight expression around his mouth. Then he said:

"Ay t'ink Ay am going to resent it."

"You let them alone," ordered Henry. "You came down here, knowing that they would be here. Josephine is old enough to know what she wants. If she prefers Julius, that is entirely her business."

"Hanry," said Oscar, "have you ever been in lofe?"

"I—why, Oscar!" Henry's eyes filled with tears. "Are you in love?"

"You bat you!"

Henry had turned away, but now he looked at Oscar, his

eyes nearly screwed tight, tears glistening on his cheeks. Then he shifted his eyes to the lanky Jospehine, stiffly sitting in a chair, feather erect, her lips pursed defiantly.

"God bless you, Oscar," whispered Henry, "I—I have never seen a Swedish Cupid, but you have my blessing."

"I'm goin' to git me a seen-yuh-reeta and rattle m' hoofs," declared Frijole. "Play me a fan-danger, and I'll show yuh a sight."

"Don't look now," said Henry, "but Frijole is about to lose his pants."

Both Oscar and Frijole lurched away. Jimmy Miller said:

"Shore stormy out tonight. Big thunder storm comin' down the valley. But we need rain."

Henry wiped away his tears. "And I used to laugh at professional comedians!" he said huskily. "Oscar and Frijole could get top-billing on any circuit merely on their appearance. And Josephine! Judge, I am afraid there will be trouble before we can ever get Oscar away from Julius. If those two mammoths ever lock horns in here, there will not be a wall or ceiling left."

"Dumb brutes," muttered Judge. "I would not be adverse to leaving Oscar and Frijole here. There is no earthly use of us endangering our lives by staying with them. You have the information you were seeking."

"Wait a minute," said Jimmy Miller. "You can prove that the bank forged my fathers name to that check; and the man who forged that check must have known that my father would never know it had been forged."

"True, Jimmy," replied Henry. "The evidence seems conclusive. But it doesn't help your case at all, because it doesn't show who killed Ed Clay and stole that gold."

"What about the gold that Thunder and Lightning found?"

"Someone moved it away. No doubt it was the men who kidnapped the two Mexican boys, and forced them to tell where it was hidden."

"In that old cabin in Red Wall Cañon, wasn't it, Henry?"

"Yes, Jimmy."

"Red Wall Cañon is on the Circle M spread."

"Yes, I have thought of that. But it has little significance."

"Wait a minute!" exclaimed Judge.

THEY TURNED TO follow his gaze. Oscar was leaning on the table, talking to Josephine, who was not even looking at him. Suddenly he reached out and deliberately plucked the feather from her hat. Julius, still seated, scowled at Oscar, but did not get up. Slowly Josephine got to her feet. Swinging half-way around, she balled her right fist and took a tremendous smash at Oscar's jaw. But he bobbed his head and the blow merely sent his derby hat sailing across the room.

There was a commotion in the cantina, and they turned to see Jack Tallant coming into the dancehall, a gun gripped in his right hand. He saw Jimmy Miller with Henry and Judge. With his free hand he strong-armed a waiter, whose tray and glasses went flying, and came straight to the table.

"Some of them damn coyotes kidnapped Gila Jim!" he panted. "They left a ransom note, askin' for twenty-three thousand dollars, if I ever wanted to see him alive. King Colt's outfit, as sure as hell! A couple of 'em followed me across the Border."

Jimmy Miller was on his feet, a gun in his hand.

"We better get out, Jack," he said quietly. "All this bunch belong to Colt or Pancho Lopez."

"No way out, except through the cantina, Jimmy. Are yuh game to shoot a way through?"

"Start shootin'—I'm with yuh, Jack."

"My goodness!" exclaimed Henry. From the middle of the room came a Viking yell, and they turned to see Oscar and Julius locked in mortal combat. Josephine was dancing around, a chair in her hands, seeking for a crack at the head of one of them, presumably Oscar.

The whole room was in an uproar. A bottle whizzed past Henry's head and shattered against the wall. Jack Tallant whirled and fired a quick shot at the huge kerosene lamp hanging in the middle of the room, and the light went out in a shower of broken glass and kerosene.

"Hurrah for the Swedes!" yelped Frijole's voice above the commotion.

In the dim light Henry could see Jack Tallant and Jimmy Miller ploughing their way toward the cantina doorway, knocking everyone out of their way. Judge was down on his knees under the table. Someone crashed into Henry, knocking him off his chair, and others walked across him.

From the front of the cantina came the rattle of pistol shots. Henry got to his feet and made a diving run toward the doorway leading into the cantina, but collided with a heavy body and they both went down. It was Josephine. She gasped:

"What in de ha'al is going on around here, anyvay?"

While Henry pumped air into his aching lungs, Josephine got to her feet, the light of battle in her eyes, and when a frightened waiter tried to go past her she vented her wrath in one right swing to his jaw. He fell across Henry, bumped his head against the wall, and did not move.

"My goodness!" gasped Henry. "This is—er—real interesting, Judge! Oh, Judge!"

"Present," wheezed Judge, stumbling up to the doorway. Henry shoved the inert body off him and got to his feet. Most of the fighting seemed to have moved outside.

"I—I believe we should go, Henry," quavered Judge.

Slowly they went through the deserted cantina. Those pistol shots had sent everyone to cover, it seemed. Josephine was on the porch, and she turned to look at them, as they came out.

"Did you see Yulius?" she asked painfully.

"Not after the battle started," replied Judge. "Where is Oscar?"

"That yug-head! If yentlemen were vorth ten cents apiece, you could buy a cor-load of Oscar Yohnsons for a nickle."

"He—he loves you, Josephine," declared Henry hoarsely.

"Ya-a-ah! He does, eh? Look at my yaw! Ay vars trying to hit him vit a chair, and he sucked me on the yaw. Love!"

"Well, it must be a species of love."

"Oscar Yohnson vars only a trouble-maker. He came ha'ar to show off his clothes and make poor Yulius yealous."

SOMEONE WAS COMING through the cantina, and they turned quickly. It was Oscar Johnson, a split in ever seam, minus his hat, his muffler and part of his shirt, one eye completely closed and his jaw swollen. His huge right hand was locked in the collar of Julius' shirt, and Oscar was dragging him through the cantina. Julius was unconscious, a huge, limp figure, his clothes nearly torn off his body. Oscar dragged him out on the sidewalk, looked squarely at Josephine, and let go of Julius, whose chin bumped hollowly on the sidewalk.

"Ha'ar is your yentleman, Yosephine," he said calmly.

"T'ank you," she replied just as calmly.

Oscar dusted off his hands, pretended to flick some dust off his dusty and torn green suit, and grabbed at a porch-post for support. He had a lump as big as an egg on the side of his head.

"Ay t'ank Ay have leever trouble," he announced. "Where is Free-holey?"

"Spots before your eyes?" queried Henry.

"Yah—su-ure."

"Well, well!" exclaimed Frijole, who stepped out of the darkness. "It has been quite an evening. Look at that green suit!"

"It evidently did not stretch much," said Judge.

"It shore didn't. Julius looks kinda put out, as yuh might say. How about goin' back to Tonto City, Henry?"

"What is the matter, Frijole; did you get hit in the stomach?"

"Hell, no! But some sap-sucker grabbed my suspenders and busted 'em; and I've got to hold up my pants. Ready to go home, Oscar?"

"Yah, su-ure. Yosephine, you vant to ride home vit us?"

"Ay came vit Yulius, and Ay vill go back vit Yulius."

"Yust as stubborn as a mule," said Oscar. "Alvays Yulius. Yust a knot-headed hurse-vaterer. Oll head and no brains. Coom on, yentlemen."

They reached the vehicle, just as the rain started in earnest. To the north were the flashes of lightning, presag-

ing a heavy storm—and there was no top on the spring-
wagon. Oscar announced his intention of doing the driving.

"Then don't you try to do any guidin' in this dark," said
Frijole. "You let the team foller the road."

"Ay am de best driver since Ben Hor," declared Oscar.

"Shut up and do some driving," ordered Judge. "Do you
want to keep us soaking in this rain. Henry, when I think
of my rheumatism, I shudder."

"Hey!" said Frijole, turning in the front seat. "I got a
couple of quarts as I went out; the bartender wasn't lookin'.
It'll help waterproof us on the way. Oscar, you knot-head—
slow 'em down a little!"

"Free-holey, give me de odder line."

"I ain't got no line. How would I; yo're drivin'."

"Va'al, Ay am sorry, Free-holey, but Ay only have von."

"What's that?" gasped Judge. "He only has one line?"

"What's the difference?" chuckled Frijole. "He couldn't
drive with two lines if he had 'em. Anyway, if we get off the
road, we'll know it."

15

TWO WANDERING MANIACS

SHE HAD RIDDEN quite a distance out of Tonto City before La Mariposa realized that they were not on the road to Scorpion Bend. There had not been a word of conversation. The only sound was the hissing of the rain, the rattle of wheels and the thud of hoofs in the mud. She was about to question Tommy Roper when a flash of lightning gave her a faint glimpse of the profile of her driver.

It was not Tommy Roper's rugged, good-natured face— it was the profile of Pancho Lopez, the last man on earth she wanted to be with. He did not realize that she had recognized him. At first she was urged to try to leap from the buggy, but they were going too fast, and she was afraid the wheels might go over her, hampered as she was by her long dress and coat.

She realized now that he was taking her to Agua Frio. She had no weapon of any kind. Mesquite and sage whipped against the wheels, as they went swiftly along. La Mariposa, frightened and helpless, crouched low in the seat, her shoulder bumping against the shoulder of Pancho Lopez. She thought of trying to grasp a line and throw the horse off the road, chancing an upset; but she did not have the nerve. It was evident that Pancho was going to take her into Mexico before revealing his identity.

In spite of the darkness and rain, Pancho drove swiftly. The chance of encountering the Border Patrol was slight, because of the drenching rain. She had not the slightest idea of what Pancho might do with her, once she was in Agua Frio.

Suddenly the horse swerved partly off the road. Pancho surged on the lines, and the next instant there was a crash, the rending of wood, and the light buggy turned completely over, throwing La Mariposa headlong into the brush. She dimly heard several voices yelling, the crashing of brush and the rattle of wheels.

The brush had cradled her fall and she crawled out, unhurt, except for a few scratches, and stood there in the blinding rain and darkness. There was no sign of Pancho or the team and buggy. A lightning flash illuminated the country, but she could see nothing except the wind-blown brush. Apparently she was all alone out there, but that did not frighten her half as much as being with Pancho Lopez.

She stumbled into the road and started walking back the way they came, going slowly and listening closely in case Pancho came back in the buggy.

THE CRASH FLUNG Judge and Henry into the bottom of the wagon. The front seat jumped loose on one side and deposited Frijole into the bottom with them. The team was running away in earnest now, but they left the road, crashed off through the mesquite, where they tangled in the brush and came to a stop. Frijole got out and managed to find both lines this time, while Henry and Judge read-justed the front seat.

"My goodness!" exclaimed Henry. "Where is Oscar?"

"Well, I'm a son-of-a-gun!" blurted Frijole. "I never saw him leave."

"Never mind Oscar," groaned Judge. "Get this equipage back on the road to Tonto City."

"I wonder what we hit back there," said Henry.

"Possibly a stump," suggested Judge.

"There ain't a stump between Tonto and Agua Frio," said Frijole.

"No matter," said Henry, "we will not go back and investigate."

"I shore hate to lose Oscar," mourned Frijole.

"Do you think that much of him, Frijole?" asked Judge.

"No, but the big jug-head had both bottles of whisky."

... They got back to Tonto City and slopped their way into the hotel, seeking dry clothing. John Harper was in there, looking for them. He said:

"They found Tommy Roper, out there beside that old fence behind the Tonto Saloon, all tied up with ropes. Somebody had hit him over the head, and he hasn't been able to tell us anything yet. Doc Bogart says he'll be all right by morning."

"That is rather queer, John," said Henry. "I cannot quite figure out an attack on as harmless a person as Tommy Roper."

"And another thing, Henry," said the lawyer. "A man told me a while ago that La Mariposa is missing. She failed to show up for her song, and an investigation disclosed that her clothes are missing, the window was open, and a ladder led to the ground. I went to talk the matter over with King Colt, but he is out of town."

Henry shook his head slowly. "John," he said soberly, "I have always said that anything can happen in Arizona. To that I will add: everything seems to happen in Wild Horse Valley. Someone has kidnapped Old Gila Jim Tallant and left a ransom note for Jack, demanding twenty-three thousand dollars."

"Twenty-three thousand? Why, that is the amount stolen from the bank and from the Tonto Saloon, Henry."

"Yes, I have pondered over that, John."

"But why would anyone kidnap that poor, old cripple? Do you think that Jack Tallant robbed the bank and the Tonto?"

Henry shook his head wearily. "I haven't a ready answer, John. I feel that the Board of Commissioners discriminated against me when they gave me the additional thirty days—because the last thirty days seems to be the hardest. If you will excuse me now—I feel the need of dry clothing, and a soft spot on which to lay the weary bones."

"I'll talk to you in the morning, Henry. Something must be done."

"I believe you are right, John," agreed Henry. "The thing to do is to find out just what to do, before we try to do anything."

"Here comes Doctor Bogart," said Judge.

The old doctor hurried in, saw them and came over to the desk.

"Tommy Roper regained consciousness a few minutes ago," he told them, "and was able to talk a little. He say that La Mariposa engaged him to drive her secretly to Scorpion Bend tonight. He brought the horse and buggy out behind the Tonto, placed a ladder up at her window—and that is all he remembered. Apparently someone slugged him, Henry."

"My goodness! I wonder why she was running away from the Tonto."

"Tommy doesn't know, except that she asked him to take her to Scorpion Bend," replied the doctor. "I was over at the Tonto, but King Colt is not there tonight. Perhaps, when he comes back—"

"Yes, perhaps," said Henry. "It does not appear that we can do anything tonight; so we may as well get a good sleep and make a fresh attack in the morning."

HENRY AND JUDGE went up to their room and threw off their soaked clothes. Judge groaned dismally over the prospect of rheumatism, but grunted in amazement, when he saw Henry changing into dry clothing.

"Are you going to bed with your clothes on, Henry?" he asked.

"We, my dear man, are not going to bed," replied Henry.

"Not going to bed? Are you losing your mind, sir?"

"I hope so," replied Henry seriously. "We will take slickers, in case the rain continues, Judge."

"*We?* We are going out in that damnable rain again, Henry?"

"On horseback," nodded Henry.

"Well, of all the asinine—why, Henry? Give me one reason why we should go horsebacking in the rain on a dark night?"

"I have a feeling," replied Henry, drawing on his trousers, "that the obstacle we struck with our equipage was the buggy that contained La Mariposa. Someone knocked out Tommy Roper and stole the girl. I felt at the time that it was a buggy. She may be hurt, lying out there in the rain. Anyway, it is our duty to investigate. Come to think of it, we really should find out how Oscar survived his landing."

"Well," said Judge dismally, "I do not see what good we can do—in the dark. Why, you cannot see your hand before your face."

"I realize that, Judge. But we shall carry a lantern."

"Lantern?" Judge sat there in his wet underclothes, looking very much like an old rooster which had been plucked and thrown in the creek.

"A lantern, you said, Henry. Two damned old fools and a kerosene lamp. A lightning-bug in a million acres of dripping brush, sir. Looking for a woman who *might* have been thrown from a buggy—in case we did hit a buggy, which we very likely did not. Henry, this move of yours strikes me numb."

"It may be those wet flannels, Judge. Come, come! I am half dressed. You forget that a very beautiful young lady may be in need of succor."

"Two suckers, I suppose," groaned Judge. "Well, I can see that you have one of your stubborn streaks, Henry; so neither common sense nor any flow of oratory can swerve you from your ridiculous ideas. It is really a pitiful situation, when a man of my age becomes a slave to a—well, the vagaries of a—a—"

"Wandering minstrel?" queried Henry.

"Wandering maniac," groaned Judge. "Well, I may as well peel."

Clad in warm, dry clothing, but still groaning, Judge managed to saddle his horse. The heavy rain had turned to a dismal drizzle as they rode away from the main street, with Henry carrying a lighted lantern. They found the road to Agua Frio and turned south. The lantern did not cast any amount of illumination ahead, and they were obliged to trust to the horses to stay on the road.

About a mile out of Tonto City they met Oscar, standing beside the road, soaking wet and muddy, his round face barely visible in the weak lantern light. In their slickers, with the collars turned high, and their hat-brims turned low, Oscar did not recognize them.

"Who in de ha'al are you?" he asked hollowly.

"I am the spirit of the storm," replied Henry dramatically.

"Va'al," remarked Oscar, "oll I can say is dat you have made damn bad valking. Gude night."

Chuckling, they rode on. Judge said:

"Do you think he recognized us, Henry?"

"No," said Henry. "When the crash came, Oscar had two quarts of whisky in his possession. Right now, I will wager that he has at least a quart of it in his stomach."

"Even the Swedes have better luck than I," groaned Judge.

THEY SEARCHED ALONG the road, nearly to the Border, but found no sign of anyone, and it was nearly daylight when they came back to where a road forked to the Tallant ranch. Here, in the lantern light, they found the imprint of a woman's shoe in the mud. The tracks were on the road to the Tallant ranch.

"That poor girl must be lost," said Henry, "Evidently, heading back for Tonto, she got off on the wrong road. Well, she will be all right if—but will she? I just remembered that Gila Jim Tallant has been kidnapped. I wonder if Jimmy Miller and Jack Tallant—but no matter. It is getting light, so we will not need this lantern any further."

They were a queer-looking pair in the cold, gray light of that wet morning. The pudgy Henry, atop a tall roan horse, a huge sombrero on his head, making him resemble a toadstool; while the lanky Judge, riding a small, short-coupled gray, splayed his feet wide in the stirrups to keep from dragging them in the low brush.

"We may as well go to the Tallant ranch," said Henry wearily. "Even if there is no one at home, we may find more trace of that lost girl."

"Our hero," groaned Judge. "A modern Don Quixote."

"And Sancho Panza in the flesh. All we need is a pair of tin hats and a spear."

"All we need is brains," corrected Judge, shivering under his glistening slicker. "I shall be thankful when this fool's pilgrimage is over. At your age, Henry, you should be more considerate, even if only of yourself."

"I am afraid, Judge, that I may have to get a younger deputy—one more my own age. Once you had legs—but they are merely limbs now."

For once, Judge was too miserable to form a retort. They slogged along the muddy road until they came in sight of the Tallant ranch. A trickle of smoke came from the sagging stovepipe, and at sight of it Henry essayed a cheer.

"Smoke means the presence of human beings, and human beings means a possible breakfast, Judge."

"I reserve judgment," grunted Judge.

They rode up to the kitchen doorway, dismounted and walked into the house. A disheveled La Mariposa was trying to coax a fire with wet wood, a smudge across her nose, her evening gown torn and bedraggled. She turned quickly, her eyes full of fright.

"Thank God—the sheriff!" she gasped. "I—I am glad you came."

"We were looking for you," explained Henry. "You see, we found your tracks on the road."

"Did you? I thought I was on the road to Tonto City. But how—why did you look for me down here?"

Henry explained about the accident on the road, the finding of Tommy Roper, and his subsequent explanation.

"It was Pancho Lopez," she said. "He tried to take me to Agua Frio."

"My goodness!"

"What did King Colt say?" asked the girl anxiously.

"As a matter of fact, he knew nothing about it when we left town. He has been away, it seems. You were—er—running away, were you not?"

"Yes, Pancho threatened me and I thought I better go. You see—"

La Mariposa stopped, her eyes widening, as she looked at the doorway.

"HOLD IT, FOLKS," ordered a voice. Henry and Judge turned quickly. Joe Hake was in the doorway, his six-shooter covering them. Then a man stepped past him and took the guns from Henry and Judge. Hake scowled at the girl, puzzled at her presence, but turned and called to someone out of their view.

Two of Hake's men came in, carrying Old Gila Jim Tallant, and put him on his chair in the main room. Old Gila cursed them bitterly. Then two more men came in, driving Jack Tallant and Jimmy Miller ahead of them.

Both men had been beaten severely, it seemed; but Jimmy grinned at Henry. Hake motioned for Henry, Judge and the girl to follow them into the main room.

"What is the meaning of this?" demanded Henry. Hake snarled at him:

"It means that the whole damn bunch of yuh are prisoners, Conroy; and yuh can take it or leave it."

"Oh, I'll take it, of course," said Henry. "Where is King Colt?"

"He's gone to Tonto, if it's any of yore business."

"No, I merely wondered."

"Yuh won't need to wonder long—not with this bunch of coyotes," shrilled Old Gila Jim. "They'd slice out yore heart for a dime."

"Shut up, before I cut yore ears off, you old rattler!" snapped Hake. Then he turned to La Mariposa. "Where'd you come from?" he asked.

"I do not believe it is any of your business," replied the girl.

"That's the stuff!" applauded Gila Jim. "He's nothin' but a hired killer, anyway—hired by King Colt, who should have been strangled in his youth."

"Keep it up," rasped Hake, "Colt will be here pretty quick—and then you'll talk."

"Will I?" shrilled the cripple. "Talk about what? Money that never existed? You fools, you believe that I could show yuh where the money is cached, so yuh brought me back here. If I had that money, King Colt would never get it. Stick pins under my nails, would he? Go ahead."

"My goodness!" exclaimed Henry. "That must hurt."

"Shut up, you fat-nosed fool!" snapped Hake. "Here!

One of you boys get a couple ropes and tie up these two jaspers."

"Do not be melodramatic," begged Henry. "We are officers of the law."

"We're not usin' any law this mornin'," replied Hake.

"I am sure Mr. Colt would not approve, Mr. Hake."

"We'll leave that until he gets here, Conroy. Tie 'em tight, boys. Yuh remember, Colt said not to underrate Conroy; so yuh can take an extra half-hitch on him."

"How about cookin' a little breakfast, Joe?" asked one of the men.

"Go ahead," said Hake. "We can't do anything else until the boss gets here."

"You are making a terrible mistake," declared Henry, as they bound him tightly. "The law will surely take cognizance of this treatment of two officers."

"Funny, ain't he?" chuckled one of the cowboys. "Talks like he'd done swallered a dictionary."

They had placed Henry and Judge on either side of La Mariposa on a rough bench beside the wall, but made no move to tie her. Jimmy Miller grinned weakly at Henry.

"Quite a night, Henry," he said. "After that ruckus in the cantina, me and Jack discovered where they had taken his dad. But they outsmarted us, ganged up on us from behind. It shore was a nice fight while it lasted."

"But why did they kidnap Gila Jim Tallant?" asked Henry.

"They think we've got that bank money and the Tonto money cached down here. They was goin' to torture Gila down there, but he swore that unless they brought him home, he'd never tell where it was cached."

"And we ain't even got it," chuckled Gila. "They had to pack me all the way down there and all the way back for nothin'. Yuh don't need to glare at me, Hake. There's a rope waitin' for yore neck—you and all yore gang, includin' King Colt."

"You won't live to see it," snarled Hake.

"Isn't it possible to talk of something pleasant?" asked Henry.

"Better save the talk until King Colt gits here," said Hake. "You'll talk plenty then."

16

CONROY'S CLEANUP

IT WAS SHORTLY after daylight when King Colt, swathed in a slicker, dismounted from his horse behind the Tonto Saloon, and entered the back door. It was too early for many customers. Swampers were busily engaged in mopping floors and cleaning up the place. King went to the bar, where he was served quickly.

"Any word of La Mariposa?" asked the bartender. King looked up quickly.

"What do yuh mean?" he asked anxiously. In a few words the bartender told him, not realizing that King Colt had been away.

King Colt shoved the bottle aside, his lips grim, as the bartender told him about Tommy Roper's statement.

"So she was runnin' away, eh?" he muttered. "Where's Pancho Lopez?"

"Nobody has seen him since early yesterday, King."

King Colt's eyes narrowed thoughtfully.

"Steve McRae and Tuck Darnell have been looking for you, too," said the bartender. "Waited around here most of the evening."

"What did they want?"

"They didn't say. And we heard a rumor that Old Gila

Tallant had been kidnapped. Didja hear anything about it, King?"

"No," grunted King Colt. "I'm not interested in him. If anybody asks for me, I'll prob'ly be in this evenin'."

He turned and went out through the rear entrance swiftly.

… Oscar Johnson had tried half the night to find Henry and Judge. He finally went to the hotel, only to discover that they had left. Their two horses were not in the stable. Oscar had lost one quart of the whisky when the lurch threw him out of the wagon; so he decided to go down there and try to find it. As he rode out of town, he saw King Colt gallop away from behind the Tonto and cut into the Agua Frio road.

Oscar was not much of a hand to wonder about things, but it did interest him to know where the boss of the Tonto was going at this time in the morning. So he trailed King Colt, staying far enough behind to not be seen by the big gambler. He saw King swing to the left on the Tallant ranch road, and after due reflection Oscar went on to try to find his whisky. He felt the need of stimulant.

He found it, unbroken, lying in the mud beside the road. Quickly he dismounted, drew the cork, and proceeded to slake his thirst. Then he rode north again toward the forks of the road, and there he saw two riders, coming south, turn and go toward the Tallant ranch. They were Steve McRae and Tuck Darnell.

"Va'al," said Oscar to his horse, "it looks like somebody vars having a porty. Ve better go and take a look."

KING COLT GALLOPED up to the ranch house, dismounted and came in through the kitchen. He stopped in amazement at sight of the people in the main room. His eyes shifted from face to face. Then he said:

"Hake, what does this mean?"

"They was here ahead of us, King," replied Joe Hake, "so we took 'em in."

"So you took 'em in," muttered King Colt. "You fool, you fool! Hake, what in hell have yuh done?"

Then his eyes searched out La Mariposa. "You, too," he said. "So yuh tried to run away, eh? Who brought you here?"

"I walked here from the main road. Pancho Lopez—"

"So he was the one, eh? Pancho Lopez knocked out Tommy Roper and took yuh with him."

"We were coming from Agua Frio in a spring-wagon last night," explained Henry, "and we ran into their buggy in the dark."

"I'm damned!" exploded King Colt.

"Undoubtedly, Mr. Colt," agreed Henry.

"Hake, do you realize what you've done?" asked Colt bitterly. "Why didn't yuh scout this place before yuh came here?"

"We thought the place was empty, King."

"With our two horses in the yard?" queried Henry.

"They'd drifted around the other side of the house," said one of the cowboys. "We found 'em later."

"And that old crippled coyote over there," said Hake, pointing at Gila Jim, "swears that he tricked yuh, King. He says there's no money cached at this place—that he lied to git back here."

"Yeah?" said King Colt. "All right, we'll take him back to Mexico with us. This time he won't come back."

"Well," snapped Gila Jim, "you crippled me for life, so yuh may as well finish the job."

So intent was everyone on the business at hand that none noticed the coming of Steve McRae and Tuck Darnell, until they entered the house. Joe Hake was taking no chances, and had them covered quickly.

"Put down that gun, Joe," said Darnell. "Don't be a fool."

"Hold it," ordered King Colt. "What do yuh want, Steve?"

"Quite a collection you've got," said Steve, scanning the room. His eyes came back to King Colt and he replied:

"As long as you've got that red-nosed sheriff, I guess it's all right. He seemed to have some bright ideas about your friendship with my dad. He wanted to know why the bank loaned you money without security, and all that. Talked about examining the books—and I thought you ought to know about it. They took the books to the courthouse and locked them up in a vault."

King Colt laughed quietly. "He's no fool—that red-nosed fathead."

"I deny that," declared Henry. "Look at these ropes."

Gila Jim Tallant was staring at Steve McRae, a queer glint in his deep-set eyes. All at once he began laughing.

Everyone looked curiously at him, as he cackled loudly, slapping a fist on his withered, bony knees.

"I've got it!" he croaked. "That face!"

He pointed a bony forefinger at Steve McRae.

"I'd know that face anywhere, I tell yuh. Steve McRae! Hell, yeah! It's the same face, I tell yuh—the face of Tex Rayburn! King Colt, I can see it all now. Tex Rayburn got the loot from all yore robberies, after they sent you to the penitentiary. Then he became a banker. Yeah, he was educated. And you came here to blackmail him out of everythin' he had."

The room was silent, except for the wheezing chuckle of Gila Jim. Then Henry said quietly:

"But McRae, or Rayburn, got even when he had his bank robbed and stole all the money, including what belonged to King Colt. It had to be an inside job, because the vault was dynamited *after* the money was taken out."

"Pretty smart, Conroy," rasped King Colt. "I didn't think you figured that out."

"Oh, my goodness, yes," said Henry. "I have been curious to know if you found the stolen money after you murdered Howard McRae, or Rayburn."

"You poor fool," whispered King Colt.

"So *you* killed him, eh?" said Steve McRae. "Damn yuh, Colt, I thought Jack Tallant and Jimmy Miller pulled that job. Well, yuh didn't get the money."

"I suppose," remarked Henry pleasantly, "that you added it to the six hundred and fifty ounces of gold that you stole from the stage, and the ten thousand you took oft the dead body of Hailstorm Miller."

Steve McRae backed up a little, his face white. Tuck Darnell's eyes shifted from spot to spot, estimating his chances to get away.

"So that's the angle, eh?" said King Colt. "Watch 'em, Hake, they're feelin' like runnin' away."

"King!" called Jimmy Miller. "Untie my arms and give me a gun, will yuh? All I want is them two killers. I won't come back to bother yuh—and I'll guarantee that they won't come back either. They belong to me more than they belong to you."

"Don't ask favors of that stinkin' grizzly, Jimmy," said Gila Jim. "Tex Rayburn was a killer, and that kid of his looks like the same breed of rattler. He'd slit yore neck for a dime. So would King Colt. That makes me laugh. King Colt! Look in the records of the Wyomin' State Penitentiary. You'll find him there, but yuh won't find King Colt—you'll find—"

The small room shuddered from the concussion of a heavy shot, and old Gila Jim Tallant fell sideways, a leer on his face, killed instantly.

"I SHOT HIGHER that time," said King Colt quietly, as he holstered his gun and fanned the powder smoke away from his face with a wave of his big left hand. La Mariposa screamed suddenly and put her hands over her face.

"That," exclaimed Henry, "was cold-blooded murder, Colt."

"Call it what yuh please," said King Colt, "it shut his mouth."

"Yes, there is no doubt of that," admitted Henry. "Things are gradually clearing up, it seems. Steve McRae and Tuck Darnell robbed that stage and murdered Ed Clay. Steve knew the gold was being shipped. They hid the gold in Red Wall Cañon, where Thunder and Lightning found it. King Colt's boys forced Thunder and Lightning to reveal the hiding place of the gold—but it had already been removed by Steve McRae. Steve, it seems, was suspicious when Lightning or Thunder remarked that gold is where you find it. Am I right, Steve?"

"Go to hell!" snapped Steve. "And I never had a hand in that robbery and killing."

"Tuck Darnell worked alone on that job, eh? Was the murder of Hailstorm Miller a one-man job, too?"

"You can't prove a thing," declared Tuck Darnell. "You say that Steve and me robbed the bank and the Tonto. We was at a show in Scorpion Bend that night; so that proves yo're all wrong."

"My goodness!" said Henry quietly. "Then that *Clarion Weekly* editor must have lied. In the last issue it said that the *East Lynn* company were obliged to cancel their one-night stand in Scorpion Bend, because of a freight wreck, which prevented them from reaching the town in time to put on a performance."

"I reckon that cinches you two," said King Colt. "But what good it'll ever do the law, I can't see."

"You surely cannot do us any harm," said Judge.

"For a feller that's supposed to be smart, you're pretty ignorant," declared King Colt. "Put yourself in my place. Do you think I'm goin' to let you put a rope around my neck? I've got to have money—a lot of money. Then I'm headin' so far south that nobody'll ever find me. I'm through in Wild Horse Valley—through with every place except Mexico or south of that. Conroy, you and Van Treece can only blame yourselves; you came to the wrong place."

"Yes, it seems that we did," admitted Henry. "Our main idea was to try and find La Mariposa."

Under cover of Henry's slicker, La Mariposa was sawing on his wrist-ropes with a tiny pen-knife, small, but sharp. Just what good freedom of hands would do him, he did not know. He could not hope to do much, empty-handed against guns. Still, it thrilled him to feel that little knife eating away at the ropes. He felt the last strand fall apart, and he managed to work the ropes away from his wrists.

"Well, what's to be done, King?" asked Hake. "We've got to make Steve and Tuck tell us where the money is cached, and then we've got to head south fast. The first thing we know, this whole valley will be on our necks."

"We're safe enough for a while," said King Colt. "We've got everybody concerned right here with us, Joe. They won't be missed for twelve hours; so we've got time. The thing to do is to figure out just how to do this thing."

"I might suggest," said Henry, "that you take the money and leave the valley. Someone will find us and turn us loose, I am sure."

King Colt laughed. "And have the Mexican officials run us down before we get as far as Hermosillo. No, we've got to figure out somethin' better than that. All right"—he turned to Steve McRae—"go ahead and tell us where yuh cached that money."

"Yo're crazy," snapped Steve. "Tell you where that money is cached, and get killed, anyway? Not a chance, Colt. You're between the devil and the deep sea right now. You don't dare let us go; we won't tell you where the money is cached; and you can't get away without money."

"I feel," said Henry, "that your best move, Mr. Colt, is to turn us all loose and give yourself up. You *might* escape the rope, you know."

King Colt laughed. "That is a fine idea—for you, Conroy. What about you, Steve—you and Tuck Darnell? Willin' to risk a rope?"

"Damn yuh—no!" snapped Tuck Darnell. "I'll make a

deal with yuh. We dig up the money and all go south—me and you and Steve."

"Well, figure out somethin'," said Joe Hake impatiently. "I'm gettin' nervous."

"Yo're idea sounds interestin', Tuck," said King Colt. "What'll we do with the rest of the folks?"

"I don't care," replied Steve, "just so they ain't able to tell what they know."

"You would make that sort of a deal with the man who killed your father?" queried Henry in amazement. "What an unnatural son!"

"Go ahead and worry about it—you won't worry long, Conroy."

"We'll send La Mariposa to Scorpion Bend with one of the boys," said King Colt.

"What's the idea?" growled Steve. "She'll talk as much as the rest."

"I said we'll send her to Scorpion Bend, Steve. Don't forget that I'm bossin' this party."

"We could take her up there," suggested Henry.

"You ain't goin' no place," declared King Colt. "Yo're too damn smart, Conroy; and you'll be the first to go, when it starts. If I was you—"

FROM OUT IN the kitchen came the sound of a blow, the scrape of a boot on the rough floor. King Colt whirled, reaching for his gun, but his hand stopped. In the doorway, flanked by two men, was Pancho Lopez, and their guns covered the room.

"Keeng Colt, my old *amigo*, you forget to post the guards," said Pancho amiably. "No one see us come. *Buena!* This ees quite a party, eh? Oh, the leetle Butterfly, too. This ees ver' nice. Meester Hake, eef you mak' leetle move weeth the hand, you die queek.

"W'y don' somebodee say sometheeng? You are so nice and quiet. This ees the firs' time that Keeng Colt ever forget to talk. I am ashame' for doin' all the talking. Ah, the shoriff, too. This ees nice. All tie up for Pancho. Well, well! Meester McRae, Meester Darnell."

"Pancho, you came just in time," said Henry. "King Colt was going to kill all of us."

"Well, that ees w'at you call the toff deal, eh? Pancho not do that. No, no. Pancho going tak' La Mariposa, and then he ees—Stop that, Colt, you fool—"

King Colt had suddenly thrown caution to the wind, and his big right hand snaked for his gun. Pancho fired twice, deliberately, rattling the windows with the double concussion. King Colt's hand fell away from his half-drawn gun; he backed slowly, buckling at the knees, and pitched into Henry. Henry's free right hand, trying to fend the heavy body away, came in contact with the butt of that big Colt .45. With a twist of his wrist he pulled the gun away, cocking it with the same motion. And as Pancho's eyes darted from face to face, Henry shoved the gun past the limp body of King Colt, covered Pancho Lopez—and squeezed the trigger.

The shock of that heavy bullet seemed to almost lift Pancho off his feet. He bumped heavily into one of his own men, throwing him off balance, and at that moment Joe Hake and his men went into action. There was also action from another quarter. Yelling at the top of his voice, Oscar Johnson, armed with a section of two-by-four, dived in through the little kitchen and was into the melee before Hake's men were able to pull their triggers more than once.

Both of Pancho's men were staggering backward, their guns blazing, when the human tornado struck. Joe Hake sprang back, raised his gun as he dodged a mighty swing; but before he could shove the muzzle against the whirling Swede, Henry's finger squeezed the trigger again. Hake was not over six feet away from the muzzle of Henry's gun, and the smashing impact of the big bullet whirled him completely around. Oscar's next swing clipped the tall outlaw behind the ear.

It was all over. Oscar stood in the center of the room, club in hand, a grinning Viking in the swirling powder smoke.

"What is going on ha'ar, anyvay?" he asked.

Henry shoved the big body of King Colt aside and got shakily to his feet. He quickly released Judge, who stood up and quickly sat down again.

"Rheumatism," he said simply.

"Weak from fright," corrected Henry. "Oscar, where on earth did you come from?"

"Oh, Ay yust drifted in, Hanry. How are you?"

"Greatly relieved," replied Henry, as he surveyed the room. Then he removed the bonds from Jack Tallant and Jimmy Miller.

"Let Steve McRae and Tuck Darnell alone," ordered Henry. "The law can handle their case. I—oh, hello, John!"

JOHN HARPER, THE prosecutor, flanked by Thunder and Lightning, came slowly into the doorway, wide-eyed. Behind them came Jim Henderson, chief of the Border Patrol, and one of his men.

"What a mess!" exclaimed Harper. "What happened, Henry?"

"How did you happen to come here?" queried Judge.

"Well, I—I don't know," admitted Harper. "You reported the kidnapping of Gila Jim Tallant and you were not in town, so I had Thunder and Lightning drive me down here—sort of looking around, I suppose."

"It looks like you've had a showdown, Henry," remarked the big Border officer. "King Colt, Pancho Lopez, Joe Hake—well, well! It seems that both sides lost. Miss McLean, I am glad to see you. We heard that you had disappeared. How are you, Jack?"

"Well, I'm all right now, Chief," replied Jack Tallant. "They shore had us in the hole, until Henry got into action. I dunno yet how he ever got loose and picked up a gun. Gee, I'm shore sorry about Gila Jim. He was a great man."

"Wasn't he your father?" asked Henry in amazement.

"No. You see, I work for the Government, Henry. I posed as his son, and was supposed to be smugglin' cattle and horses. But I couldn't find out much; so they sent Miss McLean and she got a job at the Tonto. She found out more than I could, but it wasn't quite enough to trap Colt and Lopez."

"My goodness!" exclaimed Henry. "There *are* things I did not know."

"Amazing," said Judge.

"Amazing that there should be anything that I do not know?" asked Henry.

"No, sir—amazing that you would admit not knowing everything."

"But, Henry, I would like to know a few of the things," reminded the lawyer. "I just got here, you know."

"Oh, certainly," said Henry. "Well, Tuck Darnell and Steve McRae killed Hailstorm Miller and stole ten thousand dollars. Then Tuck Darnell robbed the stage and killed Ed Clay. First degree murder in both cases.

"It seems that Howard McRae framed a robbery of his own bank, which was done by his estimable son, aided and abetted by Mr. Darnell. They also relieved King Colt of a few thousand. King Colt, knowing full well that the robbery of the bank was all a fake, had Howard McRae killed and tried to find the missing money in the McRae home.

"John, they were a bad bunch of boys. King Colt, thinking that Gila Jim Tallant instigated a lot of this outlawry when he failed to find the money at the McRae home, kidnapped Gila Jim and tried to force him to tell where the money was hidden."

"Well," said Harper, "there seems to be work ahead for the courts, thanks to you, Henry."

"You might thank Miss McLean," said Henry. "She cut my hands loose."

"She's a great girl, Henry," said Jack Tallant. "She said that just as soon as we put Colt and Lopez out of business she'd marry me."

"Well, bless you, my children," exclaimed Henry, beaming. "They are both out of business—permanently."

No effort was made to remove the casualties. The prisoners were hustled out and soon the cavalcade was on its way to Tonto City. There, while the townspeople crowded around, trying to discover what had happened, Henry found the stage-driver and drew him aside.

"Do you remember a few days ago that King Colt gave you a letter to post at Scorpion Bend?" asked Henry. The man nodded thoughtfully.

"Yeah, I 'member that, Sheriff. What about it?"

"By any chance do you remember who that letter was sent to?"

"Yea-a-ah. Wait a minute. Mrs.—Mrs. McLean, I believe."

"Thank you very much. It was of no importance."

"Pawnee Bill," muttered Henry, as he walked away. "I wondered just why he killed Gila Jim—to prevent him from letting that girl know that King Colt was her own father. At least he was a man."

He walked away, unaware that two persons were watching him interestedly. Over on the edge of a sidewalk, sitting together, wondering what it was all about, were Lightning and Thunder Mendoza. No one had explained a thing to them. Lightning said:

"Everybodee ees keeled—almost—and theese banker who owe us ten dollar een the book ees also een jail. I see these toff Jack Tallant kees the fimale feedler, and everybodee ees pound Hanry on the back. Judge he ees greening like hell, and the beeg Swid act like hees been elec' *presidente* of these *Estados Unidos*. W'at ees go on, do you suspec', my leetle brodder?"

"Too much talk," declared Thunder. "Of theese, I can not get my head nor tail. Pippel are dead, pippel are een jail. Everybody say *'Buena!'* W'at ees good about that? But I know sometheeng that ees *importante*."

"W'at ees that?" asked Lightning anxiously.

"I'm spiking weeth the drogstore, and I ask heem eef rattlesnake oil ees wort' twenty dollar for leetle beet."

"W'at he say?"

"He say 'Nots!'"

"He don' say w'at kind, eh?"

"W'at ees the deeference? They don' grow here."

"Don'be too damn sure," warned Lightning, "Hanry ees smart, and he say that anytheeng can happen een Arizona."

AN HOUR LATER Henry and Judge were preparing to drive out to the ranch when the depot agent found them and handed Henry a telegram from the editor of the Scorpion Bend *Weekly Clarion*. It read:

PLEASE SEND US FULL DETAILS OF MOST WONDERFUL ACHIEVEMENT IN HISTORY.

Henry turned the buckboard team around and drove to the depot, with Thunder and Lightning sitting in the back, their legs dangling. Judge held the team, while Henry went into the little depot. He came out in a few minutes and resumed his place as driver.

"It is rather remarkable," said Judge, "that you were able to wire full details of everything that happened today. It seems that it does not require much time for you to cover the most wonderful achievement in history, Henry."

"I made it rather short," admitted Henry blandly.

"What did you tell him, Henry?"

"I told him to reprint the Declaration of Independence."

BUCKSHOT FOR HENRY

Did you know that the Shame of Arizona has been erased? Well, temporarily. Henry Harrison Conroy is no longer sheriff; but affairs in Wild Horse Valley are dark and bloody, and after a little more prune whisky Henry will be ambling into another mystery

PROLOG

THE MAN KNELT and carefully scooped up water in a battered, rusty bucket. Then he stood up and looked all around. He was a big man, frowsy and unkempt, but wearing a fairly good suit of gray clothes, pilfered, no doubt, along with the nearly new black shoes on his feet. Myriads of insects buzzed around his head as he picked up the bucket and went toward a small, tumbledown shack, nearly hidden in the foliage at the edge of the swamp.

For several moments he stood in the doorway of the shack, watching and listening. Then, going inside, he built a fire in the crude fireplace. There were several paper sacks and cans of food on the rough table, a bedroll on the crude bunk. Leaning against the fireplace was an old sawed-off shotgun, patched of stock and rusty of barrel, but still serviceable.

Bees and other insects buzzed around the doorway, birds called from the brush, and high in the sky two buzzards wheeled on motionless wings, searching the swamp. A pair of mallards seemed to come in from nowhere, circled the place, set their wings for a landing, but took fright and climbed swiftly, their pinions whistling.

After a while there was a slight rustling in the cattails near the shack, and a man's face appeared. For a long time, only the man's eyes moved, as he studied the shack and the spiral of thin smoke from the rusty stovepipe. Then the man crawled out, looking not unlike a tiger in his striped clothes, filthy with slime and mud. With the stealth of a tiger he came to a crouched position. Inside the shack a pan rattled. After a  moment or two the striped man came forward toward the corner of the shack, halting just short of the doorway.

The man in the shack was kneeling at the fireplace, frying bacon, when the striped one leaped. The attack was so sudden that the kneeling man was nearly driven into the fire, unable to make any defense. Two huge hands banged his head against the hearth, and his body went limp.

The striped man got quickly to his feet, listening intently. But there was only the drone of insects, the calling of the birds. The man reached out and picked up the old shotgun. Snapping it open, he noted that it was loaded. With a grunt of pleasure he placed it on the crude table, broke open a can of beans with a rusty ax, and wolfed them hungrily, his eyes on the unconscious man.

Finishing the can of beans, he wiped his smeared face with the back of his left hand. The man on the floor was beginning to twist about, finally to sit up, feeling painfully of his head, a dazed expression in his eyes. He saw the striped one, and understanding seemed to flow back in to his mind. The striped one said:

"Take off your clothes—and be quick about it."

"Take off my—you almost busted my head, damn yuh."

"Start takin' 'em off, you fool, or I will bust it. I'd just as soon take 'em off your dead body, if yuh want it that way."

The striped one picked up the shotgun and carefully cocked one hammer, hunched back against the wall, watching the man remove all his garments. Still holding the gun and watching the naked man, he stripped off his prison garb, tossing it to the man.

"Put it on," he ordered savagely.

FROM SOMEWHERE FAR off across the swampland, came the faint howl of a dog. The man with the shotgun twitched nervously. Bloodhounds! Not more than a mile away. But the water would stop them for a while. The other man did not hear them. He was only a petty criminal, hiding out in the swamp.

Dressed in the prison clothes, he waited for orders from the man with the gun. After all, even if the law did find him, it would not be difficult to prove what had actually happened. The man with the shotgun, fully clad in the other man's garments, edged away from the wall, eyeing the other closely. They were about the same height, same build.

He was close to the other man now, whose back was against the wall. Suddenly the man with the gun lashed out a brawny right fist, landing square on the point of the other's chin. It was a knockout. The man with the gun did not hesitate a moment. He shoved the muzzle of the gun under the unconscious man's chin, and pulled the trigger.

The shack shook from the concussion of the heavy shell. Then the killer knelt down and removed the right shoe and sock of the dead man, placed the shotgun by the body, and stepped over to the doorway. Again he heard the baying of a bloodhound, closer this time. Without a backward glance he stepped outside, parted the cattails and went wading away from the shack.

*Thunder and Lightning stumbled happily
in—to face a six-shooter*

Less than a half hour later five men and two leashed
hounds broke into the little clearing and gingerly
approached the open doorway of the shack, both hounds
straining at their leashes. For a moment the men stopped
in the doorway. Then they tied up the two hounds and
went into the shack.

These men did not question what they saw. One of them
said:

"Well, that's the end of Tiger Smith. He was hard, Tiger
was. Said we'd never take him alive. Heard the hounds and
blowed him damn head off."

The others nodded soberly. One of them, a tall, lean,
youngish man, knelt beside the body and looked it over
curiously. Another said:

"Your hunch was right—about him mebbe holin' up on
yore brother's old shack here in the swamp. Took off his

shoe and pulled the trigger with his toe. Figured we was too close, I reckon."

"And took his secret along with him," said another. "They'll never find out where he hid that fifty thousand dollars in gold."

The tall one got up slowly, nodding, and stepped back.

"Must be your brother's shotgun," said one of them, and the tall one merely glanced at the weapon.

"I dunno," he said slowly. "Mebbe I wasn't cut out for this kinda work. Kinda gets a feller, yuh know. Houndin' a man down like this."

"Yuh ain't thinkin' of quittin', are yuh?" asked another.

"Yeah, I'm gettin 'tired of the swamps—kinda. Mebbe go west."

"Well, this ain't no time for ruminations," said the leader. "We'll go and find the sheriff."

John "Tiger" Smith, name known to be an alias, attempted to murder his wife, and escaped with fifty thousand dollars in cash, which she had received on a real-estate deal. Smith shot and killed two officers at Macon, Ga., when apprehended. Arrested later, convicted and given a life sentence, he broke jail at Macon, crippled two guards and seriously injured a spectator.

He was recaptured and sent to prison, where he served two years, mostly in solitary. Then he killed a prison guard and escaped, only to be tracked down in a swamp, where he committed suicide with a shotgun. Finger printing was not exactly unknown, but was not in general use; so Tiger Smith's case was closed.

1

THE POLITE PILGRIM

THE MAIN STREET of Scorpion Bend was dark, except
for what scanty illumination was afforded by the lighted
windows. Danny Regan, foreman of the JHC ranch in
Wild Horse Valley, came from the hotel, his spurs rasping
heavily on the wooden sidewalk.

Danny was mad. For an hour he had argued with a cattle
buyer, who finally managed to make Danny understand
that King Fisher had undersold the JHC, and that King
Fisher had informed him that he would undersell any
outfit in Wild Horse Valley, now and hereafter, in order to
keep other growers from selling on the open market.

In other words, King Fisher now controlled the market.
A fine message for Danny to take back to Henry Harrison
Conroy, owner of the JHC.

Danny was still a young man, built like a middleweight,
a capable cowman, and not at all adverse to fighting, either
with fist or gun. In fact, he was very fast with a hand-gun,
and his reputation was well known over the range country
of Arizona.

Danny surged away from the porch-post and went striding across the street to the Silk Hat Saloon. He rarely
drank anything, but right now he felt the need of a bracer.

Then he was going to get on his horse and ride all the way back to the JHC, figuring just how many ways he could kill King Fisher and enjoy each one.

As he entered the saloon he heard voices pitched higher than usual in ordinary conversation. There were five men at a poker table, four of them sitting, while the fifth was standing, leaning on the table. He was a young man, very blond, and wore glasses. His city clothes seemed out of place there.

Danny stopped at the bar. Three of the seated men were from the King Fisher ranch, and one of them was Roy Fisher, son of the man who had made up his mind to be the big boss of Tonto and of all of Wild Horse Valley. The other two were Bob Haney, Fisher's foreman, and Dish Allen, a puncher.

The blond young man was trying to explain something, while the four men watched him stonily. He told them:

"Gentlemen, this isn't at all fair to me. You invited me to play a few hands, and I foolishly accepted. I asked you how much those chips were per stack, and you—"

"We said fifty," finished Roy Fisher. "You didn't think we'd deal cards for fifty cents, do you?"

"It was fifty dollars, stranger," said the saloon keeper. "You've got ten markers over there, and that's five hundred dollars."

The young man choked slightly and there were tears in his eyes, as he said huskily:

"I—I didn't realize, but I haven't that much cash with me. I could write a check, I suppose—"

"Yore check's all right, ain't it?" asked the saloon keeper.

"Why, yes, of course. But I—"

"We'll accept it," said Roy Fisher. "Anyway, Dick will, and he can pay us for our chips. Get the gentleman a pen, Dick."

The saloon man went behind the bar to secure a pen, and the bartender said to Danny:

"What'll yuh have, Regan?"

"A little fun, I reckon," replied Danny, without turning.

The saloon man came back with the pen and handed it to the young man, who started to unfold his check-book.

"Don't sign it, stranger," advised Danny. All the men turned quickly.

"You spoke to me, sir?" queried the young man.

"Yeah," drawled Danny quietly.

"Who sold you a corner in this game, Regan?" asked Bob Haney.

"Keep yore hands on the table—all of yuh," said Danny. "Stranger, you better get out of here."

The young man backed away from the table. "I—I don't understand," he said nervously, realizing what might happen any moment.

"That's all right," said Danny. "You look kinda new, and I'd hate to see yuh get yore varnish scratched off. Me, I know these snake-hunters. They meant four-bits a stack. I know 'em well. Fifty dollars! They don't make that much a month!

"Wait a minute. You owe 'em two dollars and a half. There's ten markers at four-bits a marker. That's five dollars, but yuh can discount it fifty percent for crooked dealin'. Give 'em two and a half, and that's more than they've honestly got comin'."

THE NERVOUS YOUNG man tossed the required amount

to the table, and went quickly out of the saloon. Danny looked at the discomfited gamblers and chuckled.

"You'll pay for this, Regan," declared Haney.

"Yeah? I suppose you'll take it out in JHC cows. But remember that I don't own 'em, Haney."

"We never stole your cows!" snapped Roy Fisher.

"Matter of opinion, you scrawny sidewinder."

Roy's face flamed, but he shut his lips tightly.

"Go tell yore pa," advised Danny.

"He'll put you and that JHC outfit out of business," flared Roy. "Yuh notice that yuh didn't sell any cattle, don't yuh?"

"Forget it, Roy," advised Bob Haney.

"With a brain like his he could forget anythin'," said Danny. "And as far as puttin' the JHC out of business—that's a job, even for the great King Fisher. Wild Horse Valley was a white man's country, until King Fisher came along with all his money and his crooked ideas."

"Yo're sore because Conroy got beat in that election for sheriff," said Haney. "It was time that Wild Horse Valley had a capable man in there—and not that fat, red-nosed actor. At least, they're not laughin' at King Fisher's candidate, Regan."

"As a matter of fact," said Danny calmly, "King Fisher didn't dare leave an honest man in office. I know Vinegar Bill Hawkins, and he was an honest man."

"Meanin' that he ain't honest now?"

"We'll wait and find out, Haney," replied Danny. "Sorry to interrupt yore hold-up, gents, but it was a little too raw. *Buenas noches.*"

Just away from the doorway Danny met the young man.

"I just wanted to thank you," the latter said gratefully. "You see, it—"

"I know," interrupted Danny. "They had yuh trimmed like a lamp. Next time, insist on payin' for yore chips, or don't play."

"Thank you, Mr. Regan. You are from Tonto City?"

"Near there—the JHC spread."

"I hope your defense of me will not react against you, Mr. Regan."

"Don't worry about me. Who are you—a drummer?"

"My goodness, no! I never played an instrument in my life."

"Well, that's fine," Danny grinned. "Yo're just a visitor, eh?"

"I am on my way to Tonto City. I arrived a few hours ago, and that stage does not leave until about nine o'clock; so I was merely passing away the time."

"You almost passed away five hundred dollars, too."

"I shall always remember that, Mr. Regan—and thank you."

"Call me Danny and don't thank me. That stage leaves right after the nine o'clock train from the west. They haven't had a passenger off that train since Sittin' Bull stood up, but they always have hopes."

"Are you well acquainted around Tonto City—er—Danny?"

"Lived there since the first hill was built. What's yore name?"

"Albert Marshall Henshaw."

"They'll prob'ly cut yuh down to 'Hen.' Let's walk up to the depot and see the train come in."

"It will be a pleasure, I assure you."

Danny chuckled. "You sound like Henry," he said.

"Who is Henry, if I may ask?" queried Albert.

"Henry Harrison Conroy, the man who owns the JHC ranch where I work. Henry had been an actor most all his life—sort of a funny man, with a red nose—and just about the time his—well, the kind of actin' he was doin' had kinda played out, his uncle died at Tonto City and left him the JHC ranch.

"Henry came here, not knowin' a jackass from a juniper tree about cow ranchin', but he learned. They elected him sheriff of Wild Horse county, as sort of a joke, and they've been laughin' ever since. But he made good."

"Is he the sheriff now?" asked Albert.

"No, they beat him this last election. Yuh see, Albert, a rich man named King Fisher, bought out a lot of cattle land, was lucky enough to get control of a couple producin' gold mines, and got enough political power to run things to suit himself. He beat Henry."

"Is King Fisher the sheriff?"

"Oh, no. But he elected the man he wanted—Vinegar Bill Hawkins."

"I heard you talking about him in that saloon," said Albert.

"Yeah, that's right. That thin-faced hombre across the table from you was Roy Fisher, King Fisher's son. And if he's any good, a skunk is a geranium. Well, here's the depot, and all we need is a train."

"Did you ever know a man named James Henshaw?" asked Albert, as they sat down on the platform. "He was a prospector down here."

"No, I don't remember the name. Relative of yours?"

"My uncle. I am from St. Louis."

"Are you lookin' for this uncle?" asked Danny.

"In a way, yes. However, I have always wanted to see the West; so this gave me a good excuse. You see," explained Albert, "he was my father's brother. My father has been dead quite a while. After my mother passed away, I found some letters among her effects. My uncle mentioned Wild Horse Valley in his letters, and said that he had discovered a rich gold mine.

"He said that he did not fully trust the man who had grubstaked him, whatever that means, and that he had falsified a location notice, after discovering that ore assayed very rich. He said he did that to protect himself.

"He sent my mother a map of the location of this mine, saying that in case she did not hear from him within six months to turn the map over to some reliable party and secure the mine for herself. I know nothing about mining; so I came here to find out what I could."

THAT'S SORT OF a queer tale," remarked Danny. "I thought I knew most everybody that prospected in Wild Horse Valley, but I don't remember a man named Henshaw. 'Course, we had a lot of prospectors in here at one time or another. Yore uncle didn't say who grubstaked him, eh?"

"No, he did not say."

"Uh-huh. How long ago was that?"

"About three years ago, I believe."

"Three years. Only been two producin' mines discovered since then—the Yellow Cross and the Golden Streak. They both belong to King Fisher."

"Well, I suppose it is a wild goose chase," sighed Albert. "But I have always wanted to see the West."

"And I've allus wanted to see the East," said Danny. "All my life I've wanted to see a house more'n three stories high, and I've wanted to see the ocean. All my life I've had to save water. Well, here comes that train."

"Somebody on it, too."

The long passenger train ground to a stop at the depot, and three people dismounted from a rear coach. As the train rolled on, the two women and the man walked into the lights of the depot office.

Danny said, "Hyah, sheriff."

The big man stopped short, a valise in each hand.

"Oh, hello, Regan," he said. "Didn't recognize yuh at first. I want yuh to meet Mrs. Hawkins and her daughter, Miss Buckley."

"Mrs. Hawkins?" queried Danny.

"Shore—my wife," chuckled the big sheriff. "I kinda slipped one over on Tonto City, didn't I?"

"Yeah, I reckon yuh did," admitted Danny. Miss Buckley seemed to be a very lovely young lady in the dim lights of the depot office. Danny remembered Albert Henshaw, and introduced him.

"Well, we've got to be movin'," said the sheriff. "That stage is due to leave pretty quick, and we don't want to have to spend the night in Scorpion Bend."

They walked down to the stage depot, where Danny drew the sheriff aside and told him what King Fisher had done. The sheriff nodded gravely.

"No man ought to do that," he said. "Who's this Henshaw, Danny?"

Danny told about the poker game, and the sheriff chuckled.

"They'll love yuh for that, Danny."

"Well, I couldn't see 'em strip that kid."

"I know. Well, I'll pile in. See yuh later, Danny."

As the stage rolled out of Scorpion Bend, Albert told them about how Danny Regan had come to his assistance.

"And I had never met the gentleman," said Albert seriously. "Really, he has a very forceful personality."

"Yeah—and a quick trigger finger," added the sheriff. "Danny Regan is a good man to have as a friend."

"You make him sound interesting," said Joan.

"Don't get too interested, my dear," said the sheriff. "Danny is the sort of a feller that's goin' to ride into trouble one of these days."

"He accused those men of stealing his cattle," said Albert, "and I understand that they hang cattle thieves out here."

"When they catch 'em," said the sheriff dryly.

2

CATTLEMAN CONROY

IT WAS NEARLY two o'clock in the morning, when Danny Regan rode in at the JHC ranch house. He could see a light in the window of the main room, and there was an odor of coffee in the air.

"Henry and Judge playin' cribbage," he told himself, "and Lightnin' or Frijole makin' coffee to keep 'em awake."

And there they were, Henry Harrison Conroy and Judge Van Treece, clad in long underwear and slippers, Judge wearing an old hat, seated at a table, playing their inevitable game of cribbage by the light of a smoky lamp. Henry Harrison Conroy, erstwhile favorite of the vaudeville stage, edging close to sixty, nearly bald, short and fat, with a face like a full moon, on which grew one of the largest and roundest noses in captivity—and the reddest.

Judge Van Treece, six feet, three inches, thin, bony, with a long, lean face, a shock of gray hair and piercing eyes under thatched brows. Judge had been a Western criminal lawyer, until liquor had ruined his career. When Henry came to Tonto City to take over his inheritance, he met Judge, whose genteel manners, covered by a frock coat, gaiter shoes, and great thirst, appealed to Henry's sense of comedy.

When Wild Horse Valley, in a fit of humor, elected Henry sheriff of the country, Henry, not to be outdone, appointed Judge as his deputy, and Oscar Johnson, whom Judge dubbed 'The Vitrified Viking,' as jailer. The newspapers called them "The Shame of Arizona." But with the election of King Fisher's candidate, Vinegar Bill Hawkins, the Shame of Arizona was relegated to the JHC ranch.

"We give you good evening, Danny," said Henry soberly, not looking up from a perusal of his cards. "And give us the news, Crier of the Ranch."

"Bad news," replied Danny, sitting down at the table. "Our friend King Fisher has fixed it so we can't sell a cow to a buyer."

"Danny," said Judge reprovingly, "you must have been drinking some of that Scorpion Bend whisky."

"I didn't have a drink, Judge," declared Danny, and proceeded to tell them about the conversation with the cattle buyer. Judge got to his feet and began pacing the room, shuffling his slippers, his old hat over one eye.

"Be seated, Droop-drawers," said Henry. Lightning Mendoza came to the kitchen doorway, wiping some moisture off his scraggly mustache.

"*Buenas noches,* Danny." He grinned. "How the hell am I? Good, you hope and pray. I mak' leetle coffee, eh?"

"That's fine, Lightnin'," said Danny, and went on talking about the dirty work of King Fisher. Lightning said:

"*Por Dios!* Those damn Feesher. Always I'm saying that keeling ees too good from heem. I should have a keek in your pants—I hope."

"All right," said Henry soberly. "Things are bad enough, without your explanation, is the coffee ready?"

"Weethout crim," said Lightning. "Even weethout milk. Frijole forgeet to breeng the can cow."

"All right, let's have it," said Danny.

Lightning produced the coffee pot and some cups. "I'm theenk maybe I keel those Keeng Feesher some day," he stated soberly.

"And get hung," said Henry, pouring the coffee.

"Where's Thunder and Oscar?" asked Danny.

"Asleep," said Judge. "Frijole's sleeping with them. They sampled Frijole's last batch of prune whisky, and—well, it got them—cold."

"Today," announced Lightning, "I find a mommy."

"Whose mommy?" asked Danny.

Henry groaned. "Do not go into that again, Lightning," begged Henry.

"You mean a mummy, don'tcha?" asked Danny. "Wastin' yore time, huntin' around old cave dwellin's again, eh? You and Thunder—"

"Theese mommy ees not een cave," said Lightning. "I fin' the track of beeg lobo, after hee ees keel a colt, and I go in the bottom of Smoke Tree Canyon. Down there I am finding the mommy. I tak' look at the mommy and I am saying, 'Hm-m-m-m, these are sometheeng else, I hope.'"

"PAUSE AND REFLECT," said Henry. "You are going beyond the tale you told us. At least, be truthful about it."

"Go ahead, Lightnin'," said Danny. "Finish the tale, even if it ain't true."

"Theese mommy," declared Lightning, "had hees hands and feet tied weeth rope."

Henry jerked an elbow and upset Judge's coffee into his lap.

"Of all the damnable, clumsy—" howled Judge, leaping to his feet, and grabbing at his sagging underwear.

"There is plenty coffee, Judge," assured Henry, undisturbed. "Lightning, are you sure the mummy's hands and feet are tied?"

"Sure. I theenk eet ees a *maguey* rope."

"They never had *maguey* in those days," said Danny.

Lightning shrugged his shoulders. "I theenk so that theese are white man, too."

"My gracious!" exclaimed Henry. "A white mummy. This will startle the whole world. What do you think, Judge?"

"Damn the mummy!" snapped Judge. "Get me some axle grease, I have been burned! And I have never heard of a white mummy, and I do not believe Lightning ever found such a thing."

Lightning shrugged his shoulders. "I show heem to you *mañana.*"

"All right," said Danny. "Henry, have you or Judge ever known a prospector named Henshaw?"

Neither of them had. Lightning said:

"I am knowing two prospector name Smeeth. You like that?"

"Not so much," replied Danny.

"Maybe he ees calling yourself Smeeth."

"This mummy wasn't one of the Smiths, was he?" asked Danny.

"*Quien sabe?* His face ees not much from looking at."

"What are all the questions about, Danny?" asked Henry. "And why are you searching for a Henshaw?"

"Oh, I dunno," Danny yawned. "Seems to be one missin'.

Let's go to bed; I'm tired. How did yore game come out, Henry?"

"Judge owes me twenty cents."

"Oh, I forgot to tell yuh," said Danny. "Vinegar Bill came in on the train tonight, bringin' a bride and step-daughter."

"A bride and step-daughter?" queried Judge. "That damn maverick!"

"A very estimable gentleman, and I wish him happiness," said Henry.

"I could say the same—if I wanted to lie like you, Henry," said Judge. "I suppose you wish King Fisher well, too?"

"Why not? He won, we lost. It was merely the turn of Fortune's Wheel, Judge. Although as far as we are concerned, it seems that the proverbial wheel is stuck. But we will manage, I assure you. At least, we do not have to trail criminals to their lair, read scathing denunciations of us in the papers, and prove alibis to the commissioners. Out here, we are as free as air, my dear sir."

"Free, yes," agreed Judge gloomily. "I hope things do not come to a point where we must don steel bills and pick gravel with the hens in order to exist."

"At least," said Henry, "we can eat our beef."

"How 'bout my mommy?" queried Lightning.

Judge shuddered in his sagging underwear. "I hope we never get to that point," he said.

"He ees not on a point; he ees een a hole," corrected Lightning.

"Start adoption proceedings in the morning, Judge," chuckled Henry. "The mummy will fit in with our outfit."

KING FISHER WAS a big man, hard-eyed, two-fisted and tough. Easy living had added jowls to his heavy jaw and inches to his waistline. He owned the Diamond F, the biggest cattle spread in Wild Horse Valley, owned the Tonto Saloon, which he had renamed The King's Castle, owned the majority of stock in the Tonto City Bank; and in addition to these he owned the Golden Streak and the Yellow Cross mines, both coming into heavy production.

He had moved into Wild Horse Valley little over two years ago, and had set out to gain control of the whole valley. In the recent election his political power had been strongly evident, for the county officers elected were his men; and he was now in a fair way to boss Tonto City and the whole county.

Mrs. Fisher, who knew little and evidently cared less for Wild Horse Valley, spent most of her time at their estate near San Francisco. Roy Fisher, their son, whom King Fisher hoped to make head of his interests in the valley, turned out to be a hard-drinking, heavy-gambling liability.

It was the morning after Danny Regan had broken up the poker game at Scorpion Bend, and Roy Fisher was eating breakfast with his father at the ranch. That is, he was making a pretense of eating, to cover up the fact that he had a decided hangover. King Fisher looked at his son disgustedly.

"Drunk again, eh?" he said coldly. Roy shrugged his shoulders.

"Do we have to argue about it?" he asked.

"Roy, you are pretty much of a damn fool."

"All right, all right. We had a run-in with Danny Regan last night."

"You did, eh? What about?"

"Oh, we were havin' some fun with a tenderfoot in Scorpion Bend. We tried to make him believe that he owed us five hundred dollars, instead of five. Got him into a four-bit game. We sure had him covered with goose-pimples, until Regan showed up and got nasty about it."

"I'll have to attend to that young slick-ear," said King Fisher.

"Let him alone—I'll handle my own affairs, Dad."

"You will, eh? You fool, Regan can tie you into a bowknot with one hand, and he can go home and get a gun before you can draw one from a holster. You keep away from him."

"I didn't know you thought that much of him," said Roy.

"I'm not a fool, Roy."

"Meanin' that I am. All right. Did you know that the sheriff is married?"

"Hawkins? No, I didn't know."

"Well, he is. Brought her in on a train last night, and they came down on the night stage. I talked with Steve McCord, the driver, and he said Mrs. Hawkins has a daughter about twenty-three. Pretty, too."

King Fisher smiled slightly. "So Hawkins got married, eh? I knew he went on a trip. Well, he's old enough to know what he wants to do."

Roy said:

"That tenderfoot also came down to Tonto."

"Who is he?"

"Name's Henshaw."

"Henshaw?" King Fisher scowled thoughtfully. "What's his business?"

"Steve didn't know. Damn it, my head hurts!"

"You better go to bed. Take my advice and quit drinkin' whisky and quit wearin' a gun. They don't mix."

"That's good advice from a man who drinks as much as you do, and always carries a gun," retorted Roy.

"I've got brains enough to handle both!" snapped King Fisher angrily. "And that is more than you'll ever have. A few more smart remarks, and you'll go back to San Francisco and stay there."

"Oh, don't preach," sighed the youngster. "I'm goin' back to bed."

"And stay there until you're sober," advised King Fisher, and went striding out of the house. He stopped on the front porch, his brow furrowed in deep concentration.

"Henshaw," he muttered. "That's funny. But that isn't an uncommon name."

With a shrug of his heavy shoulders, as though to dismiss any thought of the tenderfoot, he swung down the steps and headed for the stable.

3

THE MYSTERIOUS MUMMY

HENRY HARRISON CONROY and Judge Van Treece, soaking with perspiration from their descent into Smoke Tree Canyon, squatted on their heels and examined Lightning's mummy. Perched together on another rock were Thunder and Lightning Mendoza, while Danny Regan leaned against a sandstone ledge.

The mummy, if it could be called a mummy, lay in the sand under an overhang of sandstone, where no rain could have reached it and where the blazing sun would strike it for only about two hours each day. Of the face there was little trace. The clothing was rotted away, and both ankles and wrists had been tied with *maguey* rope. There was a bullet hole through the skull.

"W'ite man?" queried Lightning.

"I believe it was," replied Henry.

"Keeled dead, eh?" said Thunder.

They ignored the question, as they searched the particles of clothing for some identification. Buried in the folds of parchment-like skin at the throat, they found a gold chain, nearly as fine as a thread, and at the back of the neck was a tiny locket of gold. Henry managed to open it with the blade of a knife, but it was empty. However, on the front were the two initials L.L. in block letters.

"If we can find someone with those initials," sighed Henry.

"Some missing person," added Judge painfully. That climb into the canyon had not helped his rheumatism.

"Theese one ees meesing," said Lightning. "How long you theenk before he ees died, Henry?"

"Oh, maybe two or three years. They dry up very quickly here."

"Anyway," stated Lightning, "a copple or two year ago I find mommy een canyon, and the man weeth the glasses in hees eye he ees saying that theese man ees died for maybe thousand year. I ask heem how in hell he can know from those ages, and he says, 'Heestry tell me.' Maybe Heestry can tell us from theese ones. He mus' de dam' smart, theese Heestry, eh—I hope."

"Very," agreed Henry soberly. "Now Lightning, you and Thunder climb out and ride to town. There you will tell the sheriff about this, and guide him here. Do not mention the chain and locket to anyone."

"I cross your heart—"

"I hope I die," finished Henry gravely.

"I hope you die," said Lightning. "Sometime I get those wrong, eh?"

"Maybe I better go," suggested Danny.

"You read my mind," said Henry smiling. "Go ahead, Danny."

THE MAIN STREET of Tonto City seemed very quiet as Danny rode in and tied his horse in front of the sheriff's office. Usually there were quite a number of people on the main street, but not today.

Danny went into the office, where he found Spook Gilliam, the deputy, sprawled in a chair. Spook was a long, lean young man, with a surprised expression, buck-teeth and a perverted sense of humor. As soon as Spook opened his mouth, Danny knew that Spook was drunk.

"Where's Vinegar Bill?" asked Danny.

"Oh, the sher'ff?" queried Spook owlishly. "Well, shir, he's stalkin' his prey."

"He's what?" asked Danny. "Stalkin' his prey?"

"It was like thish," explained Spook. "There was three of us in the boat and the oars leaked. Well, shir, it sure looked bad. You shee—"

"What happened?" interrupted Danny, "and who is the sheriff stalkin'?"

"Albert Marshall Henshaw. Fact—give em thish day un'er my hand and sheal. How'r yuh, Danny?"

"You mean, the sheriff is after that tenderfoot?"

"Tennerfoot? Not him! He's reincarnation of Billy th' Kid. I had to quit him or losh my job, don'tcha know it? Bad asshoshiations and all that, Danny. Bir's of a feather."

"Yuh mean he's drunk and gone on the prod, Spook?"

"Oh, without reshervation. You shee," Spook brightened visibly, "thish mornin' I re-ju-ven-ated him. I helped him outfit himshelf, so that he wouldn't be sho visible. Got'm shome boots, overalls, shirt, hat and a gun. My, my, I shouldn' let'm have that gun."

"You don't mean he's killed somebody, do yuh?" asked Danny.

Wham! From across the street came the unmistakable

report of a revolver shot, a decidedly tenor yell, and Danny sprang to the doorway. Out of the King's Castle Saloon came Albert, attired in a flaming red shirt, overalls, high-heel boots and a ten-gallon sombrero. Those high heels were a handicap, along with an overload of rye, and Albert managed to get his legs crossed and did a spread-eagle right in the middle of the street.

Vinegar Bill Hawkins, the sheriff, evidently intending to make a bloodless capture, dashed out of the alley beside the saloon and headed for Albert, arms outstretched to fall upon him. But Albert struggled up to a crouched position just as Vinegar Bill launched his dive, and fell backward.

Vinegar Bill made his dive into space and skidded on his nose in the gravel. Then Albert, whooping with glee at the thought of having a playmate, fell upon the dazed sheriff. In the melee Albert's gun went off again, and there was a tinkling crash as a window of the general store turned into a spider-web pattern.

"Ride'm, cowboy!" yelped Spook.

But the action was short-lived. Vinegar Bill got a strangle hold on the luckless Albert, hoisted him over one shoulder and brought him to the office. Tonto City, relieved of a menace, came out into the open again.

VINEGAR BILL WAS mad. His nose and hands were bruised and his pride was hurt. He slammed Albert into a chair, tossed Albert's gun to the desk-top and started to berate Spook, when he saw Danny.

"Bring'em in alive, eh?" remarked Danny soberly.

"Damn fool ort to be killed!" rasped the sheriff. "You, too!" he yelled, pointing at Spook. "Know what that red-shirted fool done? Well, he took a shot at himself in that big mirror at the King's Castle. Smashed it to bits. And yo're to blame, Spook! Don't deny it!"

"I never deny anythin'," protested Spook. "I got 'm drunk and I helped him buy new clothes, but I never pulled no triggers, Bill. He's of age."

"Wha's wrong?" asked Albert. "I am as innochent as—as—as a egg."

"Yo're a damn bad egg," declared the sheriff. "This'll sure cost yuh plenty. I'll bet that mirror cost a hundred dollars, and you'll have to pay for it, young feller."

"You better go have Doc fix that nose," said Spook. "My, my, you mus' have slid long ways on that nose. It's really beautiful, Bill."

"Never mind my nose!" snorted the exasperated sheriff.

"Never mind anybody's nose," said Albert solemnly, "Lettum mind their own."

"You better lay down and go to sleep," advised the sheriff. "And when you wake up, don't pay no attention to Spook. He's the biggest liar in the state, and if yuh foller him, you'll be in jail. That's my advice."

The sheriff mopped his nose and tried to grin at Danny, who proceeded to tell him about the mummy in Smoke Tree Canyon.

"That's damn funny!" exclaimed the sheriff. "Two, three years, yuh say? Well, well, we'll have to look into that. Looks like murder to me."

"And you ain't even seen it," sighed Spook. "That's ability."

"I'll get the coroner and go right out there, Danny," said the sheriff, ignoring Spook's jibe.

"Take plenty ropes," advised Danny. "I doubt if Doc Knowles can get down there, even with ropes."

"Uh-huh. Mebbe I better take Spook along. Sober the darn fool up a little, climbin' down a rope in the hot sun. Says he's been under a strain, runnin' the office while I was away. Nothin' to do; so it must have been mental strain, I reckon."

As Danny turned toward the doorway, King Fisher and the bartender of the King's Castle came in. King Fisher was mad.

"There's the damn fool!" he exclaimed, pointing at Albert, who was nearly asleep in the chair.

"He's harmless now," assured the sheriff. "I got his gun."

"But he will pay for that mirror!"

"Well, that's between you two," said the sheriff. "Let him sober up, King; he won't run away. I've got to go and get a mummy out of Smoke Tree Canyon."

"A mummy?" queried King Fisher.

"Well, I reckon he's pretty well dried up. It was a murder."

"Oh! A murder, yuh say, Bill?"

"Hands and feet tied and a bullet through the head. Spook, go get the horses, while I find Doc Knowles."

"Where's Smoke Tree Canyon?" asked King Fisher.

"Out on the JHC," replied Danny. "Yuh see—oh-oh!"

Albert fell off the chair, sighed contentedly and went on snoring.

"Yuh see," continued Danny, "somebody tied his feet and bands, and shot him off the rim of the canyon."

King Fisher nodded grimly. "Any way to identify him?"

Danny shrugged his shoulders. "Mebbeso; yuh never

can tell. Checkin' back a couple years, mebbe we can find a missin' man."

Then Danny walked out, mounted his horse and headed back for the ranch. The bartender went back to the saloon. Spook brought the horses to the front of the office, where he waited for the sheriff and coroner.

"So Vinegar Bill got married, eh?" remarked King Fisher.

"He shore did," agreed Spook. "Got a good-lookin' wife, too. I ain't seen her daughter yet, but Bill says she's a dinger. Her name is Joan Buckley."

"Buckley?" queried King Fisher.

"Yeah. Bill says her father died several years ago."

"How old a girl is she?"

"Oh, I dunno. Mebbe twenty, twenty-one, I reckon."

King Fisher crossed the street toward the King's Castle, as the sheriff and Old Doc Knowles came down the street from the doctor's office.

"Nosey devil," muttered Spook to himself. "How old is she? What the hell's it to him how old she is? I think I'll file on that claim my ownself. Hyah, Doc."

THE BRINGING OF the mummified body of a white man to Tonto City only caused mild interest. It was impossible to identify the body. The doctor could only hazard a guess as to how long the man had been dead, but placed it at not over two years.

"If we can only find that some feller is missin'," said the sheriff. "Henry Conroy says we must find a man who had no friends and no relatives around here—a man nobody would miss."

"So Conroy is workin' with yuh, eh?" King Fisher smiled.

"No, he ain't workin' with me. Two years ago he was the sheriff; so he's kinda interested, yuh know."

"And a hell of a sheriff," laughed King Fisher.

"I guess that's true… First time yuh get a chance, I want yuh to meet my wife and step-daughter, King."

King nodded. "I didn't know you went away to get married, Bill."

"I kinda slipped one over on everybody," laughed the big sheriff. "I went to Denver. Oh, we've been writin' to each other a long time. I'll have yuh up for supper some day, King. She's a fine cook. Her daughter is a mighty fine girl. Her name's Joan Buckley."

"That's what Spook told me. Well, I'll see yuh later."

"When are yuh goin' to invite me up to supper?" asked Spook.

"Oh, some hard winter," replied the sheriff. "Do yuh think I want a feller like you hangin' around her? Unreliable, unrefined, and anythin' else yuh can think of."

Spook's eyebrows lifted in dismay. "You act like you'd raised her, instead of getting' her in a marriage deal with her ma."

"It don't matter how I got her. I shore don't want you for a stepson-in-law—not if I can help it."

"I s'pose I should expect that from you, Bill. Sour old rawhider like you. No wonder they call yuh Vinegar Bill. Go ahead and poison her young mind against me. Belittle me to her. But remember this, Bill; some day, when I've got a hunk of two-by-four plank in my hands, and I catch you hung up in a bob-wire fence—don't plead for mercy. Jist take it like a man, and if yore vertebray is found to be six inches shorter than it was, say to yourself, 'Well, I shouldn't have done what I done.'"

"And you'll still be single," reminded the sheriff.

"Uh-huh, that's right, ain't it? Well, mebbe yo're right, Bill. If I was to marry her, I'd have to call you papa."

Spook shuddered visibly. "That'd be awful," he said.

4

DANGER: VIKINGS

DANNY REGAN HAD related to Henry and Judge what Albert had told him about the letters from Jim Henshaw, his uncle. This gave those two estimable gentlemen much to discuss over their cups of Frijole Bill's prune whisky, as they sat on the shaded porch at the JHC.

"If that dehydrated human from Smoke Tree Canyon is Jim Henshaw, he had fears that were well founded," declared Henry.

"Exactly," agreed Judge soberly. "But identification is impossible. The initials L.L. are most certainly not the initials of Jim Henshaw."

"Ay t'ink," remarked Oscar Johnson, who was seated on the steps, putting a rawhide hondo on a new rope, "das ha'ar faller might be Larsen, who vars here a coople years ago."

"Larsen," said Judge, "was six feet, three inches tall and would weigh over two hundred. And he went to Chicago with a trainload of cows."

"Yah, su-ure," agreed Oscar, "but he might have coom back, Yudge."

"What was his first name, Oscar?" asked Henry.

"Yulius."

"That doesn't account for the L.L. You do not spell Julius with an L, Oscar."

"Ay give oop," said Oscar. "Ay am not great defective."

"I question that," said Judge dryly.

Henry squinted thoughtfully at his empty cup, but laid it aside.

"If this young Henshaw has a map," he said, "no doubt he will be able to locate that mine."

"And I believe we should cultivate the young man," said Judge.

"For mercenary reasons, my dear Judge? Fie on you, sir!"

"Mercenary, indeed!" snorted Judge. "You do not seem to realize that our income has perished, and that we cannot sell a pound of beef. Are we going to sit here and—er—dehydrate in the sun?"

"My goodness!" exclaimed Henry. "Is it that bad, Judge?"

"We are," declared Judge, "facing a panic."

"That *is* serious," agreed Henry soberly. "The only panic I have ever seen was during a summer season, in Syracuse, I believe, when one of Barney South's trained bears was stung by a migrant bee during the act. It was the last stunt, and I was in the wings, ready to follow. I never want to face another panic, if you please."

"This," said Judge, "is a financial, not a physical, panic. Unless we can discover ways and means to break the strangling grip of King Fisher on Wild Horse Valley, we may as well—" Judge drew a deep breath and reached for the jug of prune whisky. "We may as well have another drink, Henry."

"True, my dear Judge, true. What are a few hardened arteries between old friends? Frijole Bill did well with this batch. It has a tang and aroma not found in commercial liquor. It not only warms the cockles of your heart, but it broils them to a crisp, and the devilish machinations of King Fisher fade to nothing. To you, my dear Judge."

"A confusion to King Fisher and all his tribe, Henry."

"Ay t'ink," said Oscar, "de confusion is on de odder foot."

"And with that sage remark," said Henry, "Oscar Johnson went to the stable and hitched up the buckhoard team, while Henry Harrison Conroy prepared to go to Tonto town."

"Oll right," nodded Oscar, getting to his feet. "Ay am de best driver in Vild Hurse Walley, you bat you."

Oscar was a giant Swede, powerful as a grizzly, and ready at any moment to fight anybody or everybody; but as a driver he had wrecked every vehicle on the ranch and nearly every vehicle in the livery stable at Tonto City. Roads meant nothing to Oscar.

"Some day," said Judge, as Oscar started for the stable, "that Vitrified Viking is going to kill you, Henry. He has no conception of proper driving. In fact, he is a road maniac."

"But he gets you there on time, Judge. Four wheels or no wheels, you arrive at your destination when Oscar drives. Well, I must be presentable."

"Why this sudden trip to Tonto?"

"Do you remember what killed the cat, sir?"

"Curiosity, I believe"

"So they say. Well, I hope I have better luck."

WHILE HENRY WORE overalls and high-heel boots at the ranch, when he went to town he wore a pearl-gray suit, white shirt, bow tie, the latest in oxfords, and a pearl-colored derby hat. He also carried a gold-headed cane. Except for an occasional smile, Tonto City paid little attention to the little, rotund man with the red nose and quizzical eyes.

For once in his life Oscar managed to reach town with all four wheels intact. Oscar's light o' love was Josephine Swensen, maid of all work at the Tonto Hotel. Josephine was over six feet tall, raw-boned, two-fisted. She had stringy blond hair, prominent cheekbones and a large nose. As a fighter, Josephine was a close second to Oscar.

"Be reasonable in all things, Oscar," advised Henry, as he got out of the buckboard in front of the courthouse. "Remember to turn the other cheek, and do not drink too much. I shall be ready in perhaps an hour."

"Ay vill be oll right," assured Oscar. "Ay am a yentleman."

Henry entered the courthouse and went to the recorder's office, where he perused the mining records carefully.

"Find what you wanted, Mr. Conroy?" asked the clerk.

"I find a record of the Glory Hole mine, located by a man named Henshaw, Dick. Do you remember him?"

"Henshaw? No, I can't say that I do. We had a lot of locations to put on record at that time. The valley was full of prospectors."

"True." Henry nodded. A further search showed that the Golden Streak, one of King Fisher's properties, had been located and recorded only a short time after the recording of the Glory Hole.

Henry went from the courthouse to Tom South's assay office. South had been in Tonto for several years, and was now handling all the assay work for King Fisher. Henry leaned against a fly-specked showcase full of ore samples, and wrinkled his red nose against the smell of acids, as he questioned the assayer.

"Henshaw?" queried South. "No, I don't remember him—much. It seems to me that he did have some rich ore, though. That was a couple years ago, Henry. I don't remember what he looked like, but I remember that name."

"Was he a large man or a small man?"

"I just can't remember. There was so many prospectors around, and I done work for most of 'em."

South glanced at a clock on the back counter.

"I'm pretty busy on some stuff for Fisher," he said, "and he's due in today."

"Thank you very much, Tom. Good day, sir."

Henry met the sheriff outside the courthouse.

"My dear Mr. Hawkins, allow me to congratulate you," said Henry. "I have been informed that you have a wonderful wife. I wish you both all the best in the world, I'm sure."

"Well, thank yuh a lot, Conroy," said the sheriff. "I didn't know how yuh felt about—well, the election and all that."

"Oh, my dear man!" exclaimed Henry. "I surrendered gladly. In fact, just between us, I was ready to quit. Yes, indeed."

"Well, that's shore nice, Conroy. Yes, I am married. Sorry I didn't get married before. Got a fine woman."

"Wonderful! Good luck to both of you."

"Well, thank yuh again. Yuh know, I was talkin' to Danny Regan about—well, about that cattle buyer, who said that King Fisher wouldn't let him buy your cows. Yuh see, I don't approve of—"

"My dear sheriff! It really doesn't matter. I hold no grudge against Mr. Fisher. Really a fine character, they tell me. Must cultivate him. Now that I am out of office,

I must be neighborly—visit around. We are having fine weather, don't you think?"

"Yeah, it's pretty good, Conroy. Well, I must be movin'."

Henry watched the sheriff disappear, and chuckled to himself:

"Henry, you are either entering your dotage age, or you are the biggest liar in Arizona. And I do not believe it is dotage."

HE SAW KING FISHER enter the assay office of Tom South, and went down to the general store. King Fisher accepted the penciled notations from the assayer, a pleased smile on his lips. South said:

"Henry Conroy was in here a few minutes ago, asking about a prospector named Henshaw. Didn't he do some work for you at one time?"

King Fisher looked up quickly: "Henshaw? No, I—why, yes, he did, too. Located me in on a mine. Wasn't worth anything, though."

"That was the Glory Hole Mine?"

"Why, yes, I believe so."

"Conroy mentioned it. Said he saw it in the records."

King Fisher accepted the assay reports and walked out. After a few moments of indecision, he went to the recorder's office at the courthouse, where he asked to see the mining records.

"That book is getting popular," remarked the clerk. "Henry Conroy was looking it over a while ago. Did you ever know a prospector named Henshaw?"

"Yes," replied King Fisher gruffly.

Someone came in to occupy the attention of the clerk, and in a few minutes King Fisher walked out. In the hallway he met Vinegar Bill Hawkins. The big sheriff grinned, as he told Fisher about his conversation with Henry Conroy.

"Is he a liar, or is he just plain dumb?" asked Fisher.

"He may be a liar," said the sheriff, "but he is not dumb. Records show that, in spite of what people say about him, he was an efficient sheriff and a smart one. Nobody ever understood him, except Judge Van Treece."

"So yuh think he's smart, eh?" mused King Fisher. "How smart, Bill?"

"Smart enough to take care of himself, I reckon."

"M-m-m, I wonder."

Henry had gone to the buckboard. He was waiting for Oscar, seated comfortably in the shade, when a horse and buggy came down the street. As they passed, Henry recognized Josephine riding with a big man, wearing a black suit and a black derby, at least two sizes too small.

Henry's eyes shifted to the front of the King's Castle Saloon, where Oscar had appeared. He was leaning against the doorway, watching the equipage, which drew up at the hotel. The big man got out and assisted Josephine to alight. After a few moments of conversation the man entered the buggy and drove over to the livery stable.

Oscar was halfway down there when Henry looked again. Henry climbed out, untied the team and got back in the buckboard. Swinging the team around, he drove swiftly to the front of the stable, but he was too late to interfere.

Oscar was backing out of the wide doors, an ankle in each hand, and the ankles belonged to the big man who had squired Josephine. Ignoring Henry's command, Oscar dragged his victim straight to the watering trough, where he immersed him completely, dusted his hands off on his knees and came straight to the buckboard. The man was floundering, clawing his way out of the dirty water, spouting like a whale.

OSCAR HAD ONE swollen eye and a skinned nose. He took the lines from Henry, chirped to the team, and they headed for the ranch.

"What happened?" queried Henry.

"Yulius coomed back," replied Oscar.

"So Julius wasn't the mummy, eh?" said Henry, after a long pause.

"Yulius vill be, if he don't stop taking adwantage of Yosephine."

"Oh, he took advantage of her, eh?"

"Va-al, today vars her day off, and Yulius inweigled her into taking a boggy ride. Yosephine has a veakness for boggies."

Oscar drove one wheel over a roadside boulder, and almost threw Henry out of the buckboard.

"Keep your mind on the road," said Henry sharply.

"It is hord to think of love and boulders at de same time," said Oscar apologetically. "Sometimes Ay get so damn mad, Ay yust yerk on de wrong line. By yee, Ay am going to ta-al Yosephine a few t'ings, you bat you."

"Be a gentleman," advised Henry. "Always be a gentleman, Oscar."

"When Ay am calm, Ay am yentleman. But when Ay get mad—to ha-al wit' yentlemen. Ay yust turn Wiking, and feel for fight."

"Yes, I know."

"Hanry, have you ever been in love?"

"Every spring when I was younger, Oscar."

"Not now?"

"At my age, Oscar, there is no spring—only hard bumps."

Oscar caressed his swollen eye and smiled wryly.

"Ay get a few boomps myself, Hanry. Two times Ay have had Yosephine olmost to de preacher. Somet'ing olvays bosts it oop. Next time, Ay hope, ve might make it."

Henry wiped his eyes and nodded violently.

"I hope you make it," he said huskily.

"You catch cold?" queried Oscar.

"No, just dust," breathed Henry.

Judge was curious to know what Henry had done in Tonto City, but the fat man merely smiled enigmatically. After supper he said to Thunder and Lightning:

"You two go to Tonto City and find Albert Henshaw, the stranger. He is at the Tonto Hotel, I believe. Ask him to come out here with you. Tell him that Danny Regan wants to see him."

"Are you going to let them have that buckboard and team, Henry?" asked Judge.

"Why not? They can drive as well as Oscar."

"Well," sighed Judge, "as long as everything else is going to the dogs, we may as well smash up the rolling stock."

Thunder and Lightning Mendoza were more than pleased to go to town on the errand. It was a rare occasion for them to have sole charge of the buckboard team.

Thunder said:

"You see, my leetle brodder, you amount to sometheeng. You mus' be proud from me—personally."

"Look out for the stomp!" yelled Lightning. *"Por Dios,* you are not driving ships! Stay on the road, beeg mouth."

"You know these stranger we are looking for?"

"I'm never see heem," declared Lightning. "But we fin' heem all right. He leeve een hotel."

"How much *dinero* you got?" asked Thunder. "I theenk we need dreenk pretty good, eh?"

"I am not having even *cinco centavo*. Theese ees one time we stay sobber."

"You theenk so, my leetle brodder?" queried Thunder. "Een my pocket I have two peso. Wa't you theenk from those, eh?"

"*Buena!* We 'ave leetle fiesta, eh? Two bottle tequila. Get heem down at Mostano's place—beeger bottle for the money."

5

HOW AM I TONIGHT?

AND THAT IS exactly what they did. They tied the team in front of the hotel and bow-legged their way to Mostano's cantina, where they invested the two dollars in a poor grade of tequila, the potent distillation of the *maguey* plant. An hour later they found the Tonto Hotel and squeezed their way into the lobby.

Taking off their sombreros they bowed their way to the desk, where Old Matt Corrigan, the clerk, looked them over suspiciously.

"You spik weeth heem, Lightning," said Thunder. "I can't remember your name."

"Sure," said Lightning. "Theese ees how it happened. We are looking for sometheeng wheech ees a stranger to you."

"That sure sounds loco to me," replied Old Matt.

"Hanry send us," declared Thunder. "You know heem?"

"Henry Conroy? Sure, I know him. What'd he want?"

Lightning became inspired. "You got something name ees Hanshaw?"

"Henshaw? Sure. He's up in number twenty-six, I reckon."

"Hanry want heem."

"He does, eh? Well, yuh can go up and talk with him.

Right up the stairs and straight down the hall. It's at the far end."

"*Gracias,*" bowed Lightning. "*Mucho gracias.* How am I this evening? Well, I hope and pray. Come on, brodder from mine."

They managed to climb the stairs and reach the long hallway. It was none too light up there, and neither of them could have told a twenty-six from a forty-four, even in the daylight, but they understood, "at the far end of the hall."

Those two bottles of tequila had blunted what little sense of etiquette they had ever acquired; so they did not bother to knock. Lightning merely turned the knob, stubbed his toe on the carpet edge, and they both fell into the lighted room.

"*Madre de Dios!*" gasped Thunder, on his hands and knees, staring into the muzzle of a six-shooter, held by a masked man. On the bed was Albert Marshall Henshaw, tied and gagged, and the room was strewn with clothes, bedding and other of Albert's personal property.

But the masked man did not hold them long in suspense. He stepped past the two Mexicans, jerked the door shut behind him, and was gone.

Thunder and Lightning sat up and looked at each other foolishly. Albert was jouncing on the bed and making queer noises through the towel over his mouth.

"I theenk theese ees a hold-off," said Lightning.

Thunder got to his feet and made a quick inspection of the luckless Albert, who blinked at him furiously. Thunder shoved his big hat to the side of his head and looked around the disordered room.

"I look like eet," he decided, finally answering Lightning's conclusion. "I theenk we must fin' the shoriff, my leetle brodder—queek!"

They bolted out of the room, went onto a balcony, where they practically fell all the way down an outside stairway. Then they went galloping through an alley, neck and neck, heading for Vinegar Bill's modest cottage on the edge of town.

There was a huge sycamore in the front yard, and the fence was heavily lined with poplar trees, screening the house from the street. Thunder and Lightning were nearly to the front gate, which was about fifty feet from the front door, when a shot crashed out.

The two dumpy Mexicans skidded to a stop at the open gateway, and a moment later a man bumped into them, running at top speed, sending them spinning. In the darkness they only had a momentary glimpse of him, and he was gone.

A woman screamed, the door banged and another man came running. Luckily both Thunder and Lightning were not in his path. As soon as he passed, they got to their feet and headed back for town.

"*Madre de Dios!*" panted Lightning. "Sometheeng happen—bad! You hear those women scrim?"

"You theenk you are deef?" countered Thunder. "Sure, I'm hear. I theenk I got piece skeen gone from both your knees. W'at you theenk now?"

At that particular moment Lightning did not know what to think, so he let the question go unanswered. He merely scratched his head and wondered.

The alarm had been given, and they could hear men

running, questioning; so they moved in against a fence and let the group go past. They heard someone call:

"Doc will be here in a minute."

"That sound like seekness," said Lightning.

"Biffore, that sound like shotgun," remarked Thunder. "We better look."

They joined the group and heard a man say:

"Somebody blasted a load of buckshot through Bill's window, while they were eatin' supper, and hit Bill's wife."

"Is she dead?" asked another.

"I reckon so. Doc will be here in a minute. Ain't that a terrible thing?"

"Prob'ly meant for Bill. Nobody knows his wife."

"Yeah, I reckon that's what it was."

INSIDE THE HOUSE Doc Knowles knelt beside the still figure on the floor, while Bill Hawkins steadied himself against the disordered supper table. Doctor Knowles shook his head and got up.

"I'm awful sorry, Bill," he said quietly.

"Gone?" whispered the big sheriff.

The doctor nodded and picked up his bag. Big Bill Hawkins lifted his agonized face and looked around. There were faces in the doorway and at the smashed window, but they all seemed blurred, indistinct.

"Who done this to me?" he asked hoarsely. "I want that man. The law can't never have him—he's mine, do yuh understand."

"Take it easy, Bill," said the doctor. "You'll find him. Keep your nerve."

Hawkins clenched his fists, raised them high above his head.

"Keep my nerve? Doc, you don't understand. My God, who could do such a thing to me, and to her. She never harmed anybody."

King Fisher shouldered his way into the room, looked at the still form on the floor, and then at Bill Hawkins.

"They told me what happened, and I didn't believe 'em, Bill," he said.

"She's gone, King," said the sheriff slowly. "Nothin' can be done now."

King Fisher shook his head slowly. "Nothin', Bill. But who would do a thing like that? Do yuh suppose it was meant for you?"

"If it was, God knows I wish it had been me instead of her. Doc, will you go into that room with Joan. I reckon she needs yuh."

King Fisher examined the smashed glass, and the buckshot holes in the plaster behind the chair.

"Didn't scatter much," said one of the men. "Buckshot at fifteen feet is shore bad medicine."

Fisher merely nodded.

Thunder and Lightning, sobered now, listened for a while and then went back to the street.

"I theenk the shoriff ees busy," said Lightning. "We turn heem loose."

There was nobody in the hotel lobby, as they went through and up the stairs. Albert had managed to paw the gag loose, but was unable to get his hands free. They cut the knots and let him up.

"We go to get the shoriff," explained Lightning, "but he ees busy biccause hees wife ees keeled."

"His wife was killed?" exclaimed Albert.

"Sure." Lightning nodded. "Just a few minutes from now. Danny Regan ask for me to breeng you home."

"Danny Regan wants me?" queried Albert.

"Cross my heart, I hope you die," said Lightning soberly.

"I really thought I was going to die when that masked man came," said Albert. "I have never had such an experience. Wait until I get some things together, and I will go with you."

Thunder and Lightning got Albert between them on the buckboard seat, and headed for the JHC ranch. They were on the road at least sixty percent of the time, which was very good for them, and they eventually pulled up at the ranch house, with all four wheels intact, and harness on both horses.

Henry greeted Albert warmly, after Danny had introduced them.

"Hell ees being paid een Tonto," declared Lightning. "Albert ees held off by a man weeth rag over your face, and somebody ees keeling the sheriff's wife. My, my, I am all excited over you!"

"What happened?" asked Judge.

ALBERT TRIED TO explain, assisted by both Thunder and Lightning, who clouded the issue badly. But finally everyone understood. Albert had been tied and gagged by a masked man, and the sheriff's wife had been killed.

"I have no explanation," said Albert. "I am completely in a fog."

"Undoubtedly," agreed Henry. "What did you miss after he was gone?"

Albert looked puzzled.

"Miss? Why, I—I—really, I had nothing that a robber would desire."

"What about the letters Danny said you had?"

"Oh, those letters. Well, they are—" Albert reached to an inside pocket of his coat, and a blank expression came over his face.

"They are gone," he said. "I remember, the man had my coat when Thunder and Lightning—er—fell in on us."

"The map?" queried Danny quickly.

"The map," replied Albert, "was in the envelope with the letters."

"Never mind the map and letters," said Judge. "What about the sheriff's wife?"

"She is keel—" Lightning began.

"Shut up," said Judge, "I asked Albert. What about her, Albert?"

"I only know what Thunder and Lightning told me," said Albert.

"And what a mess they can make of the telling," sighed Judge.

"I believe I'll go to town and get the story," said Danny. "I can't believe that someone shot through a window and killed her. It don't sound reasonable."

"You theenk you are lying to me, eh?" said Lightning. "I see everytheeng weeth my own eyesight. I see the hole in the weendow and I see the doctor. *Por Dios*, the man who keel her run over us! W'at more can I ask, you hope and pray."

"Anyway," replied Danny, "I reckon I'll go in and listen to somebody else."

"Should I go back with you?" asked Albert.

"No use of that," said Henry dryly. "You haven't anything left that is worth stealing."

After Danny went to town, Henry said to Albert:

"In that letter you had, your uncle did not mention the man he was working for, did he? I mean, the man who grubstaked him."

Albert frowned.

"No, he did not mention any names, Mr. Conroy."

"But you have lost the map," said Judge. "You had a chance to get rich, if you had kept it."

"I am not worried about riches, Mr. Van Treece," said Albert, "but I am worried about what that man said to me. He warned me to get out of this valley and stay out. He said I would not live but a short time if I did not obey that order."

Henry rubbed his red nose and looked reflectively at Albert.

"Do you believe he meant it?" asked Albert.

"There is only one way to prove it," said Henry.

"Oh, I realize that. But why should I run away? I haven't harmed anyone."

Lightning said, "He who fights and gathers no moss, ees wort' two in the brosh."

"What on earth does he mean?" queried Albert.

Henry shook his head, "Your guess is as good as mine."

"My onkle learned me," said Lightning.

"But what am I going to do?" insisted Albert. "I am not a coward. When that masked man told me what they would do to me, something arose up inside of me, and seemed to say, 'Albert, you must see this through in spite of anything.'"

"Are you sure it wasn't something you ate?" queried Judge.

"No," replied Albert soberly, "that came up later."

"I would not care to advise you," said Henry.

"You see," explained Albert, "I am the last of our branch of the Henshaw family."

"The last of the Henshaws," said Judge. "Well, if you stay, you must take the chance that the Henshaws will *all* be gone, Albert."

"If you do not mind, I shall stay," said Albert firmly.

"Buena!" applauded Lightning. "Weeth all of us and Henry behin' you, you weel otherwise leeve or die, and that ees all I hope. *Viva* Bolivar!"

"Never mind Bolivar," said Henry. "Go help Frijole wash the dishes."

KING FISHER WAS in a vile temper when he came down to breakfast next morning. He swore at the Chinese cook for being slow, and drank a big hooker of raw whisky. He discovered Roy on the porch, and Roy said:

"I've got to have some money today, Dad."

King growled.

"More money? What for? To pay gamblin' debts, eh? Well, you won't get it and that's that."

"I only need five hundred dollars. My gosh, that—"

"Only five hundred, eh? Well, you won't get a dime. You think I'm made of money, don't you? I think that this is a good time for a showdown, young man. I brought you away from the city to try and make somethin' out of you. Did I? Roy, you're a damn fool, and you'll never be anything more. From now on, you'll draw forty a month, just the same as any puncher on this spread. When you show me you're worth more—but you won't."

"Forty a month!" sneered Roy. "You must have slept badly."

"Forty a month—take it or leave it."

Roy got to his feet, his face gray with anger.

"Take it or leave it, eh? If you think I'm just a white chip in this game of yours, you're all wrong. You can't cut me down to forty a month. Just try to do that and you'll be sorry."

"Well, that's what you've got comin'," declared King Fisher.

"Yeah? Well, you watch my smoke."

Roy walked off the porch and went straight down to the stable, where he found Bob Haney, the foreman.

"What's eatin' you?" asked Haney, noting the expression on Roy's face.

"The Old Man cut me off with forty a month," snarled Roy.

"What was the quarrel about, Roy?"

"Oh, I wanted to settle up a poker debt," replied Roy bitterly. "The Old Man thinks he's a tin god around here. If he does me dirt, I'll sure throw somethin' into his machinery. I know a few things."

"What do you know?" asked Haney coldly.

"So you're backin' him, are yuh? Well, Haney—"

"I'm workin' for him," interrupted Haney, "and don't you forget that."

His voice remained cold.

"I never forget anythin'," retorted Roy hotly. "With both of you against me, I ought to do real well. To hell with both of yuh."

6

THE FRIENDLY DICE

HENRY AND JUDGE went to Tonto City that morning. The tragedy had sobered the town, and men spoke quietly on the streets. They found Spook at the sheriff's office, and for once his sense of humor had faded.

"Bill's down at the house," he told them, "and he won't see anybody. He shore took it hard, gents. Jest sets there."

"Any clues?" asked Henry.

"Only a busted window and buckshot in the walls. I—I tried to tell Bill that the load was meant for him, but he won't have it. Bill was at one end of the table, Joan was at the other end, and Mrs. Hawkins was in the middle. Her back wasn't over ten, twelve feet from the muzzle of that shotgun. They're havin' the inquest tomorrow."

"Rather a puzzling case," said Henry. "Did I understand rightly when I heard that she came from Denver, Spook?"

"That's right, Henry. Lived in Denver quite a number of years."

Henry looked thoughtfully at Judge. "Have we ever known anyone from Denver, Judge?" he asked.

Judge shook his head slowly. "Not to my knowledge, sir."

"Her daughter might know if she had a bitter enemy," said Henry.

"She says no," replied Spook. "She says her mother didn't have no enemies."

"Well," said Henry dryly, "a load of buckshot in the back isn't exactly a friendly gesture. At least, I would not designate it as a mark of great friendship."

"It is a terrible thing," sighed Judge. "No one should rest until that murderer is apprehended. If I were Bill Hawkins, I would hire the best detective—"

"That's jist what I told him," interrupted Spook. "But he's too upset to do anythin'."

Henry and Judge sauntered up to the bank, where they talked about the murder with Harvey Olds, the banker. When the conversation lagged, Henry said:

"Mr. Olds, I have two hundred head of beef, ready for market, and I need some money. Would they be security for about five thousand dollars?"

The banker shook his head, his lips pursed. "Sorry, Conroy, but I am unable to make such a loan."

"Of course," said Henry, "you would be in a position to know that King Fisher coerced the buyers into refusing my cattle."

"Well, yes, I did hear something about it. Your assets, as you might say, are frozen, Conroy."

"Frozen—very true. And frozen by the man who owns control of this bank. Of course, I can make a deal with some other packing outfit, but I need ready cash."

"Mr. Conroy, I am not interested in the methods used by Mr. Fisher. My job is to operate this bank—under orders from my board."

"Thank you very much, sir," said Henry courteously.

"Why not take the matter up with Mr. Fisher person-ally?"

Henry blinked and caressed his red nose. "Mr. Olds," he said quietly, "can it be possible that you are suddenly developing a sense of humor?"

"No, no, it was merely an idea."

"And a very good one," said Henry soberly. "Shall we go, Judge? Good-day to you, Mr. Olds. It has been nice seeing you, sir."

They left the bank and crossed the street to the King's Castle. Business was rather slack at that time of day, but there was the usual crowd of loafers, miners off shift, cowboys and saloon girls. One poker game was in prog-ress, surrounded by the usual crowd of onlookers.

There were many smiles as Henry and Judge approached the long bar. Drinking, with them, was a ritual. Dignified, courteous and quiet, they drank to each other. Judge always said, "A very good health to you, my friend," and Henry would reply, "And to you, sir; a gentleman and a scholar."

ROY FISHER WAS in the poker game, evidently losing. When his father came in from his private office, Roy left the game for the bar, where he swallowed two full-sized drinks of whisky, scowled at Henry and Judge, and left the saloon. It was not unusual for King Fisher to sit in a game in place of his regular dealer. He spoke to the dealer, warning him not to give Roy any more credit, and then took the dealer's seat.

King Fisher saw Judge and Henry at the bar, and a smile flashed across his thin-lipped mouth, as he said:

"An empty chair, Conroy."

The sheriff charged out, to find Danny crouched on the man pinning him down

Henry turned and looked at King Fisher for several moments, while every eye was upon Henry.

"I rarely play penny-ante," said Henry.

King Fisher flushed when someone had the temerity to laugh.

"You can make your own limit," said King Fisher.

Henry came over and sat down in the vacant chair, resting his chubby hands on the table-top, his cane between his knees.

"Mr. Fisher," he said calmly, "you persuaded a cattle buyer to not buy anything except your cattle. You undersold every rancher in Wild Horse Valley, in order to try and freeze us out. I have two hundred head of beef ready to ship. What are they worth as a gambling stake?"

King Fisher's color flared again, but he remained silent for several moments. Then he said:

"About five thousand dollars, Conroy."

"I would estimate that they are worth twelve thousand," said Henry calmly. "But, as I say, I never play penny-ante."

"You—" King Fisher hesitated. "You want to play for five thousand?"

"Of course," Henry nodded.

"All right," said King Fisher slowly. "What do we play?"

Henry smiled slowly. "To prevent skull-duggery," he said, "we will roll one die—once—for five thousand dollars."

King Fisher scowled thoughtfully. "One die—one roll, Conroy?"

"If you have that much nerve, Fisher—yes."

The audience gasped and moved in closer. One of the gamblers took the dice from the crap table and tossed them over in front of King Fisher. Henry looked at them and shook his head.

"Not those," he said.

"What's the matter with them?" demanded Fisher.

"That," replied Henry, "would require the opinion of the man who made them. It is very difficult for a layman to find anything wrong, before or after his money is gone. I really prefer ordinary dice, such as are used at the bar."

King Fisher got to his feet and went over to the bar where the alert bartender, masked from the audience by King Fisher's broad back, gave Fisher two of the ordinary-looking transparent dice. A whispered word, and King Fisher came back to the table, palming the extra die.

"Who gets the first roll?" he asked. "Do you want us to cut for it, Conroy?"

"We will roll that die, sixes high, aces low—and I shall

waive the right to draw for first roll, Mr. Fisher. You may shoot when ready."

"Sixes high, aces low," said Fisher.

With a twist of his wrist he spun the die out on the green-covered table. Every eye in the place was on that die, which showed a five. A sudden mutter went up from the crowd. Fisher picked up the die, laughed huskily and handed it to Henry.

"Try and beat that one, Conroy," he said. "The odds are against you, my friend, and I believe I own the cattle."

Henry, his eyes narrowed, a half-smile in his lips, shook the die in his left hand. Then he cast it out on the table, and a roar went up from the crowd.

"A six!"

KING FISHER LEANED back in his chair, staring at that die. The bartender, who had left his post to watch the match, went back, licking his lips, a puzzled expression in his eyes. Henry sighed and lighted a cigar.

"I will thank you for the cash, Mr. Fisher," he said.

King Fisher paid, his face stony. Henry folded the great wad of bills, thanked King Fisher very gravely, and walked out with Judge, whose face was gradually resuming its normal color.

They went to the bank, where Banker Olds looked with amazement at the pile of bills which Henry had placed on the slab in front of the teller's window, along with his almost depleted bankbook.

"You—you must have taken my suggestion, Mr. Conroy," he said.

"Yes, thank you very much," said Henry pleasantly. "I did see him in person."

As the teller made out the deposit, Henry took a transparent die from his pocket and rolled it along the ledge. Three times he sent it rolling, and each time it came up—a deuce. Judge watched him, puzzled over it all. Finally Henry threw it into a wastebasket.

Over at the King's Castle, in King Fisher's private office, Fisher and his head bartender leaned over the desk and carefully rolled a transparent die. Time after time they rolled it, and time after time it showed a six.

"Damn him!" muttered King Fisher. "He's a crook! He shifted dice on me. That's why he wanted those bar dice. But what became of our dice?"

"Maybe," said the bartender, "when you rolled a five, he suspected that the companion die would roll a deuce—so he used his six-dice."

"The dirty crook! Well, forget it. I'll get even for that one."

While Henry and Judge were driving back to the ranch, Judge said:

"I died a dozen times between Fisher's roll and yours, Henry. You had a five to beat. Gad, man, you have nerve! And just to think that in the all those rolls in the bank you did not do better than a deuce."

"Quaint, wasn't it?" Henry smiled. "One never knows one's luck, does one?"

After a few moments of reflection Judge said:

"That five thousand dollars saved our life, Henry. It was a great triumph, indeed. It was a case of your luck against the luck of King Fisherand you won."

"I am not exactly proud," sighed Henry, "but I am grateful, Judge."

They were nearly back to the ranch, when Henry said:

"I forgot what we went to get at Tonto, Judge. We need flour and potatoes."

"Send Frijole in after them this evening," suggested Judge.

"In case he is sober enough to drive," agreed Henry. "Danny may want to go in, too."

But there was nobody at home when they arrived. Danny had left a note on the table, saying that he and Oscar had gone to repair a windmill at Jonah Wells, while Frijole, Albert and Thunder and Lightning had gone to haul poles to repair the corral fence.

Henry and Judge secured Frijole Bill's supply of prune whisky, took easy chairs on the front porch, and spent the rest of the day in complete relaxation. It was nearly dark when they realized that Frijole was not getting supper.

"Unreliable, diminutive creature," said Judge. "Traitor to the stomachs of men. Malefactor—"

"Something must have happened to them," decided Henry. "They should have been back long ago. I suggest that we go and search for them."

"A stimulating suggestion," Judge agreed. "This is no time for inaction. Let us go at once."

Rather than hitch up the team or saddle horses, they started walking down an old road, and about a mile from the ranch they met the four men who had gone to haul poles. They were walking and driving the team.

"Firs'," explained Lightning, "we break theese haxle from the wagon. Eet ees the front haxel, which ees behin'. Then we get heem feexed pretty damn bad, and then the tire lose the wheel. So we walk home and push the horse."

"My goodness!" exclaimed Henry. "But why didn't some of you ride the horses?"

"Albert he ees trying," said Thunder. "Theese pintado throw heem into brosh-pile. We ask heem if he likes for trying more, but he ees more rady for walking t'ree, four mile."

"That spotted horse lost his temper," said Albert wearily.

"Me, too," declared Frijole Bill, a little, thin-faced rawhider of sixty summers, whose mustache was far too big for a face so small.

"What irked you?" asked Judge, standing on one foot to ease his corns.

"Tryin' to keep the rollin'-stock together," replied Frijole. "If we ever run out of bailin'-wire this whole spread will fall apart."

They walked back to the ranch in the semi-darkness. Frijole hurried to the kitchen door, anxious to get a belated supper. Danny and Oscar were at the stable, unsaddling their horses, when Frijole yelled at the top of his voice:

"What's been goin' on around here?"

7

WHO'S DEAD?

FRIJOLE WAS STANDING near the kitchen door, looking at a dark object on the ground. The rest of them hurried up there.

"King Fisher's kid!" called Frijole. "Looks plenty dead t'me."

The young man was flat on his back, dirty, bloody and motionless. Henry discovered that Roy was not dead, and turned to Danny.

"Get a blanket off a bed, Danny; we will take him into the house. Frijole, you bring a lamp."

"Madre de Dios!" gasped Lightning. "The law ees among us."

Henry looked up quickly. Vinegar Bill Hawkins and Spook Gilliam, the deputy, had just dismounted from their horses and were coming over to them. Frijole came out with the lamp, but nearly dropped it when he saw the officers.

"Roy Fisher!" exclaimed the sheriff.

"We found him—just now," replied Henry, realizing that his explanation sounded very weak.

The sheriff made a quick examination and turned to Spook.

"Get Doc Knowles—quick, Spook."

Spook ran to his horse and a moment later he was galloping toward Tonto. The sheriff straightened up and helped them slide a blanket under the unconscious young man and take him into the house. They placed him carefully on a cot. Then the sheriff said:

"Conroy, I need more explanation than you gave me."

"I really do not know any more about it, Hawkins."

"Well, some of yuh do!" snapped the sheriff. "Out with it!"

No one offered any explanation, so the sheriff said:

"We all know that there's bad blood between yore outfit and King Fisher. No jury in the world—"

"My goodness!" exclaimed Henry. "Why speak of a jury?"

"I'm no fool," said the sheriff coldly. "There's eight of yuh here. Some of yuh know what happened. Go ahead and talk."

"None of us were here," replied Henry. "Judge and I were gone about a half-hour, looking for the boys with the load of poles. Danny and Oscar had been working on a windmill over at Jonah Wells, and we all got here at the same time, which was a few minutes ago."

"You was gone about a half-hour, eh?"

"Was or were," said Henry, "I suppose either is permissible."

"And Roy wasn't here, when you left, eh?"

"No, I do not believe he was, Sheriff."

The sheriff nodded grimly and looked at the wounded man.

"King Fisher will raise hell about this," he said.

"Well," said Danny, "Fisher can blame himself for this.

He let the kid run wild, drink all he wanted, run gamblin' bills and all that. He gave him a fast horse and a six-gun, and wasn't particular what kind of women the kid associated with. It's a wonder he didn't run into the hot end of a bullet before this, Bill."

"Yeah, I know," sighed the sheriff. "Did Roy say why he came here?"

"No, he don't," said Danny. "He's just like he was when we found him; so yuh might as well bark up another tree. We didn't shoot him."

"I hope he lives to say who did shoot him."

"His holster is empty," remarked Frijole. The sheriff nodded.

"You heard about my game with Fisher, I presume," said Henry.

"Yeah, I did," replied the sheriff. "Fisher told me."

"I'm sorry," said Henry quickly. "Hawkins, I—I wanted you to know how we felt about what happened at your home. It was a terrible thing, and you have our deepest sympathy."

The sheriff's face hardened and seemed to turn gray in the lamplight. His shoulders slumped and he sat down on the edge of a chair.

"Thank yuh," he said huskily. "In the excitement, I—well, I kinda forgot my own troubles, Conroy."

"Yes, I know." Henry nodded. Frijole cleared his throat raspingly.

"I'll heat some water," he said. "Doc'll need a lot, I reckon."

IT SEEMED HOURS before Spook came back, bringing Doctor Knowles and King Fisher. The big rancher ignored everyone in his haste to take a look at his son. The doctor went right to work on the wound, while King Fisher, his jaw shut tightly, watched him work. The others stood back.

"Lost a lot of blood," informed the doctor. "Young, though—might pull 'through. More water, Frijole."

"We'll take him home right away," said King Fisher.

"Hurt badly," said the doctor. "Might not be well to move him."

"I'll take the chance!" answered Fisher. "You don't suppose I'd leave him here, do yuh?"

"Well, I don't know," said the doctor.

"You could use our light wagon," suggested Henry. "We could pile it full of hay and—"

"I'll furnish my own vehicle, if yuh don't mind!" snapped Fisher. "I'm not askin' anythin' of you and yore outfit, except—who shot my boy?"

"We have told our story to the sheriff, Mr. Fisher," replied Henry. "It is no secret that we do not like you, nor do we like the way you do business, but we did not harm your son."

"And," added Danny, "if we wanted to do some shootin', we'd take a crack at you—not yore kid."

"We'll find out about this," snarled King Fisher. "Conroy, you or one of your outfit did this; so I am asking that the sheriff arrest you for attempted murder."

"Wait a minute, King," said the sheriff. "You haven't any evidence."

"I'll get evidence. Haven't I any rights in this matter?"

"You better talk with John Campbell, the prosecutor," counseled the sheriff.

"And in the meantime, the killer rides away free, eh?"

"Ain't nobody ridin' away," said Danny. "We may not like the smell of a polecat, but we don't run away from 'em, Fisher."

"Why, you damn—" Fisher started toward Danny, but the sheriff blocked him neatly.

"Cool off," he advised. "Danny is eggin' you into throwin' a punch or reachin' for a gun."

Thudding hoofs stopped outside the front of the house. Before anyone could reach the door, Bob Haney, Fisher's foreman came in.

"How's Roy?" he asked quickly.

"Hurt pretty badly," replied King Fisher. "We'll—"

"Wait a minute," said Haney. "They told me in town what happened. Two of the boys from Scorpion Bend were on their way to the Golden Streak, and they found Sig Foster near the forks of the road—dead. The buckboard and team were about a half-mile further on, tangled up in the brush. They told me at the mine to tell you that the bedroll was gone."

"Sig Foster dead and the bedroll gone," repeated King Fisher.

"What's the bedroll got to do with it?" asked the sheriff.

"Got to do with it?" said King Fisher harshly. "That bedroll had over a hundred pounds of raw gold inside it. Sig Foster was takin' it to Scorpion Bend. Twenty-five thousand dollars worth!"

"Sig Foster was a fine man," said the doctor.

"To hell with all that!" roared King Fisher. "We've got to find that gold!" He turned and looked at Danny. "Where was you this afternoon?"

"None of your damn business!" snapped Danny.

"Mr. Fisher," interrupted the doctor, "I believe we should plan to move this boy as quickly as possible. He has very little fever now."

King Fisher turned and ordered Bob Haney to ride to the ranch and bring a vehicle. Haney left at once. The sheriff said:

"King, I suppose I better ride to the mine and get what information I can on that robbery. Nothin' I can do here."

"And take King Fisher with yuh," advised Danny warningly.

"Some sense in that, too," admitted the sheriff. "C'mon, King."

"All right," Fisher nodded. "But I'm not through with this outfit. Just remember that, will yuh?"

"Thank you very much, Mr. Fisher," replied Henry calmly. "We are not at all through with you; so we are pleased to know that it is not one-sided."

King Fisher stopped, but the sheriff urged him along, and the door closed behind them.

"I DIDN'T KNOW that *anybody* talked like that to the great King Fisher," said the doctor, as he wiped his hands.

"Henry ees tell the devil to go home, right in your face," declared Lightning proudly.

"I was really afraid there might be a fight," said Albert.

"Was that why you picked up the poker?" asked Henry.

"I—I did not realize that I had been seen," replied Albert. "While I have had little experience in fighting, I might have been able to deal at least one telling blow."

"Good boy!" applauded Danny.

"How much of a chance has Roy?" queried Henry. The doctor smiled.

"Very good, if they do not bounce him too much on the way home. I really wanted to find out whether King Fisher cared a whoop about anybody—even his own son; so I made it worse than it is. But he was more concerned over the loss of the gold. And he was not interested in the killing of Sig Foster, who was a fine fellow, as honest as a dollar. I am just a bit afraid that King Fisher is self-centered."

"And as yellow as a Jim Hill mustard in full bloom," added Danny.

"Damned if I don't believe I'll make some coffee," said Frijole.

"That is the most constructive thing I have heard today," said Henry. "And you might add some ham and eggs, too, Frijole. How about it, doctor?"

"And I shall remain eternally yours." The doctor smiled.

It was over an hour later, when Bob Haney and a couple of the men from the Diamond F came after the wounded man. They all helped to load him into the wagon, and the doctor went with them. Spook headed for Tonto, and everyone at the ranch sighed with relief.

"It has all been very exciting," said Albert.

"Sure," agreed Lightning quickly. "One man ees keeled, somebody ees stealing more gold than I am ever seeing, and some people are shooting Roy Feesher couple times or two. Theese countree ees toff like a basket from snakes, and that ees all, I hope and pray."

"After that," said Henry dryly, "we may all go to bed, feeling that everything has been fully covered."

8

THE LAW LIKES WHISKY

THE INQUESTS OVER the bodies of the sheriff's wife and Sig Foster brought no new developments. Everyone turned out for the funerals, which were held on the same day. King Fisher, still fuming over the loss of the twenty-five thousand dollars in raw gold, was there.

Roy had recovered consciousness, but did not accuse anyone of shooting him. He admitted that he had been too drunk to know what happened. Why he was at the JHC, he did not know.

Vinegar Bill Hawkins was like a man in a daze, sitting alone much of the time. He came out to see Henry and Judge, officially, and the three of them sat on the shaded porch. Hawkins seemed to want to talk about his wife; so they let him ramble on.

"Yuh know, it's a funny thing," he remarked. "Her first husband was a notorious criminal. His name was Pelkey. They lived down south, where she had a lot of city property. Right after they was married he argued her into sellin' a lot of it. I think she got about fifty thousand dollars in cash, and then Pelkey tried to murder her for the money. He got the money, but she recovered. Then he took the name of Tiger Smith.

"Well, he left a bloody trail for a while, before he got sent to the penitentiary. I was workin' on a farm for a feller who owned several bloodhounds, which he rented to the penitentiary at times. When Tiger Smith escaped, they called for the dogs, and I went along on the hunt. My brother, who wasn't such a good citizen, owned a shack deep in the swamp where Tiger Smith had gone, and I just had a hunch that he might be headin' for that spot.

"Well, we trailed him to where he took to the water, and then I told the boys about that shack, so we went there. We heard a shot before we reached the place, and we found a man dressed in convict stripes layin' in that cabin, his head and face shot away with a shotgun. He had pulled the trigger with his toe."

"You say," reminded Henry, "that you found a man, but you did not say it was Tiger Smith, Bill."

"No, I didn't, Henry," replied the sheriff quietly. "I didn't know Tiger Smith, but I had read a lot about his case."

"Then you didn't know whether it was Tiger Smith or not?"

"I knew it wasn't, Henry—it was my brother. I recognized a scar on the back of his right hand."

"You did not tell anyone?" queried Judge.

The sheriff shook his head. "No, I didn't, Judge. Maybe I wanted to get him myself. Anyway, I went to see Mrs. Pelkey, who was a young woman. I wanted a description and a picture of Tiger Smith. She didn't have a picture, but I got a good description.

"Later she married a man named Buckley. He was Joan's father. He died later and they moved to Denver, where I ran into them a year or so ago. Well, we got to writin' to each other, and yuh see—well, I—" Bill shrugged bis shoulders dismally.

"That is an interesting story, Bill," said Henry quietly. "You never found Tiger Smith?"

The sheriff shook his head. "No, I don't know where he went. The world is a pretty big place. For years I bummed from coast to coast, always listenin' and lookin' for Tiger Smith. But I never heard of him. He'd change his name, of course."

"He may have died years ago," said Judge.

The sheriff looked up quickly. "I hope not, Judge. I want him. You see, the guard he killed, when he made his escape from the penitentiary, was another brother of mine. I was the only one of the family left; so I went out to get him— and failed."

"Bill," said Henry, "could the shooting of your wife have anything to do—"

"No, Henry. I've tried to figure it out from that angle. Tiger Smith ain't in Tonto City nor in Wild Horse Valley. No, there must be some other angle. God only knows what it is."

"Could it have been possible that the shot was meant for you?" asked Judge.

"I've tried to think so, Judge, but it don't work. The room was lighted, and the curtains were drawn apart. Only a blind man could have made that mistake."

"What about the killing of Sig Foster?" queried Judge.

The sheriff shook his head. "King Fisher says that only four of them knew that the gold was goin' out in that bedroll—him and Foster, Jim Stuart, the mine superintendent and Olds, the banker. It sure wasn't Fisher, and

Stuart never left the mine. They'd sent one other shipment that way."

Henry told the sheriff about the masked man who had tied Albert Henshaw up in his hotel room and stolen the map and letters. It was the first time that the sheriff had heard about it. Henry called Albert from the main room, and Albert supplied the details.

"So this was the Jim Henshaw you was tryin' to trace, eh?" said the sheriff. "Tom South asked me about him, too."

"We thought at first," said Henry, "that the mummy we found in Smoke Tree Canyon might have been the missing Jim Henshaw, but a tiny gold locket on the mummy rather changed our ideas."

"I never heard about the locket," said the sheriff quickly.

"I know you didn't, Bill. We thought it might be a clue to the man's identity. On it were the initials L.L., which most certainly do not help identification."

Albert started to say something, but closed his lips momentarily. Then he said:

"The initials L.L.? Why, that works out! My uncle's wife, my aunt Laura, who died several years ago—her maiden name was Laura Lyman. Uncle Jim wore her locket!"

"My goodness!" exclaimed Henry. "Is that possible? Then the mummy *was* Jim Henshaw—bound hand and foot, shot through the head and dumped over the rim of Smoke Tree Canyon. Sheriff, you have a first-class murder mystery on your hands."

"Henry," replied the sheriff slowly, "I had two before this one came up."

"True, William—true. Do you know, there are times when I could shout and dance with joy."

"Why in the name of God would you want to shout and dance?" growled Judge.

"To think that I am not the sheriff of Tonto town."

THE SHERIFF'S STORY of the identification of the Smoke Tree mummy brought John Campbell, the prosecuting attorney, out to the JHC ranch. The big, grizzled lawyer was anxious for more details. Henry and Judge greeted him warmly.

"It seems," he remarked, "that Wild Horse Valley has turned savage."

"It also seems," added Henry, "that I got out in time, John."

"At least, you are in a position where the newspapers can't write of your inability to cope with crime, Henry. Very soon they will take the hide off Bill Hawkins, I suppose. We have three murders on our hands, and not a single clue to the murderers. Henry, what do you think of the situation? Have you any idea?"

"My goodness!" exclaimed Henry. "You ask *me?*"

The prosecutor nodded soberly. "Yeah, that's right. What do you know about the letters this Albert Henshaw brought with him—and that map?"

"Little or nothing, John. Albert was robbed of them the night Mrs. Hawkins was murdered. From what Albert told us, Jim Henshaw, his uncle discovered a rich prospect. He was, I believe, grubstaked by King Fisher, and—"

"You know that to be a fact, Henry?" interrupted the lawyer.

"Someone grubstaked him, John. He located the Glory Hole in the name of King Fisher and himself. In this letter he told his sister that he did not trust the man who had grubstaked him, and so he filed a fake location, wanting to be sure of this man's honesty.

"In their agreement was a clause to the effect that if Jim Henshaw died, before or after development of any prospect he might discover, the full title to the property would go to the man who grubstaked him."

"Before or after, eh?" said the lawyer. "Henry, that letter, were it available, might be damning evidence against King Fisher."

"But it is not available," pointed out Judge.

"Could Albert Henshaw give any reasonable description of the man who robbed him of the letters?"

Henry shook his head. "I am afraid not, John. Judge, do you know where Albert is at this moment? We might ask him—"

"Albert, together with Oscar, Lightning and Frijole, went to Tonto in the buckboard an hour ago—shopping."

"I saw them in front of the King's Castle as I left town," said Campbell. "At least, I recognized Frijole and Oscar."

"I declared a payday this afternoon," said Henry.

"I have talked with Fisher about the murder of Foster," said the lawyer. "Some outsider knew about that gold."

"Or insider," added Henry dryly. Campbell looked at him curiously.

"Insider, eh? Meaning what and whom, Henry?"

Henry shook his head slowly. "I do not know, John. You know I am prone to foolish ideas. Mayhap I dream. However, my dreams never materialize; so they do little harm."

"Keep on dreaming, Henry," advised the lawyer. "You

didn't do so badly, while in office. In fact, I wish you were back there."

"You would wish us back in that office?" gasped Judge.

"I would, Judge. You two may have queer ideas and a queer system of procedure, but you kept Wild Horse Valley clean."

"Thank you, John—thank you," said Henry gravely. "In fact, in the name of the Shame of Arizona, I thank you. I speak for all three Shames."

"NOT THAT I have anything against Bill Hawkins," said Campbell. "He is a fine type of man to hold that office, but between us, I don't believe Bill could follow a load of hay across a snow-covered meadow.

"He can only follow orders. And the death of his wife has wiped out everything else he may have had in his mind. I will admit that it was a terrible blow. But as a—well, detective—even the range type—he is as helpless as a child."

"As far as that goes, John," said Henry, "I do not believe that I ever gave the ghost of Sherlock Holmes any uneasy moments."

"You have imagination, Henry."

"He has!" snorted Judge. "Give him three drinks of Frijole's prune whisky, tuck him in bed and then mention one of the three murder cases on your hands at present, John. Why, his summation of evidence would turn Blackstone green with envy—and disgust."

"It is early yet," said Henry soberly, "but you might get the jug, Judge. Hast ever imbibed of Frijole's distillations, John?"

"No, but I have heard a lot about them."

"The powers of a supreme court and the odors of Araby, John. Hasten, my good Judge—the wassail bowl."

As Judge Van Treece went limping away to get the jug and glasses, John Campbell took two buckshot from his pocket and handed them to Henry.

"Two of the half-dozen that Doc Knowles took from the body of Mrs. Hawkins," he said.

Henry looked at them indifferently and handed them back.

"I—er—really, collecting deadly missiles is not my hobby, John."

"But examine those, Henry."

Henry looked at them closely, tested with at thumbnail and looked questioningly at the lawyer.

"They seem to be silver," he said. "They surely are not lead."

"Pure silver," replied the lawyer. "I had Tom South assay one; and he said they were nearly pure. The question is, who shoots silver buckshot?"

"We might advertise," suggested Henry dryly. "But what would be the advantage of a silver buckshot, John?"

The big lawyer shrugged his shoulders. "Who knows what the killer had in mind? Perhaps only a fanciful idea. Tom South suggested that they might penetrate deeper, being harder."

"Rather a high-toned murderer," said Henry.

"Yes."

"Well, here comes Judge with the jug; so we may as well forget the sordid side of life, John. I can only stand so much of it. Killings depress me; so away with them, say I."

"Not a bad idea," said the lawyer, laughing.

9

SILVER BUCKSHOT

"YUH SEE," **EXPLAINED** Frijole Bill Cullison, as he leaned against the bar at the King's Castle Saloon, "we've gotta git some flour, and we've gotta git some bakin' powder and we've gotta git some dried appercots and we've gotta git some sourdeens and we've gotta git some canned salmon and we've gotta git some—"

"You've got a awful lot of gottagits f'r a feller yore size," interrupted Spook, the deputy. "Whereat's the tenderfoot and Oscar?"

Frijole grinned.

"Oscar's gone to woo Josephine and Albert's done gone to the post-office for the mail, Spook."

"Oscar better watch his wooin'," said Spook. "Julius Larsen's been hangin' around her for the last few days. He's got himself a derby hat and a pair of yaller shoes, and if that ain't a sign of love, I'm an Apache. Have another drink, Frijole?"

"I'd hate to be in Larsen's yaller shoes, if Oscar suspects that Josephine is lookin' favorably upon him," mused Frijole. "Oh, yeah, another drink? Shore. This saloon whisky ain't got no velocity any more, Spook. She's like drinkin' milk."

"This'll grow hair on yore chest," declared the bartender.

"Tastes like hair restorer," admitted Frijole, "but if yo're hankerin' on doin' a first-class job of moultin', come out and sample my prune juice. Well, here's to yore saddle—may it never slip."

Albert came hurrying into the saloon. He was wearing his cowboy clothes and having trouble with the high-heel boots. He came up to the bar and drew a sheet of paper from an envelope.

"My gracious!" he exclaimed. "This is serious! Just came in the mail. I shall read it to you. It says:

" 'You have failed to heed my warning; so say your prayers.' "

Frijole scratched his stubbled chin thoughtfully.

"Know any?" he asked.

"Any what?" queried Albert.

"Prayers. I used to know a good'n, but I jist can't remember it offhand. Used it a couple times, when I was in a tight spot, but it never got no results. Must be quite a chore for the Lord to keep check on all the incomin' prayers, at that."

"This," declared Albert, "is no jesting matter."

"Have a drink," invited Spook.

"I do such crazy things, when I take a drink. I simply can not remember what I did."

"That's why we drink," declared Frijole. "And then, if somebody shoots yuh, yuh don't even remember bein' shot. Take a drink, Albert."

"Well, I suppose so," agreed Albert dubiously. "My gracious!"

"Wasn't the letter signed?" asked Spook.

Albert gasped, choked over the drink and turned tearful eyes upon his questioner.

"It was signed Silver Buckshot," he whispered.

"Hell's delight!" blurted Spook. "Mrs. Hawkins was killed with Silver Buckshot! By golly, I've got a idea, Frijole. We'll foller Albert around and see who kills him. See what I mean?"

"Shore," agreed Frijole heartily. "We'll wait'll he shoots Albert and then we'll get him red-handed. Spook, you've got a head on yuh."

"But—but what about me?" queried Albert huskily.

"About you?" asked Frijole. "Oh, yo're just the bait. Say! Yuh don't mean to stand there and object to helpin' the law, do yuh? What kind of a whippoorwill are you, anyway, Albert? Why, the ord'nary man would jump at the chance."

"I know, but—" demurred Albert. "You do not realize—"

"I re'lize perfectly," interrupted Frijole coldly. "Yo're the kind of a man who would go to the Ladies' Aid Society meeting, packin' a white flag. Albert, I'm s'prised and pained."

"But you do not seem to realize that—" protested Albert.

"No, no!" interrupted Frijole. "Say no more, Albert. Bartender, if you can get yore mouth closed long enough to supply us with a few glasses of weak whisky—do so at once."

"I am very much afraid—" said Albert.

"Exactly!" snorted Frijole. "I knew you'd admit it. Well, here's to a brilliant scheme that went haywire, Spook."

ALBERT ACCEPTED ANOTHER drink, had difficulty with his vocal cords, but managed to smile foolishly, after which he bought a round.

"Yo're awful new to this country," said Spook tolerantly. "After you've been here a couple of years you'll be delighted to give yore life for yore state—or vicinity. I've knowed people who have been here only a month who would give their life—well, even for their cattle spread."

"Well," said Albert dubiously, "I am unable to understand—"

"That's exactly it!" exclaimed Frijole. "He don't *sabe*. Albert, I'm sorry I misjudged yuh. Shake!"

"Well, that is mighty kind of you, Frijole. I'm sure, I—well, I want to do as others do."

"Spoken like an Arizonan!" exploded Frijole. "Let's have a drink."

Albert seemed so cheerful that he hardly grimaced over the bite of strong liquor. In fact, he became expansive.

"Silver Buckshot!" he snorted derisively. "The man is psychopathic."

"My God!" gasped Frijole. "What have we done?"

"Sounded like you'd hit the dictionary," said Spook. "Well, well! Here comes Oscar. Hyah, Oscar, have a drink."

Oscar leaned disconsolately on the bar, looking at them.

"Ay am hortsick," he announced.

"Albert," said Frijole, "show him the billie-doo yuh got from the Silver Buckshot."

"Ay am not interested in bockshot," declared Oscar.

"Somebody's goin' to kill Albert," said Frijole. Oscar looked at Albert curiously and offered to shake hands, but Albert ignored him.

"And," added Spook, "when the man shoots Albert, we'll get the man who shot him. It's shore a perfect scheme."

"Von't it be hord on Olbert?" asked Oscar.

"With a load of buckshot?" asked Frijole. "Why, he won't never know what hit him."

"Yah, su-ure. Ay t'ink somebody should buy drink liquor."

Albert bought the drinks. By this time he was rather uncertain in his movements, and managed to spill part of his drink.

"What makes yuh heartsick, feller?" asked Frijole.

"Julius Lorsen," replied Oscar. "He got hord hat and yellow shoes and he is out vit Yosephine. Dey vent some place in a buggy. Ay t'ink Ay am t'rough vit vimmin. Va'al, Ay vill buy drink now."

The King's Castle was rapidly filling up with patrons, as a mining crew came off shift; so the boys went outside.

"Ay don't like crowds," declared Oscar. "Ay am like vounded animal—Ay vant to soffer alone."

"We're goin' home," declared Frijole. "For once in our lives, we're goin' home sober, too."

"Tha's good idea," applauded Albert, and he fell off the sidewalk.

"Can yuh imagine that!" snorted Frijole. He started to step off the sidewalk, caught his heel on the edge and fell over Albert.

"Ay don't even t'ink that's funny," said Oscar gloomily. Spook whooped with mirth and slid down alongside a porch post to a sitting position on the sidewalk.

"Goin' home sober," he jeered. "Yo're as drunk as a bull-fiddler at a river-pig's ball, Frijole."

Frijole helped Albert back to the sidewalk, and Albert wanted to buy another drink.

"You've had 'nough," declared Frijole. "Don'tcha remember that yo're a marked man. No use wastin' a lotta good liquor on a dyin' man."

"Where's Danny?" asked Albert. "I wan' to tell him."

"I seen him with Bill Hawkins a while ago," said Spook. "I think he's visitin' Miss Buckley. Why don'tcha go down and find him, Albert?"

"Would that be pup-proper?" queried Albert huskily.

"It'd be Arizony," said Frijole. "You know where the house is?"

"Oh, def'nitely," replied Albert. "I wish you a good-evening."

And Albert went across the street, weaving in the darkness.

"There's a fine boy," declared Frijole. "A perfec' gentleman if I ever sheen one. I hope he has nice funeral. Now, I'll buy drink."

DANNY REGAN HAD supper with Joan Buckley and Bill Hawkins. Joan was a fine cook, which Frijole was not, and Danny thoroughly enjoyed the meal, especially cooked and served by a girl as pretty and charming as Joan. She was still greatly upset over the death of her mother.

Bill Hawkins said finally, "Joan wants to go back to Denver, Danny."

"That ain't so good," said Danny, "but yuh can't blame her. Tonto City is a pretty tough place for a young woman. I was kinda hopin' she might like it here. But when yuh figure it out there ain't much entertainment for any woman."

"I have to make my own way in the world," said Joan.

Bill Hawkins nodded slowly. "Yeah, I know how yuh feel, Joan. I can only give yuh what I'd give my own daughter."

"It isn't that," she said quickly. "You have been wonderful to me, and I'll always be grateful. But there is nothing for me in Tonto City. I don't want to be dependent on anyone."

"Yuh would if yuh got married, Joan," said the sheriff quietly.

"I never thought of that." She laughed.

"Now, yuh take Danny, for instance. If he—"

"And that," said Danny quickly, "is about all a woman would take me for, Bill. What have I got to offer a woman? Sixty dollars a month, and a swell chance to be a widow, if my cinch slips or the bronc steps into a gopher hole."

"That's what I used to think," said Hawkins soberly. "Think of the years I lost. A man don't stay young very long—nor a woman either, as far as that goes. Yuh never get that youth back, Danny."

"No, that's true, Bill. But love and poverty don't mix. Mebbe, when my ship comes in—some day."

The sheriff started to speak, but changed his mind and looked toward the front door. Someone had walked across the little wooden sidewalk just away from the porch, but inside the yard. Then they heard footsteps near the back of the house and coming up on the kitchen porch.

They were all on their feet. Danny stepped away, loosening the Colt revolver inside the waistband of his trousers, when he saw a flash of a masked face and the glint of lamp light on the barrel of a shotgun outside the front window.

He stepped quickly in front of Joan, flinging her aside, and went into action. Five shots blasted from his forty-five, smashing the window to pieces. The room shuddered from the concussion of the shots.

The sheriff was on his knees, gun in hand, trying to see what Danny was shooting at. Then Danny dropped his empty gun, took the sheriff's gun from his hand and dived for the front door; he flung it open and was outside, off the porch, crashing into a man. They went down together in some shrubbery, and he sheriff piled out after them.

"I've got him, Bill!" panted Danny.

TOGETHER THEY SOON rendered the man helpless, and carried him into the house, where Joan, wide-eyed and frightened, waited for them.

"We've got the killer!" exclaimed Danny, and turned the man over.

Then Danny let loose of him and stood up, panting.

"Albert, where in hell did you come from?" he asked huskily.

Albert sat up and rubbed a swelling eye.

"What was all the shooting about?" he asked.

Danny shook his head and looked at the sheriff. "I dunno what to say, Bill. I saw a masked man with a rifle or a shotgun out there—and this is what I caught."

"Well, my goodness!" exclaimed Albert. "My eye is almost shut."

"Yuh smell like a distillery," said Danny.

"I presume so," agreed Albert. "You see, I received a warning note in the mail this evening. That is, it was a notification that I am about to die. So we possibly drank too much. I—I hope you understand what I am saying.

"Then I wanted you to know about it, and Mr. Spook told me that you came down here. I intended coming to the front door, but I got tangled up with a tree, it seems, and went to the back door, when I heard all the shooting. That right eye really must be a sight, Danny."

"Hang a blanket over that busted window, Bill," said Danny.

"There's a shade," said the sheriff, and yanked it down.

"It was signed Silver Buckshot," said Albert.

"Yore note was, eh?" said the sheriff. "I'll be darned!"

Danny turned to Joan. "I shore hope I didn't hurt yuh, when I gave yuh that shove. I had to get yuh out of line with that feller."

"It only frightened me," she said. "I—I didn't know what it was all about."

"I don't blame yuh," said Danny grimly. "After hearin' about that note, I reckon this killer was lookin' for a chance to blast Albert."

"Frijole says I am a marked man," said Albert.

Quite a number of Tonto folks had heard the shots, and were making an investigation. Among them were Oscar, Frijole, Spook and Lightning. King Fisher and several of the men from the King's Castle were in the crowd that swarmed into the sheriff's home.

Fisher said to Albert, "Why don't you leave here, young man?"

"Because I do not like to run away," replied Albert.

"Rather die, eh?"

"I am still alive, I believe, Mr. Fisher."

"You've got a fine chance against a man with a shot-gun—in the dark."

"Yes, I realize that."

Danny said to Frijole, "Bring the buckboard down here, will yuh? I don't believe that Silver Buckshot gentleman will chance a potshot."

"Ay yust vant to get a hand on him," said Oscar. "Ay vould yust yank him aport like spreeng chicken."

Frijole brought the buckboard down there and Albert

climbed aboard with Oscar, Frijole and Lightning, and they turned the corner onto the main street on two wheels.

"Oscar isn't takin' any chances on a wing-shot," said the sheriff.

King Fisher and the crowd drifted away, leaving Joan, Danny and the sheriff at the house. Joan was still nervous and excited.

"Why is this Silver Buckshot trying to shoot Albert?" she asked.

"I'm not sure," replied Danny, "but Henry's theory may be right. He says that either the man is afraid that Albert remembers that map, or that the man is afraid to locate that lost mine, thinking it will implicate him in more serious trouble. Then maybe he's lost the map. And Bill," Danny turned to the sheriff and lowered his voice, "I believe that King Fisher knows more than he'll tell."

"You mean—about the Silver Buckshot, Danny?"

"Yeah. Bill, I was watchin' his face, when the Silver Buckshot was mentioned. And if yuh think it over—King Fisher hasn't said anythin' about the murder of Foster and the loss of that gold."

"Well, yeah, he hasn't said much, Danny. Kinda dropped it. But I can't figure King Fisher in on a deal like this, Danny. I know all about him grubstakin' Jim Henshaw, the prospector, but that still don't—well, I dunno."

"It's shore a tough one," admitted Danny grimly. "We'll have to ride herd on Albert pretty close, or we'll have another killin' to work on."

"Keep him away from here," said the sheriff.

Danny grinned.

"I'd do that, anyway," he said. "I hope I'm not barred, Bill."

"Certainly not," said Joan quickly. "You are welcome any time."

She met Danny's eyes, and the color came quickly into her face, but she did not turn her glance away. Suddenly, then, Danny forgot all about the Silver Buckshot.

"That's yore answer, Danny." The sheriff grinned.

10

TAKE A MILLION, LITTLE BROTHER

HENRY AND JUDGE went to Tonto next morning, after listening to the report of Danny Regan regarding the attempt to kill Albert.

"Wild Horse Valley is going to the dogs," declared Judge. "While our regime may have been a blot on the State of Arizona, we kept the malefactors at a distance—or jailed them, Henry. Looking at it in retrospect, we were an efficient pair of peace officers."

"Careful, Judge," warned Henry. "Your old muscles haven't enough elasticity to allow you to pat yourself on the back. Unless I am mistaken, it was you who dubbed us the Shame of Arizona."

"Only in jest, my friend—only in jest. The newspapers adopted it later. However, we were able to cope with crime. If we were in office now—"

"You would be crying upon my shoulder," finished Henry. "How well I know you, Judge. No, I have no ambitions in that direction. Let Vinegar Bill Hawkins do the suffering. Let the commissioners haunt his dreams, demanding immediate action—or else.

"Let the newspapers of Scorpion Bend write editorials, saying that Wild Horse Valley is a mecca for criminals. Hank Conroy and Horse-face Van Treece are merely cattlemen, free, white and twenty-one—and slaves of no one, sir."

"I do not like that Horse-face, Henry."

Henry gestured casually.

"Merely a sudden inspiration, Judge. I happened to catch you in profile. However, neither of us are counterparts of Adonis. I wonder how John Campbell is feeling after his libations. When a man of extreme dignity will mount a horse backwards, slap the animal across the tail with his hat and yell, 'To hell with law and order!' his libations have been, to say the least—potent."

Judge cleared his throat raspingly. "He merely seemed to express the sentiment of the country, Henry."

"Do not be too hard on the country, my friend. We live here, and at least, we are honest and law-abiding."

"And still," mused Judge, "I do not understand why that die came up a six, when a few minutes later it would only come up a deuce."

"You stoop to trivialities, my dear sir," said Henry. "Bringing up the eccentricities of a die, when the country reeks with crime. Isn't there something about straining at a gnat and swallowing a camel? But you are prone to do that. Queer fellow, you."

"Perhaps, Henry, perhaps. But what to do about Albert? If this blood-hungry murderer, who calls himself the Silver Buckshot, is so intent on Albert's untimely demise, is there anything to prevent him from coming out to the ranch and accomplishing his deadly purpose, to the risk of all of us? The mere thought of a shotgun loaded with silver buckshot contracts my stomach. It is a damnable weapon."

"Why shrink from silver in particular?" queried Henry. "Lead, gold, or even diamonds in a shotgun aimed at me are equally unpleasant. But as far as prevention is concerned, I have no ideas on the subject."

"I feel that Albert should leave, Henry."

"I feel that we should get the Silver Buckshot," said Henry. "After all, Albert has done no wrong. Why should he go?"

"You have a strange philosophy, sir. Because he has done no harm, you would endanger all of us. It is all very well to say that we should get the Silver Buckshot. But how?"

"We must concentrate, Judge," explained Henry. "Suspicion and elimination. Finally—the Silver Buckshot."

"Have you suspected and eliminated anyone yet, Henry?"

"Oh, merely as a preliminary I selected you and me. Then I eliminated myself."

Judge said sharply:

"Well, what about me?"

"I needed a little more time on your case than I did on mine, Judge."

THEY STOPPED AT the sheriff's office where they found Spook. The lanky deputy wanted to know if Albert got home safely, and when Albert might come back to Tonto City.

"If he comes, I want to go," declared Spook. "I ain't never seen a shotgun yet that didn't scatter awful wide."

"Has the sheriff found any clues?" asked Judge.

"Well, I'll tell yuh," replied Spook, "until they start makin' cities six feet wide and twelve feet tall, and paintin' 'em red, white and blue, Bill Hawkins won't ever recognize one.

"If I could only convince him that my brains are wasted while I got to stay here in the office, we might git somewhere. If a feller walked right up to Bill and said, 'Lock me up, pardner, I'm the Silver Buckshot,' Bill would argue him out of it. He's the most disbelieving hombre I ever knowed. Why, he said this mornin' that if another murder is committed around here, he's goin' to resign and go dirt farmin'."

"How does Miss Buckley feel about it?" asked Judge.

"You'll have to ask her, Judge. Bill's scared she might marry me if I ever got a chance to talk with her. She might, at that. I think she's goin' back to Denver. Least Bill says she wants to."

"How is Roy Fisher getting along?" asked Henry.

"That pup!" snorted Spook. "Well, I'm sorry to say he's doin' all right. I seen King Fisher in the bank this mornin', and he said Roy is all right. That's a lie on the face of it. King Fisher drawed out a roll of bills that would choke a burro, and when he seen me lookin', he slid 'em under his coat. Mebbe he thought I might hold him up for his roll. I heard Olds, the banker, sayin', 'I've got all the numbers'."

Judge and Henry left the office and wandered up the street.

"I've got all the numbers," muttered Henry. Judge looked at him.

"What did you say, Henry?" he asked.

"Thinking aloud," said Henry. "Let us drop in and see how Tom South is doing."

Tom South, the assayer, grimy as usual, was busy with a retort, but came out to see what they wanted. South was usually short and to the point, not given to much conversation. Henry said:

"You heard that the mummy was identified as Jim Henshaw, Tom?"

"Yeah, I heard he was."

"You knew him, I believe."

"Jist like I knew a lot of desert rats and prospectors. Didn't remember much about him, except that he was in here a couple of times. I'm too busy most of the time to bother about makin' friends. Got to make a livin'. I'm busy on some stuff for King Fisher right now, and if you'll excuse me—"

"Oh, certainly," said Henry quickly. "We just dropped in, you know."

"I guess King Fisher keeps Tom busy most of the time," said Judge, as they went down the street.

"That is nice for Tom," said Henry. "Not much outside work now. They say he is a very good assayer. I do not know how he stands the odor of acids all day and half the night. I suppose one gets hardened in time."

They made a few purchases at the general store, and climbed back into the buckboard.

"Have you made any more suspects or eliminations, Henry?" queried Judge, as they drove out of town.

"No, I am still working on your case, Judge," replied Henry.

ABOUT TWO MILES north of Tonto City there is an old abandoned adobe beside the road to Scorpion Bend. It was an old stage station, and marks the original site of Tonto City. There are no windows or doors left, some parts of the thick walls have fallen in and many of the hand-made tiles are missing from the roof. The once-cleared yard is grown up with cactus and desert growth partly screening the ruin from the road.

It was siesta time, being just short of mid-afternoon. Thunder and Lightning Mendoza had dismounted in the broad shade afforded by the rear wall of the adobe, and were stretched out on the ground.

"W'at you are theenking of theese Seelver Bockshot?" asked Lightning sleepily. Thunder brushed a bug off his nose and settled to a more comfortable position in the sand.

"*Quien sabe?*" he muttered. "Nobody ees knowing heem. Me, myself personally I am theenking he ees a bom."

"He keels from quite a few peoples, my leetle brodder."

"For wheech, I am asking? He don' get no money from keeling. I theenk he ees crazy yourself. Hm-m-m, I theenk I seet on some ant."

"Maybe he ees scorpion or sidewinder," said Lightning, yawning. "I theenk I tak' leetle sleep. Last night I have *mucho* tequila, and I ween feefty *centavos* playing weeth jomping-bean. I weesh I am having too much money for the time being."

"Sure," said Thunder. "I like for being reech one time or another. Never have for work, fine clothes, vino for my deener and tequila for breakfast. Plenty beef and frijole on the table. W'at you do weeth too much money?"

But only a snore was the answer. Lightning was asleep. Thunder brushed away a few more crawling bugs, yawned luxuriously and started to turn over, when he heard a sound. It was the slow hoof-beats of a horse, and they stopped at the front of the adobe. There was an old window opening only a few feet away; so Thunder moved over quietly and poked an inquisitive eye around the corner.

For nearly a minute he remained motionless. Then a horse went galloping away, and Thunder turned, a quizzical expression on his coffee-colored face. He rubbed his nose and looked at the sleeping Lightning. He started to call to him, but changed his mind, turned back and crawled through the window opening.

There was no floor in the building, and the ground was littered with broken adobe and debris. But Thunder went straight to a large hunk of adobe, turned it over and picked up a paper package, which had been wrapped tightly. It was quite a sizeable package, at that. Then he went back through the window and hunkered down in the shade; he cut away the wrappings and disclosed the contents. For a moment he stared wide-eyed at the contents of the package. Then he yelled:

"*Dios Mio!* Lightning! W'at in the hell!"

LIGHTNING SAT UP like a jack-in-the-box, blinking, his mouth sagging. His eyes shifted to Thunder's two hands. He brushed a lock of black hair away from his eyes and took another look.

"You are not driming, I hope," he said foolishly.

"One meelion dollar!" whispered Thunder. "We are reech!"

Lightning crawled over close and touched his fingers to the package of currency, trying to make sure that it was real. He looked closely at Thunder and said:

"Look me square in your eye, my leetle brodder. Who you keel?"

"I keel nobody. Leesten! A man hide theese money

under piece dirt in the adobe. I see heem. When he ees gone—I tak' heem."

"So-o-o? You are a thiff, eh? That ees not my money. Don' you know eet ees wrong for stealing?"

"Sure. Judge ees saying that thiff never go to Heaven."

"I know. But how he ees knowing? He neyer go there. Hm-m-m-m. You theenk theese man throw that money away?"

"I theenk he don' want heem no more—I hope and pray."

"Sure. Maybe he got so much money he got no place put heem. W'at we better do?"

Thunder thought over the question. Finally he said:

"How much you wan'?"

"Oh, I go feefty-feefty weeth you. I am no hog, you hope."

"Sure. I theenk we better go way from here, biffore we count heem. Go quick."

"You got lot brain in my head. Come on."

They mounted quickly and rode away to a spot about a mile from the adobe, where they sat down in the shade to count their spoils. But the process was not a success, because neither of them could count to ten. Finally Lightning made the separation by the simple process of "one for you and one for me," regardless of the fact that one might be twenty dollars and another a dollar.

"Now," stated Lightning, "we are too reech for working. I theenk we queet the job and go to *Mejico*."

"For the brain," declared Thunder, "you have lot sawdust. Maybe that man ees coming back weeth more money. He got plenty."

"How you know he got plenty money?"

"I know heem." Thunder grinned.

"You know heem—sure? Who he was?"

"Keeng Feesher."

"Good! He got so much money that eef he come back and never find those money under the dirt, you weel never mees heem."

"I theenk," said Thunder, "that we better keep your mouth shut. We got sicrit, my leetle brodder."

"Sicrit? W'at eesra sicrit?"

"A sicrit ees sometheeng you do not know, biccause nobody ees telling me. You onnerstand?"

"Oh, sure. I hope my shirt-tail don' pull out, biccause I'm lose lots money. I theenk I buy pocketbook. You wan' sleep leetle bit?"

"I am too reech to sleep now on the ground. I buy me damn nice bed. How are you filling, my reech leetle brodder?"

"I am filling just like *Presidente* of *Mejico.*"

"How he ees filling, huh?"

"Weeth hees finger. Ho, ho, ho! Good joke, eh?"

"Sure," agreed Thunder, "but how he ees filling?"

11

SHAKE HANDS WITH THE ENEMY

HARVEY OLDS, THE banker, Tom South, the assayer, and King Fisher sat in the main room of the Diamond F, smoking, saying little. A small fire of mesquite roots burned in the fireplace. There were glasses and whisky on the table. A huge lamp swung from a beam in the middle of the room. Harvey Olds lighted a fresh cigar and said:

"King, I don't believe he will come."

King Fisher drew a deep breath, pursed his lips and blew softly.

"No reason why he should," he admitted, "After what I've done to him, why should he come? Why should he interest himself in me enough to accept my invitation to meet me here in my own home? After all, the man is human."

"Kinda queer," added Tom South.

"We're all queer, Tom. I'm queer, and so are you; but the queerest thing I have ever done is to ask help from a man that I've wronged. I hope he comes, though. Damn it, I— well, I just hope he comes."

Bob Haney, the foreman, stepped into the room from the rear.

"He just came through the gate, King," he said.

"Good. That's all tonight, Bob."

"Buenas noches," said the foreman, as he went out.

King Fisher threw open the big front door, as Henry came up on the porch. As usual, Henry was immaculately dressed.

"Come in, Conroy," said King Fisher. "I'm glad you came."

Henry stepped inside the room and saw the two men near the fireplace. He said, "Good evening, Tom, and you, Mr. Olds."

Henry walked over and sat down in an easy chair, his eyes roving around the room. King Fisher sat down and sighed with relief.

"Is this a party?" asked Henry. "You gave little information in your note, you know."

"Conroy," said King Fisher, "I wouldn't have blamed you if you had not come. After the things I have done to you, there is no earthly reason for you to grant me any request."

"But still I came," said Henry soberly. "Perhaps that marks me as a very great fool. In fact, I was told at home that I am a very great fool. But it seems to become me, don't you think?"

"I seem to remember," said Olds, "something I read along that line. I believe it was Paul, who said something about a man only being wise when he realized what a fool he was. Something to that effect."

"Then I must be a very wise man," smiled Henry.

King Fisher laughed nervously and threw his unlighted cigar into the fireplace.

"Conroy, you wonder why I sent for you. You wonder

why Olds and South are here. They are here, because I can trust both of them. I trust few men, Conroy."

"You needed comedy relief, I suppose," suggested Henry.

"Comedy has no part in this," said King Fisher quietly. "In fact, I believe you would call it tragedy. As I said, I have two men I can trust; so I sent for a man who is my enemy. But I feel that you are also a man I can trust, Conroy. And right now I need men I can trust."

"I hope," said Henry, "that this is within the law."

Fisher ignored that.

"I hope you can see things my way, Conroy."

"Suppose you enlighten me, Mr. Fisher. Frankly, I am curious."

King Fisher opened a bill-fold and took out two pieces of paper. He handed one of them to Henry. It was printed in pencil on cheap paper and read:

YOU KNOW AS WELL AS I DO WHO KILLED
SIG FOSTER.

There was no date, no signature. Henry looked curiously at King Fisher.

"Here is the next one," said King Fisher, handing Henry the paper. It was also printed in pencil and on the same grade of paper.

THE PRICE OF MY SILENCE IS FIVE THOU-
SAND DOLLARS. TAKE THAT AMOUNT IN BILLS
OF NOT LESS THAN FIVE NOR MORE THAN
TWENTY DOLLARS, OLD BILLS TO THE OLD
ADOBE NORTH OF TOWN AND PLACE THEM

The masked man fell back before Henry's charge

UNDER THE LARGE PILE OF ADOBE IN THE
CENTER OF THE ROOM. THEN RIDE ON AND
DO NOT COME BACK FOR AN HOUR. SAY NOTH-
ING TO ANYBODY BUT OBEY THIS ORDER. I SAW
THE KILLING OF SIG FOSTER AND THE THEFT
OF THE GOLD. PLACE THIS MONEY TUESDAY
AFTERNOON AND GO ALONE. AFTER THAT
THE SECRET IS SAFE WITH ME.

HENRY READ THE note carefully and gave it back to King
Fisher. "This is Tuesday," he said quietly.

"I placed the money there," said King Fisher. "I was gone
an hour, and when I came back the money was gone."

"Marked bills?" queried Henry. King Fisher and Harvey Olds exchanged glances. Olds said:

"Marked and the numbers noted, Mr. Conroy."

Henry rubbed his nose thoughtfully. "It appears that this blackmailer saw the murder and robbery," he said quietly. "It also appears that your own son did the job, Mr. Fisher."

"You suspected that before?" queried King Fisher huskily.

"Not openly. Back in my mind there was such a suspicion. But why would he do such a thing? Surely he does not need money badly enough to resort to robbery—and murder."

King Fisher winced, shifted his position, before he replied:

"Roy has bad habits, Conroy. In order to try and break him of gambling and drinking, I cut his allowance to forty dollars a month. He was very angry, because he owed gambling bills. I cut off his credit at the King's Castle, too."

"Hm-m-m-m," mused Henry. "A rather wild young man. I understand that he says he was so drunk that he does not know who shot him."

"No one would believe that," said King Fisher quickly. "Conroy, I can't turn my son over to the law. Everything points to his guilt—but I still believe him innocent. This damn blackmailer isn't through. He'll hound me all his life. I realize that. But I can't let him talk."

"I doubt that he *would* talk," said Henry. "But that would be a dangerous chance to take. But why do you call me in on such a conference?"

"Because I want you to help me catch this man."

"I? Why, Mr. Fisher! After all the things that have been said about me? You jest, man."

"Not a damn bit of it!" exploded King Fisher. "I want your help."

"I believe I see the idea," said Henry quietly. "Because you realize that there is no friendship between us, you fear that I might work against you. Rather than to have me against you, you call me here, tell me the whole story, knowing damned well that after such a confession, I am too much of a gentleman to refuse to help you. Is that it, Fisher?"

"I don't blame yuh, Conroy. If you refuse to help me, I won't blame yuh. My son is faced with a murder. After all, he's my own son, even if he isn't worth much. I believe the sheriff suspects him, and I'm sure the prosecutor does, too. My only hope is to disprove their suspicions. I'm not offering you money nor friendship—but I do need your help. You've got brains and imagination, Conroy."

"And I'm funny looking," added Henry. "All I have to offer the voters of Wild Horse Valley is a red nose, a thirst, and—something to laugh at."

"All right," said King Fisher soberly. "I said all those things during the campaign. Maybe I said worse than that."

"Yes, I believe you did," answered Henry. "As far as being a help to you, I am afraid that I am not quite capable of doing that, Fisher. But I do appreciate you confidence. Just now I haven't any ideas that would do you any material good. If the boy is innocent, I want to see him cleared, naturally."

Henry got to his feet and picked up his hat. King Fisher held out his hand and they shook hands gravely.

"Thank you, Conroy," said King Fisher. "Mighty nice of yuh to come over here—after the way I've treated yuh."

"Yes, it was," agreed Henry quietly. "But I am that way, Fisher. Old Forgive-and-forget Conroy, that is I. By the way, what became of my die?"

King Fisher fumbled in a vast pocket for a moment and tossed a transparent die to the table top. A six blinked up at the light.

"Thank you," Henry beamed. "I hated to split the pair, you know. Without thinking, I tossed your deuce-die into a wastebasket at the bank."

"I got it back the next day," said King Fisher.

"Good. Well, gentlemen, I give you good evening. It has been a pleasure, I assure you, and I sincerely hope that everything may turn out right."

"Thank yuh for comin', Conroy."

"It was a pleasure, I'm sure."

JUDGE WAS WAITING up for Henry's return, anxious to know why King Fisher had asked Henry to come to the Diamond F. But Henry refused to tell Judge the details, because he knew that it would mean an argument with Judge over the fact that Henry was concealing a crime from the law.

"Mr. Fisher and I became fast friends," stated Henry. "He can see the error of his ways, and asked my forgiveness and friendship."

"Your nose shines unduly, my friend," said Judge, "and that signifies that you are mishandling the truth. I crave an honest statement, sir."

"The conference was entirely confidential, Judge. There is nothing to be disturbed about."

"Then I shall disturb you, sir," declared Judge loftily. He took a folded twenty-dollar bill from a vest pocket and spread it out on the table between them. "That bill, if you please, sir, was presented to me less than a hour ago by Lightning Mendoza, as a token of friendship. He also paid Oscar Johnson five dollars, which was borrowed money, and made a loan of ten dollars to Frijole Bill. Thereupon, Oscar, Albert, Frijole, Thunder and Lightning went to Tonto City."

"Well, my goodness!" exclaimed Henry, examining the bill. "Lightning Mendoza? Why, where on earth did he get that money?"

"He told me," replied Judge, "that he won it from Juan Rodriguez, at five *centavos* a corner, playing with jumping beans."

Henry looked curiously at Judge.

"Jumping beans, eh?" he muttered. "Thirty-five dollars? Why, Judge, it takes at least fifteen minutes to complete a jumping-bean game."

"That is the minimum," nodded Judge.

"The piece of currency appears to be of honest manufacture, Judge."

"Yes. And Oscar said that Lightning informed him that they had much more of the same. The question is: Where in the devil did those Mexicans ever procure that currency? Henry, they never got it honestly."

"I am afraid not," agreed Henry. "Did Lightning offer any reasons for his extreme generosity?"

"He seemed to think that I needed a new necktie."

"No doubt of that, Judge—but twenty-dollar ties… May I borrow that piece of currency?"

"Certainly. But why, Henry?"

"An idea just came to me, Judge, and I can not divulge it now. You will trust me with the money, I hope."

"Certainly. I rather had a feeling that your invitation to the Fisher ranch might have had something to do with those dice."

"No, Judge, And I have a feeling that from now on we will have no more trouble with King Fisher."

"You did not shoot him, did you, Henry?" gasped Judge.

"No," said Henry, "but that might have been a better way out of the situation. At least, safer. I believe I shall go to bed. I think more clearly on my back. And leave Lightning and Thunder to me, Judge. This is all part of the experiment."

12

PARDON OUR HEARSE

OSCAR, ALBERT, FRIJOLE, Thunder and Lightning were not home next morning when Henry and Judge awoke; so they cooked their own breakfast. The buckboard and team were gone, and Judge complained mightily over having to ride a horse to Tonto City. Judge hated a saddle.

"I would most certainly fire Oscar and Frijole," declared Judge. "Those two Mexicans haven't any more sense than to not come home; so I would let them off with a kick in the pants."

There was no sign of the missing men in Tonto City, but Spook Gilliam, the deputy sheriff, was sure they went to Scorpion Bend.

"Tell yuh what makes me think so," he said. "Julius Larsen hired a rig at the stable and took Josephine Swensen up there to a dance. I heard Oscar arguin' with Frijole about it, and in a few minutes they all pulled out. If they didn't go home, they shore went to Scorpion Bend."

"We shall be fortunate to get our team and buckboard back," said Judge gloomily. "Five of them in that light rig! And with Oscar at the lines. Henry this is insufferable."

"I am more sorry for Julius Larsen," said Henry soberly.

"Now I have a private matter to take up with Mr. Olds, at the bank. I shall be back shortly, Judge."

Henry was nearly to the bank, when he saw King Fisher hurrying over to him from the King's Castle. They went into the bank, where Olds told them to go back to his private office. King Fisher had a letter, which he had just taken from the post office.

It was from the Silver Buckshot.

YOU FAILED TO OBEY MY ORDER SO I AM DOUBLING THE ANTE. RIDE TO THE DESERTED SHACK ON THE SOUTH RIM OF SMOKE TREE CANYON AND TOSS TEN THOUSAND IN CURRENCY THROUGH THE BROKEN WINDOW TOMORROW AND RIDE AWAY. IF YOU FAIL THIS TIME THE PROSECUTOR WILL HAVE A STATE-MENT OF THE MURDER OF SIG FOSTER BEFORE MIDNIGHT AND YOU WILL PROBABLY BE IN THE MORGUE.

SILVER BUCKSHOT.

Henry and Harvey Olds read it together, while King Fisher, grim-faced, stood back and awaited their reactions. Henry said:

"You told me you left the money in the old adobe, Fisher."

"Damn it, I did!" declared King Fisher huskily. "Harvey can tell you I did."

"I handed you that amount, King," said Olds. "I know you intended to leave it there."

"I left it there!" snapped King Fisher. "That bloodsucker is tryin' to bleed me for more."

"Hm-m-m-m," mused Henry thoughtfully. "You say the bills were all marked?"

"Not only marked, but the serial numbers noted," said Olds.

"How would it be," suggested Henry, "if you threw a dummy package through that window, after several men were posted around there to grab him when he comes to get it, Fisher?"

"We don't know who to suspect, Conroy."

"He has you very neatly cornered."

"Exactly!" snapped Fisher. "No, I'm afraid your idea is a little too crude, Conroy."

"Thank you very much. But have you a better one?"

"I haven't any at all. What about you, Olds?"

Olds smiled and shook his head, "I am a banker—not a detective."

"Well, what would you advise, Harvey?" asked King Fisher.

"You cannot ask for help from the law, King."

"Damn the law. They can't help me. Shall I throw away ten thousand more good dollars?"

"You have until tomorrow," said Henry. "Perhaps in that length of time, we can make some plan to frustrate this fiend."

"I hope so," sighed King Fisher. "If I only knew who he was, I'd smash that snake. Well, I don't. Harvey, go ahead and fix up that money. Mark it and take the numbers. I'd spend fifty thousand to put my hands on that blackmailin' coyote."

"All right, King," said the banker. "I shall have it ready."
THEY WALKED OUT of the private office and Henry asked for change for twenty dollars. As Olds gave him four five-dollar bills, Henry examined the twenty-dollar bill closely.

"Looking for marked money?" smiled the banker. Henry said:

"One would, I suppose."

Olds glanced at the four corners of the bill and at the serial number, before placing it in the drawer.

"This one is all right," he said, "but we shall watch closely from now on. I have placed a list in the King's Castle and in the general store. I also sent a list to the bank at Scorpion Bend."

"I am glad," said Henry. "We want to catch him."

King Fisher and Henry walked outside and stood in front of the bank.

"I don't know what to do," said King Fisher wearily.

"That last threat was against your life as well as against your money and your son," said Henry.

"That's right. But if I pay that money—"

"You will get another demand next day," finished Henry. "If you—what on earth have we here?"

A cloud of dust appeared at the upper end of the main street, and out of it came—of all things—a hearse. The two horses were at a stiff gallop, the tall, black-plumed vehicle swaying. Behind it was fastened a buckboard, and to the buckboard was attached a top buggy.

"Oscar Johnson driving!" exclaimed Henry. "That—that is Josephine on the seat with him!"

Oscar brought the team over toward the front of the

King's Castle. There he swung them in a U-turn to the left, with the buckboard and the top buggy like the tail of a kite behind the hearse. In the buckboard was Frijole Bill, and Albert sat in the buggy.

But that U-turn was negotiated at too much speed and without regard for the tail of the kite. The top buggy crashed into porch posts in front of the King's Castle, tore loose from the buckboard and ended up with the broken shafts sticking through the doorway of the saloon.

The hearse, with Oscar and Josephine on the seat, toppled with a great crashing, landed flat on its side when the turn was nearly completed. That upset the buckhoard. The team, belonging to Henry Conroy, tore loose and headed for the JHC.

Frijole Bill was flung twenty feet away, to come down on the seat of his pants, while Josephine landed on her feet and then fell flat on the sidewalk.

It seemed rather undignified.

In a few moments the street was filled with curious people, but Henry merely leaned against a post and considered the scene calmly. Josephine got to her feet, her plumed hat down over one eye, and went toward the hotel doorway. Oscar picked himself up from the middle of the street, got his bearings and headed for the hotel doorway, too, intending to speak to Josephine. They met near Henry, and Oscar said:

"Ay vould yust like to say—" Then Josephine hit him on his button-like nose with a right swing. Oscar was bowing to her, as he spoke, and the force of the blow put him on his knees.

Oscar got slowly to his feet, but Josephine was gone

inside the hotel. The crowd had opened the back doors of the hearse, and out crawled Thunder and Lightning, little worse for their accident. Oscar Johnson considered Henry Conroy for a moment. Then he said:

"Ay am t'rough wit' Yosephine."

"Where," said Henry calmly, "did you get the hearse?"

"Lightning buy it for von hundred dollars."

"Lightning bought it for a hundred dollars, eh?"

"Yah, su-ure. Dey bought a new von in Scorpion Bend, so dey haf a auction sale last night. It looks opset."

Vinegar Bill Hawkins joined them, rather indignant over the incident.

"What the hell were you tryin' to do, Oscar?" he demanded.

"Torn around," replied Oscar calmly.

"Who owns that hearse?"

"Ay am not quite sure, but Ay t'ink Lightning Mendoza."

THE CROWD MANAGED to put the hearse back on its wheels, but the tongue was busted, the plumes torn off one side, and the glass sides badly cracked. In the excitement both Lightning and Thunder disappeared. Judge was indignant.

"Look at our buckboard, Henry," he said. "Tongue cracked, seat broken. What is this all about, anyway? It doesn't make sense."

"Who cares about sense?" queried Oscar.

"Certainly you do not," declared Judge.

"I believe we had better go home," said Henry. "After all, Judge, it was merely an accident—a diversion in our humdrum life."

Albert limped over to them, grinning foolishly.

"Perhaps you have brains enough to tell us what this is all about," suggested Judge.

"Really, I do not know," replied Albert. "It was all very sudden."

"I see. You rode in that top buggy all the way from Scorpion Bend, and still it was all so sudden that you do not know what happened."

"Oh, yes—that buggy. Well, as I understand it, Julius Larsen drove it to Scorpion Bend last night, taking Miss Swensen to a dance. The rest of it is rather vague. You see, Frijole Bill took a gallon jug of prune wine along and—"

"Prune *wine!*" snorted Judge.

"You are hereby excused, Albert," said Henry. "Coming, Judge?"

They found Thunder and Lightning at the ranch. The two Mexicans had caught the runaway team and ridden the horses home.

"Nobody ees home," said Lightning blandly, "so you are wondering eef sometheeng never happens."

Henry and Judge sat down on the porch.

"You like leetle peelow for your head and some sleepers?" inquired the solicitous Lightning.

"Never mind the pillow and slippers," growled Judge.

"Lightning," said Henry soberly, "I understand you purchased a hearse in Scorpion last night."

"You mean those beeg, black boggy weeth windows?"

"That is exactly what I mean."

"Damn pretty theeng," declared Thunder. "High-ton boggy."

"What did you pay for it?" asked Henry.

"Oh, I buy heem chip. Five piece money."

"Who counted that money for you?"

"Frijole count those money. Damn nice boggy. I geeve you ride."

"Lightning, where did you get all that money?"

"Oh een leetle game. I play jompin'-bin game weeth Juan Rodriguez and I beat heem."

"Ah-hah, I see. Five *centavos* each game."

"Sure," said Lightning. "I am locky."

"He is lying, Henry," declared Judge, but Henry ignored him.

"Juan Rodriguez lives down near the Border, does he not?" asked Henry.

"'Bout half-dozen or seex feet from Border," Thunder nodded.

"All right," said Henry firmly. "You two get your horses and ride down to Juan Rodriguez's home. Unsaddle your horses and give them something to eat. Then you stay at Juan Rodriquez's rancho until I send for you. Do you understand?"

"No," replied Lightning. "This ees damn nice place, too."

"Do you want to go to jail?"

"Por Dios—no! Nobody ees liking jails."

"All right. If you stay here, you will go to jail."

"You can take my peek?" queried Lightning soberly.

"You can take your pick," replied Henry. "Choice is a better word."

"I peek Juan Rodriquez," decided Lightning. "Come on, my leetle brodder."

THEY HURRIED DOWN to the stable. Judge was about to protest, but he noted the expression on Henry's face. A few minutes later the two Mexicans rode away across the hills, heading due south. Judge sighed and shifted in his chair.

"I suppose," he remarked, "it would do me no earthly good to ask for an explanation."

"After I get through explaining it to myself, perhaps I shall try and explain it to you, Judge," replied Henry. "Right now, it might be a good thing to see if Frijole took all his prune *wine* with him last night.

"Do you know, Judge, Josephine is a hardy soul. She landed on both feet, bounced over and went flat on that sidewalk. Then she got up, cuffed her hat over one eye and started for the hotel, but Oscar intercepted her and she knocked him as cold as a bartender's heart."

"*You* would probably call that love," remarked Judge.

"I am not so sure, Judge. She seemed to swing with malice aforethought, her jaw set tightly."

"I just wonder what became of Julius Larsen."

"We will know when Oscar Johnson comes home with the story, Judge. Please seek the prune juice—I need artificial stimulation. A hearse in Tonto City! Judge, that is our first step in civic advancement."

Judge got wearily to his feet, glancing down the road.

"Unless my old eyes deceive me, yonder comes Oscar and Frijole and Albert, walking home. It serves them right."

"Amen," muttered Henry.

The three prodigals arrived at the porch, sore-footed and limping. Frijole tried to smile, but his mustache only twitched painfully.

"Ay vish to t'row myself upon de morcy of de court," said Oscar hollowly.

"The court has gone to get the prune juice," replied Henry.

"Balm in Gilead," sighed Frijole.

"Well, Oscar, what have you to say?" queried Henry solemnly. "Until the court has heard the evidence, no mercy will be extended."

"Ay am sore at hort and Ay have damn sore nose," declared Oscar.

"I understand the sore nose," stated Henry. "I saw what happened."

"Ay am also t'rough vit vimmin."

Judge came out with a jug of Frijole's prune distillation, sat down and looked at the three weary men.

"Court has already convened, Judge," explained Henry, "and we are already in possession of the fact that Oscar is through with women. He has also declared a sore heart and a sore nose. Proceed, Oscar."

"As a matter of fact," interposed Judge, "you discovered that Josephine had gone to a dance at Scorpion Bend with Julius. Whereupon, and with malice aforethought, you all went to Scorpion Bend to try and interfere with their pleasure."

Frijole giggled and Judge turned quickly.

"What is so funny, if I may ask, Frijole?"

"You fellers jumpin' on Oscar thataway. Why don'tcha find out what happened, instead of crawlin' him? We caught up with Julius and Josephine this side of Scorpion Bend. They'd got into an argument and Josephine had shoved him out of the buggy. Oscar went to her aid, and him and Julius had a fight.

"Julius stood all he could and then he went gallopin' up

the road, headin' for Scorpion Bend; so Oscar and Josephine had it out, and she wanted to come home. Well, Oscar got into the buggy with her and they started back, but the rest of us went on to Scorpion Bend. That's what happened."

"All very clear," agreed Henry. "But what about the next chapter?"

"Va'al," said Oscar heavily, "Yosephine von't talk vit me, and den de damn hurse balked. He von't go no place. Ay got out of de boggy and Ay yerk and Ay yerk, but de hurse von't go. Den Ay unhitch de hurse, and Ay say to him, 'Ay bet you vill go now,' and he vent."

"He went, eh?" said Henry. "Well?"

"He vars unhitched," reminded Oscar.

"And the horse left you?"

"De last I seen of him he vars leaving. So Yosephine and me sat in de boggy."

"Love in the moonlight," said Henry quietly.

"Lofe!" snorted Oscar. "Ay am t'rough. For t'ree, four hour I listen to vat makes a yentleman."

"What about you gentlemen, Frijole?" asked Henry.

"Oh, us!" exclaimed Frijole. "Well, they auctioned off that hearse—and Lightning bought it. I reckon we was a bit drunk. Anyway, we hitched the team to the hearse, coupled the buckboard behind, and came back to where we picked up Oscar and Josephine. We tied their buggy on behind and let Oscar do the driving. Everythin' was fine until Oscar made that turn."

"Did you," queried Henry, "ever wonder where Lightning got that hundred dollars to spend for a hearse?"

"He won it," replied Frijole.

"Playing jumping beans," added Henry.

"With Juan Rodriguez," finished Albert. "I remember that."

13

DISASTER HOUSE

IT WAS EARLY next afternoon. Judge and Henry were on the porch, and Henry said, "Would you like to take a ride in the hills with me, Judge?"

Judge shuddered. "A ride in the hills—in this heat? Thank you so much, but I have no such desire. My rheumatics, you know."

"Yes, I know."

"You jest, my friend," remarked Judge, yawning.

Henry got to his feet and went down to the stable. Judge looked after him, wrinkled his nose, yawned and went back to sleep. It was siesta time, anyway—and why ride into the hills?

Henry had an old roan horse, short-coupled, pot-bellied, but reliable, which he saddled. He buckled on his gun, climbed heavily aboard and headed for Smoke Tree Canyon. He had no idea of encountering the Silver Buckshot, or of helping King Fisher save ten thousand dollars, but he did want to take a look at that old shack. Anyway, it was on his ranch; so he had a perfect right to investigate.

It was a long, hot climb up that series of broken hills to the level mesa above the canyon. Henry had never seen that shack, but he knew the approximate location. The brush was heavy and there were no defined trails, but he found the shack in a little clearing.

It was a one-room affair, without door or window, with the desert growth flourishing even under the sagging porch-top. Henry sat and watched the place for at least ten minutes. Bees buzzed in the sage, and there were humming-birds in profusion. A road-runner crossed the front of the shack, and Henry could hear quail calling back in the mesquite.

But Henry was cautious. He rode in a half-circle, intending to watch the shack from all angles before approaching closer. He had no desire to be hit with a load of silver buckshot. Of course, it was possible that King Fisher had already been there. Or he might never come. It was also quite possible that Silver Buckshot was nowhere around. A man demanding that ransom be thrown through the window would not wait inside the shack.

"One must grant the man a modicum of common sense," Henry told himself.

There were no windows or doors at the rear, and Henry was about to head for the shack, when he saw a rider coming down through the brush. Henry quickly reined behind some mesquite. He was about a hundred yards from the cabin, as he peered through the tangled brush.

"King Fisher!" he murmured.

The horse and rider passed from Henry's vision, around in front of the shack. Henry had stopped on much lower ground than the shack, and if someone left it by going along the rim of the canyon, Henry would not be able to see him.

Fifteen minutes passed, but King Fisher did not appear.

Henry began to get inquisitive. Again he was about to ride out of the mesquite, when he saw another rider, following approximately the same route as that taken by King Fisher.

"Our estimable sheriff!" grunted Henry. "Now, how does he figure in this deal?"

The sheriff was riding cautiously now, watching the shack. Finally he, too, passed from Henry's vision. A moment later the report of a rifle clattered through the hills, echoing and re-echoing, until the sound died away.

"My goodness!" exclaimed Henry.

Forgetting that he might be riding straight into danger, he spurred his horse up the slope, through the brush, and around the corner of the shack. Vinegar Bill Hawkins was flat on his back near the doorway, his horse fifty feet away, the reins tangled in the brush.

HENRY DISMOUNTED HEAVILY and made a quick examination. The sheriff had been shot through the right side, just below the breast. He was unconscious and breathing with difficulty. As tenderly as possible Henry half-carried, half-dragged him into the shade. Then he turned his attention to the shack.

It was empty and there was no scent of burned powder inside the one room, which was unfurnished, the old floor-boards broken in places. The dust and sand had been disturbed on the floor, showing that someone had been there recently. Henry did not know exactly what to do. He went to the doorway and tried to figure out what had become of King Fisher.

Was King Fisher lying about the ransom, he wondered? And did King Fisher shoot Bill Hawkins? Henry went back into the one room again. He got on his knees and pulled out some of the broken flooring. The shack had been built over a sort of ravine, and was high enough above the ground to allow a person to crawl under easily.

Then he went outside, walked around to the end of the shack and slid down into the little ravine, tearing aside the brush. Here the shack was so high above the ground that Henry could easily go under on all fours.

Under there, hanging on nails on one of the half-rotted stringers, wrapped in a section of old yellow slicker, was a double-barrel, muzzle-loading shotgun of large gauge. Henry unwrapped it; the gun was in fine condition.

"The weapon of the Silver Buckshot!" muttered Henry to himself.

He examined it closely. The ramrod was equipped with a screw end, with which to withdraw the loads, and with little trouble Henry drew out the paper wadding from over the shot. He allowed the dozen sizeable buckshot to roll out into his cupped hand.

"Silver!" he breathed. The other barrel yielded the same results.

In a few minutes Henry came from under the shack, minus the shotgun, which he had replaced. The sheriff was unconscious. Henry knew that he would be unable to put the sheriff on his horse; the best thing to do would be to get hold of a doctor as quickly as possible. He decided to ride back to the ranch and send Oscar or Frijole; so he climbed into the saddle and rode off as fast as the old roan could travel.

IT WAS NEARLY dark that evening when Spook Gilliam and Frijole Bill rode in at the JHC. Henry and Judge were on the porch, waiting to hear about Bill Hawkins. Frijole had gone to notify the doctor, and no further word had come to the ranch.

The two men dismounted and came over to the porch. Spook said:

"Bill's gone, Henry."

"You mean the doctor got there too late, Spook?"

"Bill was dead when he got there. He'd been shot twice."

"Twice?" queried Henry. "Why, Spook, he had only been shot once."

"Once before yuh left, and once afterward," said Frijole. "The last shot was square through the head, and the gun-muzzle was so close it burned his hair."

Henry drew a deep breath, but said nothing. Judge remarked:

"We are living in a hell of a country."

"It ain't the country, Judge," said Frijole, "it's the people."

"It is a person," corrected Henry. "Spook, have you any idea why the sheriff should have been out at that old shack?"

Spook shook his head. "No, I don't, Henry, but I've got the strongest hunch that it had somethin' to do with King Fisher."

"Just how do you figure that?" asked Judge quickly.

"I'm setting out in front of the office," explained Spook. "I seen King Fisher go into the bank. Bill came out of the courthouse and stepped inside the bank. He wasn't hardly in there, when out he comes. He came down to the office, kinda lookin' back once or twice. Then out comes King Fisher and went over to the hitch-rack. Bill says to me:

" 'See which way he goes, Spook,' just like I knew who he meant, and Bill went trottin' back to our stable.

"In a couple of minutes Bill rides out and I says, 'He went toward the JHC.' Bill nods and heads out the same way. I don't know what he had on his mind, Henry—but I know what he got."

"I am very sorry, Spook," said Henry.

"Yuh know," said Spook quietly, "Bill was worried. Yesterday he gave me the description of a man to look for. He didn't give me a name. He said the man was almost six feet tall, brown hair, blue eyes and might weigh anywhere from one hundred and eighty up to over two hundred.

"He has a bullet scar on his left hip, the little toe of his left foot is missin', and he's got a knife scar in the shape of a crescent on his right shoulder. I said, 'Bill, I can't go around undressin' people.'

"He said, 'Spook, that's the man who shot my wife. He's got to be the man—and I want him. You watch for that man, Spook.' Yuh know, Henry, he was kinda like a feller that's locoed, only Bill was as smart as anybody. But the death of his wife got him."

"I know," said Henry.

"Do yuh think that same man got Bill?" asked Spook.

"I do not know what to think, Spook—except that a killer is about at the end of his rope. Just take it easy."

"At the end of his rope?" queried Judge. "You speak as though you knew something, Henry."

"A killer," said Henry, "is always close to the end of his rope."

SPOOK WENT BACK to Tonto City. King Fisher, Harvey Olds and Tom South met him at the office. They wanted to know more about the murder of Bill Hawkins. Spook told them all he knew.

"I just got back from the JHC," he told them. "Henry Conroy says that Bill had only been shot once when he put him in the shade."

"Did Henry have any ideas on who did it?" asked King Fisher.

"He didn't say, but I've got a hunch he has. He did say that the killer was mighty close to the end of his rope. Yuh see, he was in pretty close when Bill was shot. Mebbe he knows who the killer was."

"Did he say what he was doing up there, Spook?" asked Harvey Olds.

"No, he didn't. I don't even know what Bill was doin' up there. Fact is, the whole deal has me fightin' my hat."

"In fact," said Tom South, "there's no evidence that Conroy didn't fire the shot himself."

"Aw, Henry wouldn't shoot Bill," protested Spook.

"Never be too sure of any man," said Olds.

"No, I couldn't believe that," said King Fisher. "If Conroy is a killer, he is also the world's best actor."

"That was his business for years," remarked Olds.

"But why would he kill Bill Hawkins?" queried Spook. "Yuh got to have a reason."

"All right," said South, "look at it this way, Spook. Why did Hawkins and Conroy meet at that deserted shack? It would be easy enough for Conroy to have shot Hawkins, and when he found that Hawkins wasn't dead, he could have shot him again, pulled him into the shade of the shack and sent for a doctor. Yuh can't prove that he didn't."

"We better take it up with John Campbell, the prosecutor," said Olds. "Spook can't do a thing unless Campbell wants to make the arrest."

Doctor Knowles walked into the office and placed two battered bullets on the desk.

"They're not silver this time," he said quietly. "One is a forty-five, seventy rifle bullet and the other is from a forty-five revolver."

The three men looked gloomily at the battered chunks of lead that had killed Bill Hawkins.

"Most everybody shoots a forty-five," said Spook.

"I guess it is up to you now, Spook," said Doctor Knowles. "You are the sheriff."

Spook took a deep breath and shook his head.

"Not me," he said. "I turned my resignation in the commissioners today. I'm lockin' up the office and givin' 'em the keys. I don't know a darned thing about runnin' it— and I don't want to learn. I took the job, because me and Bill was friends. I'd rather punch cows for forty a month. It's safer."

"But you can't quit now, Spook," insisted King Fisher.

"A fine state of affairs," growled Harvey Olds. "No sheriff."

"I'm going to find the commissioners," said King Fisher.

14

HENRY, GET YOUR GUN

IT WAS NEARLY midnight when King Fisher and Doctor Knowles came out to the JHC. Henry and Judge were intent on a game of cribbage; Oscar and Frijole were playing pinochle. Frijole opened the door for the two men.

"My goodness—another murder?" Henry queried.

"One a day is enough, Henry," said the doctor. "Mr. Fisher has something to discuss with you, I believe; so I came along to add my few words of encouragement."

"It's pretty simple, Conroy," said King Fisher. "With the death of Bill Hawkins, Spook Gilliam became sheriff. Spook resigned today, and there is no sheriff in Wild Horse Valley. I found three of the five commissioners, and I have your written appointment as sheriff. Like to read it?"

King Fisher handed the document to Henry, who squinted at it, laid it aside and leaned back in his chair.

"Rather unusual, isn't it?" he asked calmly.

"Necessary," said King Fisher shortly.

"My goodness!"

"You mean," asked Judge, "that Henry is to be the sheriff again?"

"Exactly."

"Ay vill be de yailer," stated Oscar. "Ay vill be glad to get off dis damn ranch."

"And I'll be glad to have yuh off here," declared Frijole.

"And," said Henry quietly, "I get a whole flock of murders thrown into my lap. Well, well! Gentlemen, this *is* a shock."

"You will accept?" queried King Fisher.

"In the interests of society, I can not refuse, sir."

"Good! Here are the keys."

King Fisher tossed the jail and office keys to the table-top.

"When do we start?" queried Judge huskily.

"Right now," replied Henry. "Get your boots and gun, Judge. Frijole, saddle up our horses. Oscar, you can saddle your own."

"Not tonight," protested Judge. "Man, it is midnight!"

"And Wild Horse Valley has no sheriff on the job, Judge. Tonight we take over the reins of office. Tomorrow we start where Bill Hawkins left off."

"The Shame of Arizona comes back," said Judge, creaking to his feet.

Henry smiled slowly and shook his head.

"It is really coincidental," he remarked, "but only this afternoon I noticed my insignia of office in a bureau drawer, and I—I polished it."

"Yo're kinda glad to go back, Conroy?" asked King Fisher.

"Not just to be a sheriff again, Mr. Fisher, but to try and make Wild Horse Valley as clean of crime and criminals as it was when you came in here and—er—evicted me. And, after all, Jim Henshaw was murdered during my regime, although I did not know it; so I want to clear my record."

King Fisher and Doctor Knowles rode back to Tonto

City with them. Oscar took their horses back to the little stable, while Henry opened the office and lighted a lamp. Then he sank down in the sheriff's chair and said quietly:

"Gentlemen, the sheriff of Tonto is ready for business."

As if in answer to that announcement, a man came running down the board sidewalk. Henry cocked one eye toward the doorway, and Danny Regan came charging in. He stopped, looked at the group of men, and said:

"Spook's the sheriff now, ain't he?"

"Yon are looking directly at the sheriff, Danny," said Henry.

"You mean—well, I'll be darned! Listen! There's somethin' wrong at the bank. I came past there a minute ago, and yuh can hear a pounding noise in there. Yuh can't see anythin' in the dark—"

"My goodness!" exclaimed Henry, and reached for his hat. "Come on."

THEY ALL HURRIED up to the front of the bank. John Campbell, the prosecutor, joined the group. Henry rapped loudly on the front door, and they could hear the pounding again. The door was securely locked; so they went around and tested the rear door, which was closed but unlocked.

This indicated that something was wrong. They lighted matches, until someone was able to locate a lamp. In its sudden glow they saw Harvey Olds, the banker, flat on his back inside the railing, tied and gagged. He had been pounding his feet on the floor, hoping to attract attention.

"Two men!" he panted. "Masked in black. They came to my house, stuck me up and forced me to let them in here. Then they forced me to tell the combination to the safe.

After they got the safe open, they tied me up. I don't know what they got—but it must have been plenty."

King Fisher threw the safe door open and looked inside. Then he closed it, spun the combination and turned to Olds.

"I guess they cleaned us out, Harvey," he said. "You can't identify either man?"

"Not much to tell you, King. They were average size and masked. Both talked gutturally."

King Fisher leaned on the railing, looking miserable. He said:

"The payrolls for both my mines were in that safe. Tomorrow is payday."

Harvey Olds nodded painfully and chafed his wrists. "Somebody guessed that, King," he said.

Henry's eyes were narrowed, his jaw set. Then he stepped over and put his hand on Harvey Olds' arm.

"Mr. Olds," he said quietly, "I arrest you for robbery."

"Man, you're crazy!" gasped Harvey Olds.

"I arrest you for robbery, Olds," insisted Henry.

"On what evidence, Henry?" asked Campbell. "You can't—"

"Just a moment, gentlemen," pleaded Henry. "Let us all go up to John Campbell's office and talk this over. I do not want all of Tonto City in here."

"But it is ridiculous!" snapped the banker. "Haven't I any rights in this matter. Campbell, you know as well as I do that—"

"We can talk it over in my office," said Campbell.

"You don't have to hold my arm!" snarled the banker.

"I feel that need, sir," replied Henry. "Judge, you take the other arm please. I believe this is the first time that I have ever walked arm-in-arm with a banker."

They entered the courthouse and went to John Campbell's large law office. Olds slumped into a chair, jaw tightly set, a scowl on his lean face. Everyone looked to Henry for an explanation, but Henry was in no hurry. He sat on the corner of a table, facing Harvey Olds, a half-smile on his round face.

"Mr. Olds," he said quietly, "as they say in certain parts of these United States—you cooked your own goose."

"You red-nosed fool—what do you mean?"

"In the matter of that ransom money, Mr. Olds. You lied when you said you had marked the bills and taken down the serial numbers. You accepted money from that first ransom—and it was not marked. You doublecrossed King Fisher, when you posed as his friend. You aimed to loot this bank and to help break King Fisher. You gave spurious serial numbers on those ransom bills *and they were not marked.*"

Harvey Olds choked, swallowed heavily and started to get up, but Judge shoved him back into his chair.

"Damn you!" gasped the banker. "You can't prove a thing against me."

"You helped rob that bank tonight, Olds," said Henry. "True, there were two men—you and another. You are going to the penitentiary, Mr. Olds; so you may as well make a clean breast of it. I want the name of Silver Buckshot—your partner!"

"Henry—" gasped John Campbell. "You mean—"

"I mean that this man is a partner of Silver Buckshot,

and if he does not name him, I will, sir. Olds, you may as well—"

THE OFFICE DOOR banged shut, and they all turned at the sound. Against the door stood a masked man, a double-barrel shot-gun in his hands.

"Don't move and don't speak," warned the man behind the mask. "Regan, toss your gun toward me. Fisher, take that gun out of your pocket and toss it over. Van Treece don't pack any. Conroy, if you've got one, you can keep it, 'cause you won't live to use it.

"Van Treece, Campbell, Knowles, Regan—all of you lay down on the floor. Lay down, or I'll lay yuh down—flat."

There was nothing to do but obey. The masked man picked up the two guns. Henry still sat on the corner of the desk. His face was white, and even his nose had lost its usual ruddy hue. Olds started to get up, but slid back in his chair, his face tense. The masked man came a step closer, and laughed.

"I've had an eye on you, Conroy," he said. "You're smarter than they think. I knew you spotted that bill. I should have knocked yuh off when I got Bill Hawkins. I had to get him, because he seen me. You left him just in time to save your own skin; so I shot him once more. I didn't want him to talk.

"Yeah, and I killed Henshaw a couple years ago. I tried to force him to tell where that mine was located. Well, I know now. Want to know anythin' more, before I start shootin'?"

"You neglected to state that you murdered Mrs. Hawkins," reminded Henry, his voice quite firm. "Well, Tiger Smith, it's your next move."

"So you figured that out, too, eh?" snarled the masked man.

"Simple, my dear man," said Henry. "But you cannot do this thing and get away with it."

"You think not? The rest of the town is asleep. I'll go out that back door, and there's a saddled horse ready to take me into Mexico. Well, what are we waitin' for?"

He lifted the shotgun to his shoulder, leveled it at Olds, who half-screamed and drew back. The masked man pulled the trigger.

The report of the big shotgun was ear-splitting in that room. Olds fell out of his chair, crying out sharply. The masked man was staggering back, as the heavy gun crashed to the floor, and he had both hands at his face, clawing at his mask. Henry jumped off the table, ran into the staggering man, and they crashed down against the door. Danny Regan was on his feet, diving into them, grasping the masked man's flailing arms.

Olds started to run for an open window, but Judge's long right arm reached out, grasped Olds' collar, and the banker came over backward and sat down heavily on the floor. Danny and Henry quickly subdued the struggling killer and tore away what was left of the mask.

"Tom South!" gasped John Campbell.

"My eyes!" whined South, the assayer. "They're gone! I can't see!"

"The shotgun blew out at the breech!" exclaimed Danny. "Look at it!"

Doctor Knowles backed South against the wall and examined his eyes.

"They're gone!" choked South.

"Yes," agreed the doctor, "they are, Tom."

Harvey Olds was muttering: "He—he was going to murder me!"

"To keep you from making the confession that you will have to make," said Henry. "Now, wait a minute."

Henry forcibly yanked off South's left foot and tore away the sock. The little toe was missing.

"I am sorry that Bill Hawkins did not live to see that left foot," said Henry quietly.

DANNY WAS EXAMINING the blown-up shotgun, drawing the load from the unfired barrel. "Why, he never had any shot in this gun!" he exclaimed. "Of all the crazy things. Look at this, will yuh? No shot in the gun."

"No," said Henry, "I took it out."

"You took it out?"

"Yes, Danny. And then I slipped a plug of clay into each barrel. I have heard that a gas-check will blow up a gun. You see, I discovered the hiding place of that gun yesterday. I imagined I had evidence that would have hung Mr. South, but I wanted to be sure. You see, when he loaded the silver buckshot into that gun, he wadded it down with some of his own assay blanks. Being an assayer, be was in a position to cast silver. Being more or less of a fool, he convicted himself."

"But about Roy?" asked King Fisher anxiously.

"Oh, yes." Henry smiled. "Mr. South did that job. You see, Roy drank too much and went out to the mine. That is, he started for the mine. He came on the scene at an inopportune time, and South shot him. The boy was badly hurt, but managed to cling to his saddle. The horse took him down to my ranch, and he fell off there. If I am wrong in my deductions, I am sure Mr. South will correct me."

He bowed at the assayer.

"All right," groaned South. "What do I care? I'm better off dead than blind. I did it. That sniveling banker didn't kill anybody, but he stole plenty, and you'll find the money in his house. Let me have a gun for a moment, and I'll save some money for the county."

No one seemed charitably inclined. They took Olds and South to the jail, where the doctor bandaged the wounded man. King Fisher stood beside Henry's desk, looking down at the fat, red-nosed sheriff. Conroy had faced the murderer's shotgun without a quiver, and yet he could not have been sure that South had not discovered the drawn loads and plugged barrels.

"I explained to John Campbell about the ransoms," said King Fisher. "No need for secrecy any more. You saved my son a lot of trouble, and you saved me a lot of money. Now I've got some good news for you."

"Good news?" queried Henry. "That would be a novelty."

"South just told us where that Henshaw mine is located, Henry. It's in the bottom of Smoke Tree Canyon—on your land. He traced it by that map he stole from Albert Henshaw, but was afraid to uncover it because it would implicate him."

"My goodness!" exclaimed Henry. "On my land! Well, well! But about the ransom money, Mr. Fisher? You know, of course, that South did not get that five thousand."

"I—I think I know now." King Fisher smiled.

"Yes," said Henry. "Thunder and Lightning saw you leave it at the old adobe. I do not believe they have spent more than two hundred of it, including the hundred they paid for the hearse. I will get it back from them."

"All right, Henry. And when you do, it will be my wedding present to Danny Regan and Joan Buckley. Danny said he proposed tonight and Joan accepted him. He has been waiting to tell you, but you have been pretty busy."

Henry rubbed his nose violently, cleared his throat, hooked his thumbs unto the armholes of his vest and looked up at King Fisher.

"Speaking in the vernacular, Mr. Fisher," he said soberly, "ain't this the damnedest country for unexpected things to happen?"

www.ingramcontent.com/pod-product-compliance
Lightning Source LLC
Chambersburg PA
CBHW031156020726
47499CB00002B/381